THEY HAD TOLD ADAM TALCUT HE WAS A SOLDIER. BUT THEY HADN'T TOLD HIM WHAT THAT MEANT.

Only hours before, Second Lieutenant Adam Talcut had been in command of a company of infantrymen even younger than he, kids fresh out of high school who barely knew how to shoot straight.

Now those men were either dead or captured as the army of which they were a part splintered before the force of the shattering German onslaught.

Adam Talcut wandererd alone through a nightmarish winter world of slain comrades and wrecked equipment while the triumphant enemy poured over the land like a ravaging flood.

Adam Talcut was about to learn what they meant when they said war was hell . . .

THE SILENT SNOW

THE SILENT SNOW

OLIVER B. PATTON

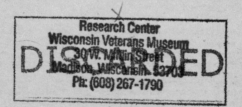

A SIGNET BOOK

NEW AMERICAN LIBRARY

PUBLISHER'S NOTE

This book is a work of fiction. Names, characters, places, and incidents either are the product of the author's imagination or are used fictitiously, and any resemblance to actual persons, living or dead, events, or locales is entirely coincidental.

Copyright © 1988 by Oliver Patton

SIGNET, SIGNET CLASSIC, MENTOR, ONYX, PLUME, MERIDIAN and NAL BOOKS are published by NAL PENGUIN INC., 1633 Broadway, New York, New York 10019

First Printing, April, 1988

1 2 3 4 5 6 7 8 9

PRINTED IN THE UNITED STATES OF AMERICA

To the men of the Golden Lion Division,
Der armer alter Loewe

 **Preface**

ABOUT FOUR o'clock on the afternoon of December 19, 1944, two regiments of American infantry surrendered to the German Army on a hill in Belgium just outside the town of Schoenberg. With the exception of Bataan, it was the largest mass surrender of U.S. troops since the capitulation of the garrison of Harpers Ferry, West Virginia, to Confederate General Jackson in September 1862.

On December 16 the Germans launched their last great offensive of World War II into Belgium and Luxembourg, bursting through two American divisions on a thinly held front in a region called the Ardennes. By desperate fighting the shoulders of the breakthrough were held, but between them some U.S. units were overrun.

By dusk on the seventeenth, two infantry regiments holding a salient into the German Siegfried Line on a forested ridge, the Schnee Eifel, were encircled and cut off. Next day they were ordered to abandon their position and break out of the trap. By the nineteenth they reached the hill just across the Our River from Schoenberg, some five miles behind their original line, and there, surrounded, their commanders surrendered what remained of the regiments.

Estimates of the number of American soldiers surrendered on that hill range from three to eight thousand. No one knows exactly because when you lose a fight like that the records get all screwed up. Even after the war when survivors of German prison camps came home, the number remained flexible.

The lowest estimate—three thousand taken on the hill—is possible because in the five miles from the Schnee Eifel to Schoenberg both regiments left behind them their wounded, their service troops, and a horde of lost and straggling men to be gathered up later by the Germans. By December 21, having pretty well cleaned up the area, the 66th German Corps reported a bag of prisoners approaching eight thousand.

What happened on and behind the Schnee Eifel was a far cry from what happened on Bataan. It took the Japanese four months to defeat and capture the American defenders of Bataan and Corregidor; the Germans bagged their quarry in four days. Historians have little good to say about the short unhappy war of the 422nd and 423rd U.S. Infantry regiments.

John Toland says that by three-thirty on the afternoon of December 19 "almost ten thousand Americans were hemmed into a few square miles of woods near Schoenberg." Under concentrated artillery and mortar fire "the mass of trapped men milled around in confusion, ignorance and terror . . . there could be no escape."

Robert Merriam's comments are similar: ordered off the Schnee Eifel, the two regiments, "lacking supplies and, apparently initiative, made one feeble, unsuccessful attempt on December 19 to get back through the German lines." Then, he adds, though many officers and men wanted to continue the fight, they were ordered by their commanders to surrender. "Over seven thousand men of these two regiments surrendered to the Germans in the largest mass surrender of American arms on the Western Front."

British historian Charles Whiting is more scathing. Visiting the wooded Schnee Eifel twenty years after the war, he found "The shame of the 106th Division is still palpable in the forest." In less than a week of combat, he reports, of the sixteen thousand men of the division who went into the Ardennes, "only some four thousand would return. . . . Naturally," he adds, "the events of that week were afterwards glossed over, perverted or conveniently forgotten."

Anyone curious enough to look into the growing number of books about the Battle of the Bulge—as the German offensive became known—might disagree with Mr. Whiting. There may be some perversion but little has been glossed over or conveniently forgotten except, perhaps, the story of the men of the 106th Division who continued to fight.

One regiment, the 424th Infantry, escaped the trap and was attached to another division to help stop the Germans lunging to turn the northern shoulder of the breakthrough. In January 1945, as part of another division, the 424th fought its way back into Germany.

Some five hundred men of the two trapped regiments evaded the surrender on December 19, dug in on a hill a few miles northeast of Schoenberg, and held out until December 21.

Of those who refused to surrender, fifty or sixty escaped through the advancing Germans to join the American troops who held Saint Vith, six miles west of Schoenberg, until December 21.

A few—no one knows how many—stayed in the forest behind the German lines and fought a lonely, desperate war to the death. One of them is a legend among Belgian villagers who heard the Germans cursing the American who ambushed couriers and mined trails around the hamlet of Meyerode. When the Germans were driven back across the Schnee Eifel in January the Belgians say they found his body—surrounded by seven dead German soldiers.

When survivors of the lost fight between the Schnee Eifel and the Our River gather, they tell "What if . . . ?" stories. What if we had stayed on the Schnee Eifel and fought it out? What if the 7th Armored Division had somehow got through the jam of fleeing American vehicles in time to help us break out?

And there is one that each man tells only to himself: What if I hadn't given up? What if I hid in the forest and fought on until the American army came back?

This is a sort of "What if?" story about two Americans: a lieutenant of the 106th and a sergeant of a black artillery battalion who stayed behind German lines and fought. There were four black battalions in the Corps artillery supporting the 106th Infantry Division.

Neither Lieutenant Adam Talcut nor Sergeant Julian is recorded in the history of the Battle of the Bulge. They were invented for this story in tribute to the unknown men who would not surrender.

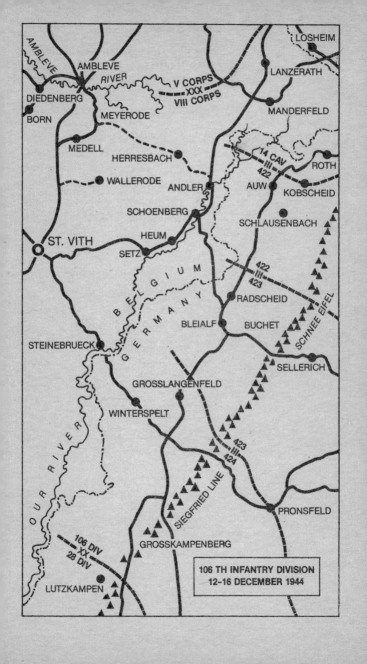

106 TH INFANTRY DIVISION
12–16 DECEMBER 1944

ONCE UPON a time, thought Adam Talcut, you went to war on a horse with flags and bugles and people cheering. Not this war—not in December 1944. Four seasick days in the English Channel and Le Havre estuary, waiting for a storm to blow over. Three bone-jarring days by truck across France and Belgium in rain, snow, and bitter cold.

Nobody cheered. Few people in the gloomy little villages even looked at the Americans spilling across their country. Only once, in Belgium, three children and a pretty girl gathered around Lieutenant Talcut in the cold rain and the girl pointed to his helmet. Puzzled, he took it off and one of the children pinned to its wet camouflage netting two little ribbons, black and red.

"We thank you," said the girl slowly and formally.

Searching his pockets, Adam found only a box of raisins to share among the children. There were two left in his palm and he held them out to the girl. She smiled at him, took one, and put it in her pocket. Adam put the other carefully between her lips, winking at the children, who giggled until she blushed.

On the afternoon of the third day the trucks carrying Adam's company stopped in the outskirts of a fairly large town. As always, they blocked the narrow macadam road. All the way from Le Havre the drivers had heeded strictly only one of the many signs nailed to roadside trees: the one that said "ROAD SWEPT TO SHOULDERS." Adam thought when the engineers swept the road for mines they must have gone a little beyond

1

the macadam but the drivers of the quartermaster truck companies had no faith in that. Veterans of the breakout from Normandy, they would not take a truck an inch off the blacktop.

"Pee-stop, Lieutenant?" called a soldier from the back of Adam's truck.

"Don't know. Nobody's gettin' out up ahead."

"Gotta go, Lieutenant!"

"All right . . . but stay close to the truck."

In minutes the side of the road was lined with men enveloped in a rising cloud of vapor of their own making. Most of them were glumly silent, only a few shouted cheerful obscenities at each other. The noisy ones Adam knew well—the only "old" soldiers in his platoon. There were not many in the 106th Infantry Division. In the six months before Adam joined it in September 1944 it had lost seven thousand trained men—sixty percent of its enlisted strength—shipped out as overseas replacements.

Ordinarily the army would have drafted and trained fillers for the looted division before it went to war, but the fighting in Europe in the summer and fall of 1944 not only swallowed individual infantrymen, it demanded more divisions. The army took drastic steps to fill those like the 106th at Camp Atterbury in Indiana and ship them overseas in a hurry.

Over seventy thousand men were expelled from the Army Specialized Training Program which had kept them in college since the spring of 1943. Thirty thousand air cadets were transferred from the Army Air Corps back to the ground forces. Few were enthusiastic about assignment to the infantry but they were fresh, healthy young men in top mental categories and the army reckoned that with training they would make good infantrymen. With this green influx came some volunteers from stateside service and antiaircraft units. Many of these were valuable men, untrained as combat infantry, but willing to learn. They had a year or more of service and that made them "old" soldiers.

A jeep made its way along the column of trucks and

slowed to a stop. "Hey, old buddy!" said the lieutenant beside the driver, and when he pulled down the scarf covering his mouth and nose Adam recognized a friend on the battalion staff.

"Heyo, Jughead. What's up?"

"We got it made, friend. Our battalion's in division reserve."

Adam looked disappointed and his friend laughed. "You won't miss anything. Nobody's got much of a fight around here. They call it the Ghost Front. Krauts haven't got diddly-squat . . . just a raggedy-ass outfit that can't even speak German."

"What are they?"

"Some kind of bohunks they drafted in Russia. They got kraut officers but they won't give us any sweat."

"What town is this?"

"Saint Vith. Division forward CP. Better load up, Adam. We're movin' out."

It was only four o'clock but already dusk. A few lights winked on in the town but as the truck column labored into the forested hills north of it there was nothing but darkness ahead.

"Shit-oh-dear," said the driver feelingly. "We musta crossed the light line."

Adam knew what that was: blackout country—so close to the front the Germans could see moving lights. A military policeman confirmed that, shouting at the driver to turn off his headlights. The trucks closed up until the cat's-eye taillight of the one ahead was visible. After a while they came to a road fork where a jeep waited and some military police with blacked-out flashlights.

"Your company's in Hochkreuz," Adam heard one of them tell the driver of the truck ahead of him. "Follow the jeep."

Something like a big outboard boat motor sputtered overhead and a fast-firing gun nearby responded with a nervous *thumpa-thumpa-thumpa,* probing the low clouds with a stream of tracer shells. The driver hunched his shoulders, swearing.

"Hope to God they don't hit it!"

Forty-millimeter antiaircraft gun, guessed Adam. "What're they shooting at?"

"Goddamn buzz bomb! Kraut flyin' bomb . . . they shoot 'em at England."

Adam remembered them. The division stopped in England for a few weeks on its way to France and he was one of the lucky ones who had a three-day pass to London. Every night heavy antiaircraft guns tried to knock down the bombs before they tipped over and dived into the town.

The trucks ground to another stop and this time the men dismounted stiffly, peering through the dark at the little village around them. A guide found Adam, led him and his platoon to a house in the blacked-out hamlet.

"This here is Hochkreuz, Lieutenant," he explained. "Battalion headquarters is about a mile from here in a place called Born."

A lieutenant wearing the big Indian-head shoulder patch of the 2nd Infantry Division appeared, grinning cheerfully.

"Glad to see you. Where's your platoon?"

"Outside. Where do we go?"

"You got this house and two more I'll show you. My people are already gone. You can move in and sack out . . . except for one squad. One of mine's on outpost up by Auw, an' you got to take over."

"Now? Hell, man, it's dark!"

"Tough shit, buddy. We're pullin' out an' you got to relieve my squad right now."

"Where is this outpost?"

"Schlausenbach Mill. Between one of our regiments and the armored cavalry in the Losheim Gap."

"All right," said Adam sourly. "If I've got to send a squad, I will but you've got to tell me more about it. What are they supposed to do?"

The lieutenant explained impatiently. Two regiments of the 2nd Division held a line in captured bunkers of the German West Wall—the Siegfried Line, Americans called it—on top of a high wooded ridge called the Schnee Eifel. To their north, a squadron of armored cavalry outposted the Losheim Gap, five miles of hilly wooded country between the 2nd and the next infantry division, the 99th.

"One cavalry squadron holding five miles of front?"

"It do be lonesome up there, friend. There's a mile between us and the cavalry and that's where the outpost is. They watch to see the krauts don't slip in between."

"What in the hell can a squad do if the krauts come through there?"

"Make a noise and hope somebody hears 'em."

"Where's your third regiment?"

"Five miles south of the other two with a mile between them and the 28th Division."

"Good Lord!"

"Right. Your outfit's takin' over twenty-two miles of front and you can forget about the book. It says an infantry division can hold twelve thousand yards but you've got almost forty thousand . . . and part of that is an eight-mile salient into the kraut line. Come on, get me a squad and I'll take 'em up there."

Adam's company commander confirmed the requirement but refused to let Adam go with the squad. "Send somebody with the truck. When he gets back he can show you how to find the place. You get the rest of your platoon bedded down and I've got a job for you tomorrow."

Adam sighed. "Yes, sir. What's that?"

"Some of our people were paid for November in England and the rest when we got to France. Battalion wants all that collected so we can change it into some kind of funny-money the army uses in Belgium. You're collector for this company, Talcut."

Adam sent his messenger, Private Ritchie, with his squad and the 2nd Division lieutenant. Ritchie was no old soldier but he was smart and capable; he had a year of college before that sanctuary was raided for infantrymen. Adam had made him his messenger, a job that included any odd task prescribed by the platoon commander.

"You know what to do?" he demanded of Ritchie after instructing him.

"Sure, Lieutenant. I go with the truck and get back here some way."

"And you remember how you did so you can show me the way."

With Duncker, his platoon sergeant, Adam got the remainder of the platoon housed and about midnight found his own billet, a house he shared with the other platoon leaders, Strahl, Kelso, and Hyatt. The company commander and the executive officer had a house to themselves.

The Belgian farmer still occupied the house and surprisingly, his wife and two children. When the American army had taken the sector from the Germans three months past, the villagers had been moved away from the combat zone but the evacuation had not included cattle so a few farmers were left to tend them. Inevitably, some women and children evaded Belgian control to come back to their men.

There was no furniture whatsoever in the room shared by Adam and his three companions. Sergeant Duncker had an explanation: either the 2nd Division or its predecessors had taken the tables, chairs, and small stoves for their bunkers in the front line. The windows were shuttered against the cold and to prevent light from escaping but there was an open one into the barn, which was part of the house. A bovine head appeared from within to inspect the new arrivals, a rope of saliva trailing from its mouth.

"Out," yelled Kelso, "you goddamn beast!" He whacked the animal on its nose and it withdrew, rumbling. "Get some planks tomorrow and close that thing."

"You city jerk," said Strahl. "You don't want to do that. Those cows keep this place warm."

Adam set up a folding cot and on the window ledge above it a photograph in a pasteboard frame. "Hello,

Miss Bitsey," said Hyatt. "Haven't seen you since we left England."

It was a blurred enlargement of a snapshot but you could tell she was a pretty girl in a modest print dress and a beribboned straw hat. She held a small book in her white-gloved hands.

"She always get dolled up like that for church?" asked Hyatt.

"Sure. Back home, they can't go if they don't wear gloves and a hat."

"She's pretty, Adam. You goin' to marry her when you go home?"

"Always thought so. Not so sure now."

"Doesn't she write to you?"

"Nope."

"Hell, old buddy . . . mail's all screwed up. I haven't heard from my girl since we left home and I know she's sending me letters."

Someone snuffed out the candle and the room fell silent except for Kelso's snoring. As soon as he was prone he slept and as soon as he slept he snored. People who shared a room with him eventually gave up trying to stop him. But it was not Kelso who kept Adam awake, it was Hyatt's casual question: You going to marry her?

He shivered and pulled the sleeping bag close around his face. The ventilator in the door of the tile stove— too big for anyone to steal—emitted a faint orange glow, enough to see his breath in the cold room and Bitsey's picture. He groaned. If she won't marry me, he thought, it's my own fault. That damnfool stunt I tried at Fort Benning. Once again he pulled that disaster from memory to make a familiar and painful tour of it.

I've known Bitsey all my life . . . we grew up together, went to Laurel City High together. Everybody knew we'd get married. The war, he thought. The war and Ma—and me—we took that apart.

I wanted to enlist right away but Ma said: You're only eighteen and they won't let you go for another year. I know you'll go as soon as you can but when your dad died he left enough money for a year of college and I want you to use it.

They'll draft me right out of college, I told her, but Ma had a friend in the governor's office in Nashville and he fixed it for me to enlist and go to the university in the Army Specialized Training Program. That way they wouldn't draft me. And Bitsey, Ma said . . . if you're going to the war as soon as you can, you oughtn't to ask her till you come home. Isn't fair. What if you have a baby? Bitsey's mother must have said the same thing to her because she wouldn't even talk about getting married. So I went to the university till Christmas, when cousin Raiford got his leg blown off fighting Japs.

I talked to Ma's friend in Nashville and he fixed me up again. They're going to pull the plug on the ASTP, he said, and you'll be in the infantry. Right where I want to be, I told him, and he said: All right, but you ought to be an officer, Adam. He got me into Officer Candidate School at Fort Benning in Georgia and I graduated in August. Asked Ma to come see me get my lieutenant's bars but she was feeling poorly and she couldn't. I reckon I was kind of glad, he thought unhappily. If Bitsey came, Ma would be a problem.

He stared at the fading eye in the door of the stove. I sure made a mess of it. Bitsey came with a girl from Knoxville who had a friend in my class and he had a hot idea . . . two rooms in a motel in Columbus, right outside Fort Benning. One for each of us.

Why two? Bitsey wanted to know. Liz and I can share one. I lied. Said we have to take two or they won't give us any. Bitsey came to the army post to see me get my commission and after the parade she kissed me. We had supper in a hotel in Columbus and if I'd stopped right there it might have been okay but the stud said take her dancing, give her some drinks, and you'll be glad you got two rooms.

Georgia was bone dry but across the Chattahoochee River in Alabama was Phenix City with a wide-open roadhouse called Beachy Howard's. You could buy beer at Beachy's or bring a bottle of whiskey in a paper bag and Beachy would sell you Coke or ginger ale with a glass of ice for fifty cents a setup.

I got a bottle of Ten High bourbon and took Bitsey to Beachy Howard's place. Couldn't hear yourself think. A couple of hundred men on their way to war raising unshirted hell. Bitsey wouldn't take a drink. There was a stand-up comic, a fat sweaty little man with an old bat playing a piano, and Bitsey watched him like he had scales and a tail. He winked at her and sang her a song:

> I used to work in Chicago,
> in a department store.
> Used to work in Chicago,
> but now I don't anymore.
> Lady came in and wanted some cake,
> What kind? I asked at the door . . .

He raised his hands and I knew what was coming. Most everybody helped him with the rest of it:

> *Layer,* she said, and *layer* I did . . .
> And now I don't work anymore!"

Bitsey's face got red and she wrote on a napkin with her lipstick, "I WANT TO GO." Cost me ten dollars for a taxi to the motel. She jumped out and said: You better get him to take you wherever you're going, Adam. I tried to say something but she just shook her head. I know what you thought, Adam Talcut, she said. And you can just forget it.

Next morning she and Liz took the bus back to Tennessee before I could get to that damn motel. I wrote to her as soon as I got to my division in Indiana. Tried to see her when I had leave before we shipped out but I didn't. I wrote to her a lot but she never answered. I quit writing but I sent her a Christmas present from London, a little gold pin I bought in an antique store. I wonder if she'll write when she gets it? If the mail's all screwed up like Hyatt says, maybe she won't ever get it.

A German buzz bomb put-putted overhead, followed noisily by an antiaircraft gun, and Adam shivered. If you can't handle Bitsey, he asked himself, what makes you think you can lead a platoon of soldiers in a fight?

In the next two days he gathered money from the men of his company, a difficult job. Some balked when they saw he had no official receipt for them, only a handwritten note on a page torn from his notebook. Others denied they had any British pounds. In two days they had learned British money was more prized in Belgium than any kind of scrip printed by the U.S. Army. Adam kept his collection in the pockets of a cloth ammunition bandolier he wore around his waist like a money belt. The thought of losing it made him sweat. He wore it even when he slept because he was sure if it disappeared the army would figure out how much money was in it and deduct it from his pay.

On the fourteenth of December he wheedled a jeep from Lieutenant Strahl, the weapons platoon commander, to visit his outpost squad and take up any money they had. Ritchie accompanied him as guide and in Auw they found a company of the division engineer battalion improving the miserable logging trails through the forest to nearby artillery positions: a battalion of 105mm howitzers supporting the 422nd Infantry, northernmost regiment of the 106th Division on the Schnee Eifel, and the division's medium artillery battalion.

"Why are the 155's here?" Adam asked an engineer lieutenant. "They ought to be in the middle of the sector so they can support both ends."

"You know what's up there on our left?" The engineer pointed north.

"The 99th Division and some armored cavalry between us and them."

"What d'you think will happen if the krauts hit that tin-can cavalry?"

"If it's big they've had it. They'll get run over."

"Right. That's why our 155's are here—to help the cavalry if they get in trouble. Eighth Corps must have thought of it. There's two battalions of corps artillery on the river right behind us—big bastards—eight-inch howitzers and 4.5-inch guns. You going to take a look at the cavalry?"

"No, I've got a squad on outpost somewhere around here. I want to find it."

"Oh, yeah . . . at an old mill on a creek up there a way." The engineer pointed at a deep-rutted track branching east from the macadam road. "If you don't find 'em, turn around quick. They're the only thing between us and the krauts."

The jeep slid and bucked on the climbing track but Strahl's driver was good, he kept it moving and less than a thousand yards from Auw they topped a rise and Ritchie said stop. The slope dropped away from the track to a clearing in the trees with a creek snaking through it, a big stone building with a red tile roof full of holes on the near side of the frozen stream.

"They're in there?" Adam asked Ritchie.

"No, sir, they're in a bunker by the road a little way on."

The jeep lurched forward and stopped abruptly as a soldier appeared beside the track, pointing his rifle at them. "Halt!" he shouted. "Who goes there?"

The ritual demand struck Adam as ludicrous this close to the front line. He wanted to laugh but the soldier's serious face stopped him.

"It's me, Renisch . . . Lieutenant Talcut."

"Yessir. I heard you comin'."

"Where's Sergeant Buell?"

"In the bunker, sir. You want me to get him?"

"No, if you're on post, you better stay here. I'll find him."

Buell was a good squad leader. Adam had chosen him for this job because he thought Buell could handle it better than any other sergeant in the platoon. The outpost position bore that out.

The bunker was on the left of the road, dug into a hill thickly covered with small fir trees. The 2nd Division must have built it but Buell had improved it with a line of deep fighting holes just below the crest of the hill, looking down into the cup containing the old mill. At the bottom of the slope he had a good start on a barbed-wire barrier—three strands of wire on iron pickets with a roll of concertina wire strung in front.

"How come you don't stay in the mill?" Adam wanted to know.

"Krauts know right where it is. Second Division people said they throw a shell at it every day or so. Besides, it ain't got no floor . . . just a cellar full of water, all froze over."

The bunker had a log-and-earth roof thick enough to absorb light artillery shells and its interior was planked with a good floor and half a dozen bunks in tiers. There was also a stove, which was a surprise. Buell chuckled.

"I reckon they put it in before they finished the bunker an' they couldn't get it out the door when they left."

"What are you supposed to do here?"

"Just sit tight, far's I can tell, sir. 422nd Infantry command post is in a village about a thousand yards south of here. They send a foot patrol to the cav'ry in Kobscheid couple times a day and it comes back by here. We're to let them know if any krauts slip in but the 2nd Division took the phone when they pulled out. I had to get one off them engineers yesterday."

"Who can you talk to?"

"422nd command post and the cav'ry in Kobscheid. Engineers said they'd string a wire to us from Auw if we stay here."

"Rations . . . ammo?"

"Engineers, sir. We draw from them."

"Sounds like you've got it made, Buell."

"No sweat, sir."

"You need anything?"

"Mail, sir. Ain't had any since we left England."

"Hasn't been any," Adam told him. "Soon as we get some I'll see yours is sent up. You got any English or French money, Sergeant?"

Buell eyed him warily. "I ain't sure, Lieutenant. You need a loan?"

"No, Sergeant. Battalion wants to take up all that stuff and issue some kind of scrip that's good in Belgium. I have to collect from our company."

Buell's squad gave him a wad of paper bills but Buell cautiously contributed only some French franc notes. Adam gave him a receipt and did not ask for more, assuming the sergeant was holding out on him.

"Anything else . . . besides mail?"

"Private Lynch, sir. He wants to talk to the Lieutenant."

"Lynch?" Adam searched his memory.

"Got a girl knocked up at Camp Atterbury an' when we got the order to ship out he married her. Simple bastard thought he wouldn't have to go, I guess."

"So?"

"He left her in a trailer camp in Indiana an' he ain't heard from her since."

"Nobody's had any mail since we left England."

"I know that, Lieutenant, but Lynch says she's due an' he wants to know if she's all right."

"Oh, hell! What can I do?"

"Talk to him, sir," said Buell patiently.

Private Lynch might have been nineteen years old but he looked younger and even in the cold wind outside the bunker he sweated.

"I've got to know, sir. She's real young. She's scared and so am I. Those people in the trailer camp won't take care of her."

"Hasn't she got any family to look after her?"

"She didn't tell them, sir. She was afraid to."

"Have you talked to the chaplain?"

"Haven't seen one since we left the States, sir."

"All right . . . I'll see what I can find out."

"The Red Cross, sir? They told us they'd help if we had to get in touch with somebody at home."

He's right, thought Adam. Why didn't I remember that? There's a Red Cross man at Division.

"I'll tell them tomorrow, Lynch." He held out his notebook. "Write her name and address and I'll ask them to find out about her."

"Thank you, Lieutenant." The soldier wrote and handed back the notebook. "Thank you, sir . . . I'm real worried about her."

Adam put his hand on the boy's shoulder. "I'll let you know as soon as I get anything. Don't worry . . . those are good people in Indiana. They'll see she's all right."

It was almost five o'clock by the time the jeep made its way down the woods trail to Auw and night was closing in. An engineer sentry said they should take the macadam road south, the way they came. Skyline Drive, he called it.

"Krauts can't see you in the dark, Lieutenant, and it sure beats the trail through the woods to Andler. Go past a village called Radscheid and there's a fork in the road called Purple Heart Corner. Turn sharp north on that and it takes you to Schoenberg and Saint Vith. Password tonight is 'Whale' and if they don't say 'Boat,' floorboard that jeep and take off."

Most of the sentries on the road were cold, sleepy, and indifferent, but at Radscheid there was an alert guard, an antiaircraft artilleryman whose battery was dug in by the road.

"Krauts were here, Lieutenant . . . hit one of the infantry kitchens right after dark."

"423rd?" Adam asked. That was his regiment, in the old Siegfried Line bunkers on the southern end of the Schnee Eifel. Where I ought to be, he thought, instead of living easy in Hochkreuz.

"Yessir, they threw a grenade into the kitchen bunker—hurt a couple of men."

"Didn't they have a guard out?"

"Nosir. Krauts tried to cross the road here. We got one."

He flicked on a flashlight, the beam searching till it found a man on his back in the snow-clogged ditch beside the road—green overcoat, worn black boots, and a terrible face, upthrust by the chin strap of his helmet. A middle-aged man with a stubble of gray whiskers around his open mouth, eyes wide, glazed. The face was greenish-yellow, the flesh already sagging from the cheekbones, tobacco-stained teeth protruding from the pale lips.

"Jeez!" muttered Ritchie.

"Cut the light, soldier," said Adam, swallowing convulsively. "What happened to the rest of them?"

"Went back, sir. We called the infantry an' told 'em to watch out but they musta got by. Didn't hear any more shootin'."

"Dumb shit . . . shinin' that light," said Ritchie when they pulled away in the jeep. "How's he know they aren't still around here somewhere?"

Lieutenant Strahl's driver goosed the jeep, wheels spinning on the slick road. "Take it easy," Adam shouted over the snarl of the motor. "Watch for the turn."

"Where the hell have you been?" demanded Strahl when Adam reached Hochkreuz. "Is my jeep all right?"

"Sure, your driver has it."

"What've you been doing?"

"Had a look at Sergeant Buell's squad at the outpost."

"They all right?"

"Haven't seen a thing, but the krauts hit our regiment tonight. Patrol jumped somebody's kitchen."

"We heard about that. How'd you know?"

"Came back by Radscheid. The krauts crossed the road and got caught."

"What happened?"

"They turned 'em back. Killed one . . . I saw him."

"Congratulations," said Strahl dryly. "A dead kraut. That's more than we've seen."

Adam turned his back to the stove and absorbed its heat gratefully. He was cold to his bones and the death mask of the German in the ditch would not leave him.

What will they do with him? he wondered. Nobody told us what to do with dead krauts. Will his people ever know what happened to him?

"First," said Hyatt, grinning, "you get a drink. Kelso drew our booze ration in Vielsalm today. You can have Scotch or cognac."

"I hate Scotch," said Adam. "I'll try the cognac." His canteen cup gave it an aluminum flavor. "First?" he said, swallowing with difficulty. "What else is there?"

Hyatt pointed at a table someone had stolen for their billet and Adam choked on his cognac. A letter and a package addressed to him. Bitsey's handwriting.

"Told you, didn't I?" demanded Hyatt.

Adam put down the fiery drink and took Bitsey's letter. He did not tear it open. He waited until his hands stopped shaking and slit the envelope carefully with his pocketknife.

Dear Adam,

I saw your mother at the A&P store yesterday and she is fine. She asked if I hear from you and I told her yes and then I felt so bad I cried.

I must be the meanest girl in Tennessee, Adam, and I'm sorry I haven't answered your letters. Just because you were so awful at that place in Georgia is no excuse. You asked if I forgive you for that and I don't but I am truly sorry that I haven't written to you. . . .

He had to read that again to make sure he understood it. She's still mad but she wrote to me. Maybe she got the pin I sent from England. No, it was Ma—talking to Ma—that made her write. He looked at the package and hoped it was fudge. Bitsey made the best chocolate fudge in Laurel City. But first the letter:

. . . Your cousin Raiford sent word he wanted to see me, so Jackson took me up to Three Forks of Flint in his pickup truck. Raiford is all right. He showed me the fancy leg they gave him at the government hospital. I never saw one before and I hope I never see another one but it works real good. He can drive the tractor and he's learning how to drive an old Chevy he got somewhere.

Mama told me he has a woman living with him on the farm, one of the Corbys from Kirkwood, and you know how Mama feels about that, but she's a real nice girl and she takes good care of Raiford. I like her and I don't care if they aren't married. He talked about what happened to him on that island. He stepped on something that blew off his leg and I'm real glad he can talk about it now. When he first got home he wouldn't say anything.

He talked a lot about you. He said maybe the army will teach you to shoot good enough so you can get a deer when you come home. Old Sebe says that buck you shot at on Bedford Mountain is still there and they are saving it for you.

He gave me a whole ham to make Christmas dinner for me and Mama and a five-gallon can of gasoline for Jackson's truck. I told him I'd get some ration coupons and send them to him but his girl, Ellen, said not to bother. He gets lots of gas for his tractor and they have plenty. She was so nice. She gave me some sausage and a dozen eggs. Mama still won't like her but I bet she uses the eggs.

Raiford gave me something to send you for Christmas and said don't send him socks or anything like that because he needs this more. I think it's wicked but maybe he's right. He said Ellen's daddy makes it and it is the best corn whiskey in Tennessee. Raiford likes it but he says he is a marine and he doesn't know what it will do to a soldier. He tried to make me taste it but it smells so awful I was afraid to . . .

Adam opened the package, lifted a flat pint bottle from it, and shuddered. Poor Bitsey, no wonder she wouldn't taste it. Corn whiskey ought to be white but this was rust-colored and the neck of the bottle was clogged with pale shapeless things. He held the bottle upside down and some of them rose slowly through the murky liquid.

"Your girl sent you that for Christmas?" asked Kelso in awe.

Adam turned Bitsey's letter over. She had covered both sides of the flimsy airmail paper with small crowded words and it was hard to read but he felt better about what was in the bottle when he got past Raiford's attempt to make her taste it.

. . . Raiford said he put some wine in to color it. To-kay wine, I think he said, and don't worry about those things in the top of the bottle. They are just canned cherries and you can eat them. He put them in to fill it up so it won't gurgle because he says if soldiers are like marines the ones who bring the mail will steal it if it gurgles.

Bud Morrison's people had a telegram from the army that he was wounded in Italy. It must be pretty bad because they haven't heard from him yet but the Red Cross wrote and said he was taken to England on an airplane. Is that where they take you if you are hurt real bad?

Adam, please be careful. Don't get hurt . . .

There was a gap and the letter began again, more neatly and carefully written.

I had to help Mama in the kitchen. She is awful. She says Raiford is a disgrace and she won't even talk about his Ellen but she's pleased about the eggs.

Oh, Adam, what a fool I am. How can you be careful in a war? I guess what I mean is be lucky.

Tomorrow is Sunday and I will pray that you are as lucky as you are bad. Dr. Parker always asks about you after church and now I won't feel so awful when he does.

I hope you have a good Christmas, Adam. I ought not to send you whiskey but Raiford says it is what you need. I couldn't let Mama know so I sent you some pecan divinity in another package and let her see that.

Be lucky, Adam, and come home just like you used to be before you went in the army. I miss you, Adam. Please don't get hurt.

Next morning, the fifteenth, he did not eat with the other lieutenants; he brought his powdered eggs and Vienna sausages to his billet and ate them sitting on his cot, reading his letter again. When the others returned, Hyatt laughed at him.

"Come off it, Adam . . . you'll get another."

There were still men in the company from whom he had collected no money: some sergeants had been sent up to other companies of the regiment on the Schnee Eifel to find out what happened on the front line. He reported to his company commander.

"If I had a vehicle, sir, I could clean it up but it'll take a week if I have to hitch rides to find them all."

"No jeep—can't spare one. How much have you got?"

Adam displayed the bandolier.

"How much money, Talcut?"

"Sir, I can tell you how many pounds and francs but I don't know what they're worth in dollars."

"Turn it in. Get rid of it but get a receipt from somebody for it."

Adam caught a ride on an empty supply truck going to Saint Vith and division headquarters. There he wandered through the echoing rooms of the Sankt Josefs Kloster, originally a complex of convent and school buildings, once used by the German Army as a hospital. When the 2nd Division occupied the town in the fall of 1944 they took the place for their headquarters, covering the big red cross on the roof with a tarpaulin. That, at least, they did not take with them when they left Saint Vith to the 106th Division—it was still stretched over the roof.

The division staff officers seemed zealous in rules and practice brought from Indiana, not yet adjusted to the proximity of a war. Nobody in the adjutant general's office wanted anything to do with his money; they sent him searching for a representative of the division finance officer. The captain who did that work in Saint Vith was appalled.

"Didn't they give you a pay roster?"

"No, sir. The company commander said take up the money and turn it in."

"My God, Lieutenant . . . how do we know who you got it from?"

Adam showed him his notebook. "I have their names and how much they gave me."

"You gave them a receipt?"

"Yes, sir. I wrote down the man's name and how much he turned in and gave him a receipt for it."

"Out of that notebook?"

"Yes, sir. I signed them."

"Were you on orders as an agent finance officer?"

"No, sir."

"Illegal! What do you think would happen if you lost that money?"

"I think about it all the time, sir. Will you have it counted and give me a receipt for it?"

"I will not! I'll report your company commander for damn foolishness. That's what I'll do!"

"Yes, sir. What do I do with the money?" Adam had a terrible suspicion the Finance Corps captain was going to say give it back to the men he got it from.

"Report to the division finance officer in Vielsalm and tell him how you got into this mess. He'll know what to do."

"Yes, sir. Captain, can you lend me a jeep to get there?"

"Absolutely not. Go to the provost marshal's office and tell him you need a ride to Vielsalm."

Adam waited until early afternoon for a jeep or truck, which never materialized. He found a Red Cross van where a tired pretty American girl handed out doughnuts and coffee. The doughnuts were armored in fried grease but just watching the girl was a pleasure.

There seemed no hope of getting to Vielsalm so he caught a ride back to Hochkreuz and told Captain Polk that nobody at Division wanted his money and the only finance officer there thought the whole affair was illegal. Polk snorted in disgust.

"All right, dammit! I'll send you to Vielsalm tomorrow. Right now I've got another job for you. Sergeant Buell got through on the cavalry phone switch. He's got a German deserter and the battalion commander wants to talk to him before the military police get him. I told Strahl to give you a jeep and driver and I want you to go get that kraut. Take one of your men for a guard and get going."

Ritchie, summoned to act as guard for the prisoner, had a suggestion. "I went to Schoenberg today, Lieutenant, and I know a shortcut to Andler. We can cross the river there and get to Auw real easy."

"What were you doing in Shoenberg?"

"First sergeant sent me, sir, with some men from the communications platoon. They strung a wire from Battalion to the division switching center in Schoenberg. They didn't go through Saint Vith. They took a trail from Meyerode to Andler and we laid the wire that way."

"It'll be dark before we can start back. You sure you know the way?"

"Always know the way home, Lieutenant."

Ritchie's track through the forest from Meyerode to Andler was scary: a deeply rutted trail winding through woods so thick it was pitch dark beneath the trees by four o'clock. In some places the road was so cut up by armored vehicles that Adam had to get out and lead the driver through the frozen ruts.

They passed through a hamlet called Herresbach and knew it only because they were stopped by engineers billeted there. They were Army Engineers, no part of the 106th Division, operating a sawmill cutting planks to build bunkers. By the time they reached Andler it was genuinely dark, a few glimmers of light from blacked-out windows marking the village, and another mile brought them to Auw.

Climbing the steep slope to the outpost got them in trouble. Both Ritchie and Adam dismounted to push, trying to keep the jeep on the track, but it slipped and skidded, finally sliding into a ditch so deep they could not get it out.

"We'll have to walk," announced Adam. "Bring the distributor cap with you," he told the driver. "If the krauts find the jeep, let's hope they don't have one."

Buell was glum. "The 422nd sent a patrol for that deserter, Lieutenant. He's been gone an hour."

"How'd they know he was here?"

"You get on the phone, sir, and ever'body in the American army gets on with you—krauts too, I reckon."

He walked with Adam and Ritchie back to the jeep and grunted. "No way, Lieutenant. Let it sit . . . we'll get a truck off the engineers in the mornin' and snatch it outta there."

"Can you get Battalion on the phone again?"

"I don't get Battalion, sir. Only line that works goes to the cav'ry in Kobscheid. If I can still get them, they'll pass a message back for you." In the bunker someone gave him coffee and Adam questioned Buell about the German deserter.

"I don't know what he was, Lieutenant. A real eight ball. No weapon, no ammunition. Corporal Holtz talks Pennsylvania Dutch and he says that dummy can't speak German."

"What do you think he is?"

"Mlotkowski got a little out of him. He talks some kind of bohunk. He says this jerk might be Russki. He

told Mlotkowski he quit because the krauts are goin'
to make a big attack right before Christmas."

"How the hell can they do that? Somebody would
have heard them getting ready for it."

"Those people from the 422nd heard a lot of noise
last night. They reported it and Division said the krauts
know we just got here an' they're playin' phonograph
records on a loudspeaker to spook us."

"You heard anything?"

"Nuthin', sir. I wouldn't believe anything that crazy
jerk said. He told Mlotkowski the krauts are goin' to
use big searchlights when they attack. Point 'em at the
sky and light up everything like the moon was out.
That's bullshit, Lieutenant. He's a deserter an' he'll
tell you anything."

He gave Adam one of the bunks, tiered two high on
the walls of the bunker, saying it would be unused.
"Sack out, sir. No sweat, we'll get your jeep on the
road first thing in the morning."

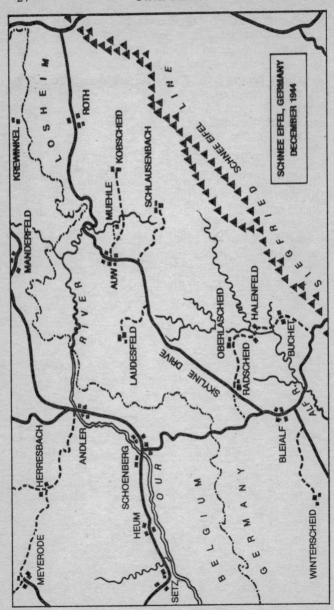

SCHNEE EIFEL, GERMANY
DECEMBER 1944

2

ADAM SAT up so abruptly he drove his head into the slats of the bunk above him. The absolute darkness of the frigid bunker was illuminated by spinning light. It diminished and he listened in awe to the crescendo of sound that had awakened him.

"Fuckin' engineers!" muttered a voice in the gloom.

The slab door of the bunker crashed open to admit more noise, a dim flickering light, and the rasping voice of Sergeant Buell.

"Off yer ass an' in yer holes! Move, dammit!"

"Jus' cause them friggin' dirt-daubers is gone on night shift?"

"That's kraut artillery, Renisch. Move, I said!"

Adam toed the door shut and used his cigarette lighter to find his boots. Shoving his feet into them, he dragged on his overcoat and lunged out of the bunker. It was no less dark outside than in it, but the rumbling explosions to the west were accompanied by a pulsing glow that reflected on low-hanging clouds. Atop the bunker in the snow-crusted firs he bumped into Buell, swearing furiously at each occupant of the shelter as he emerged.

"Riordan, you help Cotter on the .50-caliber. Get all them boxes of ammo up by the gun. Where the hell is Gumbart?"

"Right here, Sarge."

"Got your weapon?"

"Sure, Sarge."

"All right . . . take all the magazines you can carry an' get in yer hole. Don't nobody fire a shot till I tell you. Pass the word to the guys on the line and make sure every one of them meatheads is awake."

"Sarge, you sure that ain't our own stuff?"

"Yeah, Cotter . . . I'm sure. It don't sound like that goin' away."

"The infantry on the ridge isn't getting any," protested Adam. "Maybe they're just checkin' our oil?"

Buell's hand found Adam's helmet in the dark, turned his head to the north. "Lissen, Lootenant!"

Far away, beneath the crump of artillery shells falling somewhere in that direction, was the breathless mutter of machine-gun fire. "That's the cav'ry. They're catchin' somethin' an' if they bug out we're gonna get it next. Better get in my hole, Lootenant. Room enough fer two."

There was plenty of room. It was a deep hole with a roof of saplings and sandbags on top and a log step to stand on and shoot through the firing slit beneath the roof. Adam put his carbine in the slit and crouched to use the cigarette lighter to check his watch.

Five-thirty. Two hours till daylight. He shivered convulsively and remained crouched to lace and buckle his boots. Before he finished, the noise toward Auw stopped, and shortly after he stood up to peer with Buell into the darkness, so did the mutter of firing in the north. The total silence was appalling.

"What now?" he whispered to Buell.

"Beats the shit outta me, Lootenant."

"It's over?"

"Hell, no. They ain't wastin' all that stuff jus' to pick on a cav'ry outpost. I'm gonna check the holes."

"All right. I'll take the ones on this side."

"Four of 'em. There's rifle ammo under that bunk you was in. Take a couple bandoliers for each hole an' tell those bastards to stay awake."

"I don't know," Adam answered the question asked at each foxhole he visited. "I don't know what's happening but you stay awake, you hear?"

"Sheeit! I ain't ever goin' to sleep again. You think they'll sneak up on us in the dark, Lootenant?"

"Can't. Snow's frozen. You'll hear anybody coming through it. Don't shoot till you get the word though."

When Adam returned, Buell was back in his hole, muttering obscenities at something in the dark. "Goddamn rifle grenades!" he grunted, and Adam was puzzled.

One man in every squad—rarely its leader—had an adapter fitted to the muzzle of his rifle so he could fire off a clumsy arrangement of a finned tube with claws at the front to hold a hand grenade. It was difficult to assemble even in daylight and required a special crimped cartridge in the rifle. Though it hurled a grenade farther than a man could throw, accuracy was not one of its virtues.

"You like those things?"

"Hell, no! Somebody left 'em here an' I'm tryin' to take 'em apart. I want the grenades."

For half an hour there was intolerable silence and darkness, then a fresh thunder of artillery fire to the north. A strange luminescence glowed on the clouds as if they were lit from within. Adam thought it was some kind of natural phenomenon like northern lights but it moved from cloud to cloud.

"I be goddamn!" breathed Buell. "Jus' like that deserter said."

"What?"

"Searchlights! He said when the krauts attack they're gonna point searchlights at the clouds."

Maybe on open fields it made a difference but under the thick fir trees it was dark as ever. The cavalry was really catching something now: machine guns again and that booming must have been their big antitank guns. The uproar continued, rising and falling but not stopping. There was a faint edge of real dawn light now beneath the strange glow created by the Germans.

Across the creek, branches rustled and something plunged through the frozen crust of snow with a clatter. Adam's heart jumped but he heard the snort of a frightened animal and laughed shakily.

"What the hell was that?" demanded Buell.

"Wild pig. Lots of tracks by the creek." He relaxed for a moment. Just like being on stand before dawn in the Tellico mountains back home. A smart old boar would hear the dogs coming and bolt through the gunners before anybody was ready for him.

His chest tightened again. There were no hounds to drive that boar. "Buell," he whispered.

"Yeah?"

"Something spooked him. Better make sure everybody's ready."

"Yessir."

Adam felt a small glow of pride. For the first time, there was a note of respect in Buell's voice. He took the four holes to the right, as before, but this time he began at the one farthest away and worked back toward the middle of the line. He made so much noise crawling through the snow that he heard nothing else. When he reached the last foxhole before Buell's there was light enough to see the face of the soldier in it. Adam froze, and the man gestured violently.

More wild pigs? They never moved in herds large enough to make that much noise and they never moved so slowly if they were scared. Adam searched the thick wall of trees sixty or seventy yards beyond the mill and swallowed convulsively.

At the edge of the clearing stood a man in a long green overcoat, his waist belt sagging with the weight of fat black leather cartridge pouches and a couple of stick grenades. Beneath his helmet he wore a sort of ski mask snug around his face. He stepped into the open, raised a hand, and magically there were more—more than Adam could count—emerging from the firs.

It was like a slow-motion movie: the Germans wallowing through the snow. A little way into the open they stopped. Some dropped to one knee and aimed their rifles at the mill; one hurled something awkwardly and after a moment there was a muffled explosion inside the stone building. He had thrown a grenade through a window.

There was a ragged volley of rifle fire and some-

where in the forest a machine gun erupted in a breathless clatter. Snow and fragments of tile spouted from
the steep mill roof. The machine-gunner was downhill
from the building, firing through the window, and his
long burst came out through the roof on Adam's side.

The infantrymen crouching in the snow rose reluctantly, making an unenthusiastic lowing noise. A few
fired at the mill but most just resumed their awkward
wallowing toward it. Adam scrambled into Buell's hole
and the sergeant did not even look at him.

"They think we're in there!" he hissed.

"They'll get inside!" gasped Adam. "We got to stop
'em!"

"Ain't no floor, Lieutenant. Just a hole full of water. They get in there, the ice'll break and they'll
drown."

"But they'll get behind the damn thing!"

"You're right about that." Buell triggered off a wild
unaimed shot from his rifle and bawled hoarsely: "Open
up! Let 'em have it!"

The response was instant and appalling: eight rifles,
a Browning automatic rifle, and a .50-caliber machine
gun all firing as fast as possible. Adam joined them,
the popping of his carbine lost in the uproar. So many
plumes of snow spurted around the Germans they
made a mist in which they swayed and howled like
creatures in a nightmare. They disappeared into the
forest much faster than they had come, leaving half a
dozen bodies in the snow. After a moment of thunderous silence, one got up and lunged for the trees.

Buell emptied his rifle, the blast of firing ending
abruptly with the twang of the ejected clip. The German was on his knees, head down, calling urgently for
something. "Sanni . . . Sanni!" he groaned, and except for his desperate plea, there was silence.

Incredibly, a German soldier pushed through the
firs and trudged toward him. He had red cross bras-
sards on both arms and a sort of bib of white cloth
with a big red cross on it; no weapon, only a canvas
bag he held out to be seen. He kept his head down as

if watching his footing, but Adam guessed there was something else too: maybe he thought if he didn't look at the Americans they wouldn't shoot.

"Jeez!" muttered Buell. "He's got guts!" He scrambled out, calling urgently: "Don't shoot that medic! Anybody need ammo?"

I ought to go help him, thought Adam, but he could not take his eyes from the German kneeling by the wounded soldier. After a while the aid-man picked up his sack and went back to the forest. At the edge he jerked his hand in a vague sort of gesture: thanks, maybe. More likely a signal, because the machine gun erupted at once—a breathless snarl unlike any American gun.

They didn't know how to position it though. It was too close to the edge of the trees and Adam could see branches jerking in its muzzle blast. So could Cotter at the .50-caliber, and his big gun roared, throwing up snow and cut branches until he found his target and the German gun stopped. The soldier the aid-man had come out to help was on his back, overcoat and jacket unbuttoned. His bare chest gleamed in the dawn light, white except for a smudge of dark hair. Dead, Adam guessed, or that crazy medic would have dragged him off.

It took a while for someone to get the Germans in the woods in order. Like sitting at a play, Adam thought, with the curtain down—listening to stage hands moving things behind it and swearing. There was a lot of noise in the woods up the hill across the stream, and Adam supposed the Germans had their own Fort Benning somewhere to teach lieutenants how to flank an enemy position. There was a long minute of deadly silence, broken finally by a resonant explosive *Tchug!*

"Mortar," hissed Buell. "Here they come!"

He was right. On wooden bleachers at Fort Benning, Adam had sat behind a line of riflemen supported by machine guns and mortars, all blasting away in a demonstration of infantry firepower. Down-range, pasteboard silhouette targets jerked and splintered and blew away and he had wondered in awe if anything could live in that firestorm. It could—he was alive on the wrong side of the demonstration, the log-and-earth cover over the foxhole disintegrating in a howling cyclone of bullets.

The mortar gunners were better drilled than their friends on the machine gun. Their first shell burst somewhere behind Adam and they did not bracket their target—they corrected their aim and there was an apocalypse of stunning explosions directly overhead, the shells bursting as they plunged into the firs, spraying the ground with deadly fragments of steel.

Above this nightmare of sound he heard the shrill incongruous blast of a whistle and someone bellowing: "*Marschiert . . . Marschiert schnell!*"

They're coming . . . get up and shoot or they'll be all over us.

He stood up with more reluctance than he had ever moved in his life. There were Germans all over the snowy hillside, thrashing forward in frantic haste, firing their rifles and yelling—a sort of desperate screeching. The man with the whistle came behind them, waving a machine pistol and yelling: "*Los . . . marschiert!*"

The .50-caliber machine gun roared briefly and was blotted out by a salvo of mortar shells. The black empty window on the side of the mill facing the hillock flamed orange and Adam wondered how the gunner had got across the gaping hole where the floor used to be. He pointed his carbine at the mill and jerked the trigger, kept on jerking till there was no more recoil.

Buell was yelling at him, scrambling out the back entry to the hole. "Out! Get outta there!"

Adam was fumbling at the carbine. Like all green Americans armed with the underpowered little weapon, he had taped a full clip, mouth down to the one loaded in the carbine. You were supposed to jerk out the pair, reverse them, and jam in the loaded clip, but that was an operation requiring some precision. When he released the empty clip, both of them fell to the bottom of the hole. Buell was pounding his shoulder.

"Come on, Lootenant!"

"Gotta stop 'em!" There were two full clips in a canvas pocket on the stock of the carbine but he couldn't get it open.

"Nobuddy said we gotta die on this fuckin' hill!" bellowed the sergeant. "Get outta there!"

Maybe the attacking Germans were so close their machine guns had to stop. Bullets cracked viciously through the trees but not the storm of a few minutes ago. They were close, Adam knew, because he heard the flat twanging bark of exploding hand grenades. He collided violently with one of his men who had just erupted from his foxhole—Renisch, mouth open, eyes blank in terror. Adam shoved him hard.

"Run! That way . . ." He pointed at the woods track toward Auw, and Renisch shook his head numbly.

"Nah . . . nah-uh!"

For a moment Adam thought he wanted to stay and fight but that wasn't what Renisch wanted. He put his hands on top of his helmet and staggered like a drunken man toward the edge of the trees. Renisch had just declared a separate peace and Adam wondered as he scrambled down the back of the knoll if the Germans were accepting private peace offers.

He ran. He ran until he caught up with Sergeant Buell, passed him, and thought: It won't look good if I'm first out. He slowed, gasping; Buell forged ahead and Adam never caught up with him again.

The engineers in Auw lived in a big farmhouse with an attached barn and a lot of stone outhouses. He staggered into one of those to find half a dozen engineers clutching rifles and staring at him. At the back of the shed on wooden sawhorses, their company gas stove was hissing cheerfully, pots and pans atop it.

"Better get down, Lieutenant. Krauts in the woods up there."

Buell appeared with Ritchie, Adam's messenger, grinning happily. "Thought they got you, sir."

A German machine pistol uttered its characteristic burp of noise in the forest north of the village and more engineers came trotting along the road, looking over their shoulders.

"Woods is full of the bastards!" panted one of them. "God damn, Stubby, don't just stand there suckin' down my breakfast . . . get the bazooka off the truck. There's a tank on the road."

"A tank?" demanded someone, and Adam saw it was an officer, the white bar of a first lieutenant painted on his helmet under the camouflage netting.

"A hell of a lotta krauts, sir, comin' up the road from that town where the cavalry was. All I seen was infantry but they got a tank with 'em too."

"You saw it?"

"Nosir, but I heard the friggin' thing."

"All right, get the bazooka out where you can cover the road. Timothy, you help him."

Adam recovered enough breath to gasp at Buell, "How many did we lose?"

"I'll get a count, sir. Cotter's dead an' I guess Riordan got it too. Goddamn mortar put one right in the hole with the fifty."

"Renisch," said Adam bitterly. "He wouldn't come."

"He give up?"

"He was tryin' to. I don't know if he—"

"Godalmighty . . . look out!" yelled a man at the front of the shed.

There was no mistaking the clusters of men leaking out of the forest. Some wore makeshift white smocks over their green coats—bedsheets, they looked like. They were so close Adam saw the ski masks were just big knit socks with the toes cut out, pulled over their heads. They were shooting into the houses and when they saw the Americans they came at a lumbering run, making a more triumphant noise than their comrades at the mill.

Adam flung himself under a cart, got a magazine into his carbine. One engineer stayed; the rest ran out the back of the shed, taking Buell and Ritchie with them.

"Shoot, Lieutenant!" yelled Adam's companion. Three Germans ran at them, boots pounding on the cobblestones. Bayonets—they've got bayonets on their rifles, was Adam's only coherent thought. His hands shook and his breath came in panting gasps. The engineer kicked him. "Shoot, goddammit!"

His rifle blasted Adam's ear and Adam knew he was jerking wild shots from his own weapon because the carbine kicked him savagely in the mouth. The Germans scattered, yelling, and a grenade bounced and rolled over the cobbles—not the usual stick grenade but a little round one.

"Down!" yelled Adam. "Get down!"

That was a mindless warning—they were both as flat on the stone floor of the shed as possible. The grenade exploded with a snapping twang but there were no fragments, only blast. The engineer scrambled from under the cart and Adam rolled after him to crouch behind the building.

"*Schnell . . . schnell, Brandt!*" The Germans were in the shed, and through a window Adam saw one of them fumbling with another grenade. He pushed the muzzle of his carbine over the sill and emptied the weapon as fast as he could pull the trigger. Even at a dozen feet he missed. The German dropped the grenade and ran.

Squatting, Adam loaded his last magazine with shaking fingers. Another of those astounding silences had suddenly occurred. Someone in the shed coughed and groaned but that was all—no more shooting, no more yelling. Adam crawled to the door at the back of the shed, peered in, and recoiled violently.

The German was so close he could smell him—a sour odor of sweat and rank tobacco. His eyes, wild and desperate, were not looking at Adam. They stared at the tile roof. It dawned on Adam with almost sensual relief that the man was dead. Not a man . . . just a boy trying to grow a mustache, a scatter of soft black whiskers on his lip, something fat and pink clenched between his big yellow teeth. ·The engineer crawled closer to look.

"What'sa matter, Lieutenant?"

"His tongue—"

"That ain't his tongue. We had weenies for breakfast an' that sonovabitch was eatin' one when you shot him. Looks comical, don't he?"

I shot him? Adam took another quick look at the dead German. I didn't even see him. I shot at the one who ran away. There was a crowd behind the shed now, half a dozen more engineers with the lieutenant who wanted to get a tank with a bazooka. They had a prisoner, a German as young as the one Adam had killed. His helmet gone, his hands were clenched on top of his head, long blond hair falling over his face.

A soldier asked him questions in fluent German, translating the terrified answers for the lieutenant. Damned engineers have everything, Adam thought, even soldiers that speak German.

"He's in the 294th Volksgrenadier Regiment. Sounds like they came through the cavalry in the Gap. He says the Amis ran away."

"Amis?"

"That's what they call us. Short for *Amerikaner*, I guess."

"Damn! If the cavalry's gone we're wide open on that flank. The 294th is one of the regiments of the 18th Volksgrenadier Division. Were the others with the 294th?"

The young German was shivering, watching with fearful eyes. His questioner nagged at him and he muttered answers.

"He says the 295th was with them. He doesn't know anything about another regiment."

"The 293rd," said the lieutenant, writing hurriedly in a notebook. "Have they got tanks with them?"

The engineer soldier and the prisoner worked on that question for a while. "He doesn't call 'em tanks, Lieutenant. He says they're *Sturmgeschuetze*."

"Assault guns. Probably 75-millimeter gun on a tank chassis. How many?"

"He doesn't know . . . just says there were lots of them. They had to build plank ramps for them over those concrete things that stick up in front of the old bunker line. His sergeant told them they couldn't blow a gap because the Amis would hear it."

"If we did," muttered the lieutenant, "division would say they're playing phonograph records to scare us." He jabbed his pencil at the scared Volksgrenadier.

"What's the name of your regimental commander?" The youngster flinched, stammered a reply when the question was put in German.

"Doesn't know," translated the engineer linguist. "His squad leader is Corporal Steiner and the company commander is a lieutenant but he doesn't know his name."

"Sounds like they're as green as we are. All right, get him out of here."

"You old enough to smoke, bub?" asked one of the onlookers, sticking a cigarette between the German's lips. The boy took a long drag and burst into a fit of coughing. The engineers laughed at him.

"Pore little shit," said someone. "We ain't that bad off, Lieutenant."

Buell had gathered six men, all he could find of his squad from the outpost. The engineers fired up their stove again and someone gave Adam three hot frankfurters on a slice of white bread. He wolfed down the strange breakfast, trying not to think of the dead German boy with a hot dog protruding from his mouth.

The war suddenly revived with a roar of firing at the northern edge of the village. The engineers jumped for their fighting holes and Adam crouched with Buell behind the shed. For a little while there was a standoff until a tracked vehicle roared and squealed to the edge of the forest and began blowing holes in the houses. Adam saw it and thought the engineer lieutenant was crazy—if that wasn't a tank, he had never seen one.

The pair of engineers with the bazooka took a shot

at the thing and missed, but the rocket hit a tree, exploding with such a blast the German gun scuttled away. It came back though and more behind it. They shelled Auw with methodical accuracy and the engineers pulled out. Adam gave them credit—they didn't run. At least they ran slowly and some of them kept up a steady fire—at what, he was not sure. The German Volksgrenadiers hung back but the tanks or assault guns or whatever they were continued to hurl shells into Auw.

"Where the hell are the people who live here?" Adam gasped at the engineer lieutenant.

"In their cellars . . . been there all night. I should have known something was up."

"How?"

"Right before dark yesterday . . . girl went to every house in the place. She must have told 'em it was coming. I bet she's got a radio and the krauts know all about us."

The engineer company got its trucks out of Auw and loaded most of its men, leaving a squad of riflemen to cover the withdrawal. Buell watched enviously.

"We goin' with 'em, sir? They said they're goin' to Schoenberg."

"Let 'em go. We're staying."

"Here? Hell, Lootenant . . . we can't stop a whole regiment with half a dozen men! That engineer squad'll bug out soon's their trucks are clear."

Adam shook his head. "Buell, I don't think the krauts are going anywhere. I think this was a local attack. They'll back off and I want to be here when they do."

Buell gave him a black look. "Excuse me askin', sir, but what in hell are we goin' to do up here all by our lonesome?"

"Get that jeep out of the ditch. Captain Polk'll have my ass if I leave it here."

"Gentul Jeezus!" muttered Buell, staring hopelessly at the departing trucks.

It looked for a while as if Adam were right: the

Volksgrenadiers stopped in Auw—but they advanced again. Finished the engineers' breakfast, he thought grimly, and their officers kicked them out. They advanced cautiously, but they were not to be stopped by a lieutenant and seven scared infantrymen. Buell was right about the engineer squad. As soon as their trucks were gone, they faded away.

Where the trail from Schlausenbach and the Schnee Eifel joined the main road, there was an artillery outpost with a bazooka and a section of antiaircraft artillery—a 40-millimeter gun and a "quad .50," four .50-caliber machine guns in a rotating mount on the back of a half-track. Down the slope to the west a battalion of 105mm howitzers was firing in battery volleys. Adam left Buell at the outpost and went looking for an officer.

He found a captain who said the 422nd Infantry on the Schnee Eifel was calling for fire on its left flank; the cavalry in the Losheim Gap had fallen back and there were Germans on the road to Auw.

"They're already there," Adam told him, "and they'll be here pretty quick."

"Don't get panicky, Lieutenant. Have you seen any Germans?"

"Sir, I had a squad at Schlausenbach Mill and they hit us at daylight. Some of us made it to Auw and they drove us out of there."

"There's a whole company of engineers in Auw! They haven't told us they're being attacked."

"Ask your outpost on the road, sir. The engineers bugged out with their trucks an hour ago."

The irritated captain spun the handle of his field telephone and Adam watched his face with some satisfaction. "Goddamn!" he exploded. "They ought to have told us they were pulling out. Maybe we ought to get out of here too."

It was too late. The Germans were already astride the woods trail which was the only escape route for one battery and their attack south along Skyline Drive would soon cut off the other two.

The outpost on the road stopped the first assault gun. The quad .50 scattered its Volksgrenadier escort and the artillerymen broke its track with a bazooka rocket. The crippled gun continued to bark, throwing shells into the nearest battery position.

Most of the gunners ran for cover but a lieutenant and a couple of men stayed with one howitzer. They cranked the muzzle down as far as it would go and slammed a high-explosive shell into the German gun with spectacular results. The engine flamed and the ammunition racked inside the turret began to cook off. Some of it was white phosphorus and none of the crew got out.

The artillerymen buzzed like a hornet's nest overturned. They tried to get their howitzers on the road but the Germans made a deadly bowling alley of it with their guns which were out of sight toward Auw. The American artillerymen kept one battery in action, setting fuze as short as they could, plastering the road and surrounding forest. They stopped the Volksgrenadiers, who apparently would not advance without artillery support, and their assault guns had grown cautious. Maybe they couldn't move off the ridge road and they could see the smoking monument to what happened if they stayed on it.

Adam went back to his men at the artillery outpost and in a little while there was a swelling roar of firing in the valley between Skyline Drive and the Schnee Eifel.

"The 422nd sent a company to help us," said the artilleryman at the field phone. "They'll drive the krauts back so we can get out of here."

It was idle hope. The infantry counterattack stopped before it reached the road and from the noise in the valley Adam could guess why. The Germans who had taken his mill must have got to them.

By four-thirty it was dark. The gusts of rain blowing across the road turned to sleet, then snow, and there was either a hell of a fog or Skyline Drive was so high it was in the clouds. Nobody, German or American, went hunting for a fight in this misery but after a while some kind of vehicle crept up the road from the south. The artillerymen reversed their bazooka and waited for it nervously.

"Sounds like a jeep," muttered Adam.

"Yeah . . . but who's in it? Krauts maybe?"

True, thought Adam. He knew one jeep they had. A figure appeared in the swirling mist and someone hissed, "Halt! Put your hands up!"

"Don't shoot!" urged the figure, one hand high, the other jamming a flashlight under his chin. He had put the little white celluloid disk that came with a GI flashlight into the lens so it emitted only a soft glow that just lit his terrified face. He looked like a child playing a Halloween trick.

"What's the password?"

"Mule . . . mule!"

"Train," growled the artilleryman, giving the countersign. "What the hell are you doin' here?"

Sergeant Buell peered at the apparition on the road. "Voegler? That you?"

"Yeah!" The sigh of relief was explosive. "Yeah! Sergeant Buell?"

"Is the company coming up here?"

"The whole fuckin' battalion, Sarge."

"They're here? Behind you?"

"Naw, just Lootenant Strahl . . . in the jeep. I better go get him."

He disappeared, the jeep motor growled, and two tiny spots of light materialized in the dark, the cat's-eyes for blacked-out night driving. Voegler walked ahead of the jeep, his shuttered flashlight its guide.

"Turn it around," Adam heard Strahl tell the driver, "and get it off the road but don't get stuck, you hear?"

When he put his head over the edge of the sandbagged revetment, Adam rapped a knuckle on his helmet. "Hello, Dad. What's up?"

Strahl commanded the weapons platoon, a position calling for a first lieutenant but he had never received the promotion and was the oldest second lieutenant in the company. The junior lieutenants suspected he was older than the company commander and called him Dad.

"Adam! Goddamn, we thought the krauts got you. Where's my jeep?"

"They got it . . . damn near got me too. What are you doin' here? Where's the battalion?"

"Schoenberg. We pulled out of Hochkreuz this mornin'. Stopped at Saint Vith awhile and then went to Schoenberg. Battalion commander says we got orders to get the artillery back across the river and he sent me to find 'em. Where are they?"

"Right here . . . one battalion anyway."

"Yeah, I met the 155's on the road. They lost one gun section and a kitchen truck . . . missed the turn at Radscheid and ran into a kraut artillery barrage on Purple Heart Corner."

Strahl talked to the light artillery battalion commander who said he couldn't get out without infantry help so Strahl went back to Schoenberg to guide his battalion forward. It was long after midnight before the blacked-out convoy of trucks grumbled up the road. They stopped well short of the artillery position, unloaded the infantry, and somehow managed to turn around to go back to Saint Vith.

Adam found his company commander whose anger about a lost jeep had subsided somewhat. In the wet darkness, he took his platoon into the forest north of the artillery position. Somehow, a line was established and the men began digging foxholes. They were cold and wet but occasional bursts of German fire overcame that. Adam walked the line, feeling with his hands each hole to make sure it was deep enough to protect its occupants; two men in each. Ritchie found him in the dark to say the company commander wanted all officers at the artillery command post bunker.

No one seemed to believe the Germans were serious, though Captain Polk told the platoon leaders he had heard in Schoenberg that Bleialf at the southern end of the Schnee Eifel had been taken early in the day.

"The antiaircraft people on the road say our regiment took it back this afternoon," said Lieutenant Sears. He was company executive officer, Captain Polk's second in command, and the only first lieutenant in the company. He was a serious, bespectacled young officer, not given to peddling rumors.

"Damn good thing," muttered Polk. "If the krauts get that bridge in Schoenberg we've had it. So has everybody on this ridge."

"Why the hell didn't we stay there?" demanded Strahl. "We sat on the damn thing till dark."

"Because," said Polk irritably, "we got two battalions of artillery up here that are no good to anybody. Division wants 'em back where they can shoot—not play grab-ass with krauts in the woods. If the 423rd can hold Bleialf tomorrow, we're all right. There's a whole armored combat command from corps reserve coming in to hold the river crossings. Anybody know what's the story at Andler? There's supposed to be a bridge there too."

"Some cavalrymen came through here this afternoon," said Adam. "They said their positions in the Gap are gone and their squadron is trying to set up a new line from Andler to the Ambleve River. They think there's a troop in Andler."

"One cavalry recon troop? That's a fart in a whirlwind!"

"What the hell do you know about it, Strahl?"

"Ask Adam, Captain! Ask Sergeant Buell . . . in Auw the engineers got a prisoner who said two whole regiments of krauts came through the Losheim Gap this morning with a shitpot full of tanks."

"I don't think they're tanks," said Adam. "Engineers called 'em assault guns but whatever you call 'em, they're armored and they've got a big gun and a machine gun. Can't stop 'em with a rifle."

"The 9th Armored Division will be here tomorrow, I told you," said Polk. "They can stop anything the krauts have got. Sears, what's the word from the 422nd?"

"No trouble on the Schnee Eifel but Colonel Descheneaux's command post in Schlausenbach got hit this afternoon. He's going to swing his left battalion off the ridge and link up with us."

"Now?" Polk was horrified. "Tonight?"

"Yes, sir."

"Good God Almighty! I thought the krauts were between him and us."

"I don't know, sir. At Battalion all they said is the 422nd wants to get a switch position set up because they've got no contact with the cavalry up north."

"Oh, mother!" groaned Captain Polk. "Well . . . make sure everybody gets the word. If those poor bastards get off that mountain in this fog I don't want my people killing 'em. If we get any breakfast tomorrow you better make sure you aren't feedin' krauts along with your own men." He pointed at the big acetate-covered artillery map.

"Gather around. Battalion order for attack tomorrow morning: E Company on the right, F Company on the left, G in reserve. Weapons company supports. Axis of advance, road to Auw. Cross the LD at 0600."

"Where's the line of departure? Is it marked?"

"Sure . . . I'll be standing on it. In the middle of the road."

Right out of the book, thought Adam: two up, one back, an' feed 'em a hot meal. Where's he going to get a hot breakfast?

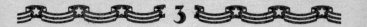

3

THERE WAS no breakfast, hot or otherwise, and that was the beginning of the trouble. Rousted out of their holes in the numbing predawn cold, the men made little fires of paper and pasteboard, trying to heat canteen cups of water and powdered coffee. Sergeants kicked out the fires and herded them into a line through the forest. They closed in, seeking company, and had to be pushed apart.

A thin light seeped through the trees and still they waited. Finally there was the *tchug!* of mortars firing behind them and the lieutenants shouted, "Fix bayonets . . . move out!" Somewhere ahead the mortar shells exploded, echoing through the forest, and the straggling line of riflemen advanced, losing all semblance of order.

Here and there a cluster of men pushed forward aggressively, others hung back, daunted by the unnatural silence ahead. A three-quarter-ton truck snarled and bucked over a logging trail, passed Adam and stopped. A soldier dropped the tailgate with a resounding clang, climbed into the back of the truck and began throwing down cases of rifle ammunition. The noise was awesome and Adam stared at him appalled.

"What the hell are you doing?"

"Resupply, sir."

"Goddamn, we ain't fired a shot!" someone exploded.

Off to Adam's right a German burp gun stuttered in astonishment, answered instantly by a ragged volley of rifle fire. A heavy-caliber gun roared, terribly close, and the shell screamed overhead—too high. The next one was not. Adam heard it punch through the wooden bows and canvas cover of the truck. Either it was defective or it was armor-piercing shell—it did not explode. The driver put his vehicle in reverse and rammed it back through the trees the way he had come.

The line of soldiers blundered into a low stone wall, a field beyond, and past the field the houses of Auw. On the road to Adam's right were two German armored guns—they still looked like tanks to him. When the Americans appeared at the stone wall, both fired and scuttled backward toward the village, turret machine guns rattling. Adam dived for the wall as the slugs cracked over his head.

Auw leaked Germans, they spewed out of the houses, milled in the street, and gradually built up a line of resistance in the farmyard adjoining the field. Their reaction was no more swift or efficient than the bumbling attack of the Americans. There was a constant shifting of clumsy running men in long green overcoats, sergeants or officers bellowed commands clearly audible, and the Americans watched, fascinated.

Exchange of fire was spasmodic: American light machine guns and automatic rifles hammered at the village and after a few minutes the German automatic weapons stammered a breathless reply, growing in volume as their machine guns joined the clamor.

"Sonsabitches been in them houses all night," snarled a soldier crouched against the wall, "whilst we been diggin' holes like a buncha friggin' groun'hawgs!" His rifle cracked and he beamed at Adam. "I got me one, by God! See 'im go ass-over-tin-cup, Lootenant?"

Captain Polk appeared, red-faced and furious. "Go!" he bellowed at Adam. "Get 'em over this goddamn wall and into that town!"

We should never have stopped, thought Adam. If we'd barreled on in, we could have had it. Too late. A few men got into the field and went flat in the frozen furrows. He got one leg over the wall and a German machine gun raked it, stinging him with rock chips, miraculously not hitting him. He scrambled back and the men in the field followed.

Like something from the Civil War—Yankees in a village, Rebels in the woods. A standoff. But the German infantrymen in the village seemed to multiply and their damned armored guns came back, scuttling through the streets to take cover in barns and sheds, blasting at the stalled American attack.

The shells screamed into the forest and exploded viciously in the trees, spraying fragments of steel. That was tolerable but now the krauts had got their mortars going—little ones, but the shells whispered down to burst with a heart-stopping *br-aack!* before and behind the stone wall. Adam's men left it, sifting into the forest.

He went with them. "We gonna leave this stuff?" A soldier pointed at the wooden boxes of ammunition scattered where they had been dumped from the truck.

"You wanta carry it, you simple bastard?" someone asked, and Adam agreed with that practical response. He turned in shamed frustration, emptied his carbine into the woods behind him. A fart in a whirlwind, somebody had said. They came back to the holes they had dug and kept going through the artillery position. The guns were gone—at least they had made that possible. There was little more credit to give their aborted attack.

Thank God, the krauts were no better. He could hear the frantic shrill of whistles and the scream of German sergeants: "*Marschiert!*" They've got their own trouble, he thought. Good thing . . . if they were any better they'd be all over us.

Adam's battalion went south, down the road from Auw to Bleialf. A retreat maybe, not a rout, he decided. They stopped, deployed in the woods on either side of the road from time to time, and waited for the Germans to appear. The krauts advanced as delicately as the Americans withdrew.

Gray figures crept through the forest, provoking a spatter of fire from the Americans, and disappeared.

Their sergeants blew whistles and bellowed orders—to attack, Adam supposed—with no visible response from their men until after a long time they got their mortars forward. The noise of firing rose but not until the growl of armored vehicles on the road announced the arrival of the dreaded assault guns did the German infantry inch forward.

Each time that happened, someone tried to stop the armor with a bazooka; if it ever succeeded, Adam did not see it. Once he saw a bazooka team cut down by machine-gun fire. The German guns clanked and rattled closer, their infantry took heart and advanced, and the American line drifted south. It went on that way all through the day until near dusk they came to a village—half a dozen deserted houses by the macadam road.

Either the Germans had given up or they had outwalked them. There was no contact, no firing. A lieutenant from the battalion staff appeared, carrying a map and full of importance.

"Dig in," he said, "block the road, make a line south of it, and lock in with the rest of the regiment at both ends. We're making a perimeter defense."

Adam's platoon went in just south of the road and again he scrambled through the snow-laden firs, marking positions, cursing tired riflemen until they hacked a shallow hole in the frozen ground. Lost in the forest, he heard a swelling roar of firing behind him, worked his way back to the road. Whatever had happened was over by the time he got there.

"What's up?" he demanded in a cautious whisper of a soldier squatting in the roadside ditch.

"Sheeit! Those dumb bastards come right down the road in a column o' fours. We got us a fifty caliber gun off a truck an' hosed their ass. Lissen to 'im, Lootenant!"

"*Sanni . . . sanni . . . !*"

Adam had heard that wail a century ago. No, only yesterday morning, but that was a hundred years past.

"He's hit . . . did the rest of 'em pull out?"

"Bet yer ass they did! We heard 'em runnin'."

"Ought to get a medic for him."

"Balls, Lootenant! They want him, they can come an' get him. Ain't nobody gonna look for that kraut bastard in the dark."

"What if it was you?"

"Screw 'im . . . I like to hear the sonovabitch yell."

Ritchie found Adam in the dark, led him to a fancy bunker dug into the shoulder of the road, log-walled, heavily roofed. Sergeant Duncker had set up a platoon command post, a Coleman lantern wheezing back the dark, and a field telephone hooked into a line to company headquarters.

"Any chow?" Adam asked.

"Not tonight. Breakfast, they said." The canvas-covered field phone rattled venomously and Duncker snatched up the handset. "Carpet White," he muttered into it. After a minute he nodded. "Roger . . . Carpet White out."

"What was that?"

"Jeep an' trailer on the road . . . droppin' off ammo, grenades, an' flares. One man from each hole pick up what they need."

"What the hell can we do with flares?"

"Grenade launcher, Lootenant. We got some."

Adam swore and retraced his line, stumbling from hole to hole on the perimeter. He had forgotten to ask for the password, but the holes were close enough together to call from one to the next, and he did not leave one until its neighbor acknowledged him. It was no way to fight a war but his riflemen were as scared of the impenetrable woods as he was, and he wanted them to know he was coming.

Near midnight he was back at the bunker and Ritchie gave him coffee and a compressed disk of dark cardboard with antique raisins embedded in it. "SWEET ROLL," said the label stenciled on the olive-drab can that preserved this abomination. It expanded in the mouth when moistened, giving off a taste of mothballs or whatever it was preserved in. He gagged, remembering mournfully the fat, rich wet pecan rolls he had at dawn in the bus-station coffee shop at home when he was working for the electric company.

Lieutenant Sears, the company executive officer, came with his messenger, a nervous boy who clicked off the safety of his rifle at every sound outside. Duncker took it away from him, soothing him with the news that there was a guard at the door.

"What's up, Will?" Adam demanded.

"Shit hit the fan, I guess. Krauts got through Bleialf this morning and joined up with the ones that came through Andler. They've got the bridge at Schoenberg."

"We're cut off?"

"That's right, buddy . . . in the bag."

"I thought there was an armored outfit going to hold that bridge."

"Didn't make it. We got new orders this afternoon . . . pull the regiment off the ridge and attack south-east. Go around Schoenberg and cross the river below it. Armor's supposed to be there to help us."

"Break through the Germans to the river?"

"Right. We can do it . . . 422nd will come with us and we've got a battalion of artillery to support us. Division laid on an airdrop of ammo and rations to-morrow morning and soon as we've got that we move out."

Adam thought of the leaden sky so near the ground you could reach up and touch it. Airdrop? How could they find us in this crap?

Incredibly, in the hour before dawn there was break-fast, hot and beautiful. The company kitchen was set up in the hamlet of Radscheid—the half-dozen houses they had seen at dusk the day before. A squad at a time, the company filtered past the kitchen truck for a messkit of hot powdered eggs, scrambled and chilled by a heaping spoonful of cold fruit salad dumped over them. There was hot coffee, though, and that was a God's blessing.

The macadam road running north from Bleialf to Auw seemed to be the heart's artery of both armies: the Germans came along it from north and south and between them the Americans shuttled back and forth in the shrinking bit left to them. Adam gathered his platoon on it and once more the battalion moved in attack formation, south this time, and again in text-book order—one company on each side of the road, one in reserve, and the weapons company supporting with mortar fire.

Shortly after what daylight there was got through the low-hanging clouds they met Germans. There was no parachute drop of supplies. If the Air Corps made one, it fell somewhere else. The Germans they encountered were no more competent than the ones who had inched through Auw the day before: youngsters as baffled and frightened as their American foe, but they were dug into shallow holes east of the Bleialf–Schoenberg road and each German position seemed to have an automatic weapon.

"Outposts," Captain Polk said. "Drive on . . . we got to get across that road to the river. The armor's waiting for us."

"They're there?"

"Christ, Adam, I don't know! Division said they'd help us get across. Keep going, man! About a hundred yards ahead there's a corduroy trail cuts west through the woods from this road to the one to Schoenberg. We go down that, cross the Schoenberg road, and drive to the river."

Adam found the logged track. Engineers had built it so you could get from Skyline Drive into the Schoenberg road without going through their ridgetop junction, the one with the sign warning it was under German observation. They called that junction Purple Heart Corner because anyone who dawdled there drew a German artillery shell and maybe the American army award for a combat wound: the Purple Heart medal. To hide their cutoff, the engineers had screened it with a tall net of burlap camouflage strips.

There was a dead German soldier tangled in the netting. One of Adam's hard-ball troopers wanted to search the body but was distracted by a burst of fire from the woods beyond. Adam's men went to ground but he was inspired by Captain Polk's strenuous order to get forward.

"You men . . ." he shouted, kneeling, "keep 'em down. Put some fire on 'em. You"—he pointed at three heads watching him—"follow me!"

Just like they said at the Infantry School—fire and movement. He took his three men down the logged road at a crouching run, protected marginally by the camouflage net, then scrambled under it and into the forest.

Miraculously, he saw the Germans before they saw him. They were wholly occupied by the rifle fire of the men Adam had left behind: two of them in a deep hole, only their heads and shoulders aboveground.

They had no machine gun but one of them had an automatic rifle of some kind. He popped up every few minutes to loose off a burst with it. They're supposed to have bolt-action Mausers, thought Adam. What the hell is that thing? The Germans didn't see him and Fort Benning's school prescription was clear in his mind: close in and throw a grenade. He scrambled forward to what he guessed was grenade range, jerked one from his belt, and thumbed out the pull-ring.

It came free reluctantly—he had cautiously bent back the legs of the cotter pin as far as he could. Standing up, he threw the grenade at the German foxhole.

"*Herr Gott . . . pass mal auf!*" shrieked one of them, pointing at him. The fragmentation grenade somehow penetrated the branches of the fir trees and dropped precisely into the hole. Both Germans yelled and scrabbled to get out of it.

The instructors at Fort Benning had more to say about throwing a grenade at an enemy position: as soon as you throw it, follow it in—be there to mop up anybody who survived it.

Adam lunged forward, carbine ready, reached the hole before the Germans got out of it, before the grenade went off. The hole was fresh-dug, wet and slippery around its lip. He lost his footing and slid into it. For one horrible moment he and the two Germans packed into the hole, wrestled and fought to get out of it, too closely jammed for anyone to use a weapon if he could think of it.

Later, Adam concluded, no one thought of such a thing because all three of them were conscious only of the grenade somewhere at the bottom of the hole. They stamped and clawed and yelled, all trying at once to get out.

The ludicrous comedy ended abruptly with a muffled explosion. Adam felt a monstrous blow under his feet, thrusting him up, then a breathless silence.

"*Du lieber Gott!*" said one of the Germans hoarsely.

"*Kamerad!*" said his companion, squirming to free his arms and raise them in surrender. The hole was surrounded at once by a dozen American soldiers, rifles jabbing at its occupants.

"You all right, Lieutenant?" someone asked wonderingly.

"I . . . I reckon so," replied Adam. "Gimme a hand up."

They pulled him from the hole and all of them stared fiercely at the two Germans still in it, both of whom held their hands high.

"Sonovabitch!" muttered one of Adam's men. "What happened to the damn grenade?"

Adam peered into the hole. "It went off . . . I felt it. Get out of there!"

The two German youngsters understood the command and climbed out with difficulty because they were afraid to use both hands. Adam knelt and stared into the sodden hole. "It's full of mud . . . we must have stomped it down so it didn't hurt anybody."

"Gawdamdest thing I ever heard of!" muttered someone. "What do we do with these bastards, Lootenant? Can we shoot 'em?"

"No! Take 'em back to the blacktop road and give 'em to somebody in company headquarters . . . and take this fancy rifle with you. Somebody ought to know they've got a semiautomatic like ours.''

They fought their way down the corduroy road—no big thing. Two more German outposts, no more deadly than the first. Adam missed the second with a grenade but the Germans in it surrendered at once. His left squad cleaned out another, reporting no prisoners.

"They gave up and you killed 'em?" he yelled at the squad leader.

"What the fuck are we supposed to do, Lootenant . . . kiss their ass?"

They broke from the forest to the edge of the road from Bleialf to Schoenberg and stared in awe at its traffic: trucks loaded with German infantry, half-tracks with antiaircraft guns, and the full-tracked things with cannon the engineers called assault guns. They still looked like tanks to Adam. The guns swiveled, blasting high-explosive shells into the trees.

A bazooka team got one, lobbing a rocket into its engine compartment that set it afire. It swerved off the road and the crew bailed out. There was room for another to pass but the flaming vehicle stalled the German column.

"We cut the road," Adam yelled into his hand-held radio. The SCR-536 handy-talky radio was a sometime thing—generally it reached company headquarters but it was just as likely to skip into a Belgian police net around Liege and get an astounded gendarme sputtering questions in French.

This time it worked. Captain Polk answered—Adam recognized his voice. "Go on . . . go on, Talcut! Get across and hold what you got! We'll follow you . . ." The remainder was lost in a gargling rush of sound.

Adam got a squad across, no more. The Germans pushing down from Bleialf spread infantry on either side of the road and jammed two flak-wagons hip to hip on the blacktop, hosing it with fire from their quadruple 20-millimeter automatic cannon. Like a man flushing leaves from his driveway with a garden hose, they swept the Americans from the road. The squad across the road was cut off; no one else could join them.

The bazooka team was cut to pieces as soon as it knelt to fire. The point-detonating shells of the twenty-millimeter guns cracked and flashed on the macadam, some of them screaming into the trees on either side to burst viciously when they hit the branches.

"Weapons company give us mortars!" howled Adam into his radio. "Get me weapons company . . . will adjust!"

The answer was a maddening rattle of noise—garbled pleas from other lieutenants and no response from company. The German flak wagons inched forward, motors roaring, guns blasting. Rifle fire snarled across the road and the men of the squad on the other side tried to come back. The first two were cut down on the road, the rest hesitated, and a young soldier a few yards from Adam got to his feet and walked into the open between the forest and the road.

Adam knew him. Private First Class Moon Scrimpsher from north Alabama, a Browning automatic rifleman. As if he were on a rifle range somewhere in America, Scrimpsher leveled his heavy weapon and held back the trigger, spraying the German flak wagons. His .30-caliber slugs did them no harm but he drove the gun crews down, methodically hauled fresh clips from his belt and searched the woods right and left of the road with fire.

His insolent bravery stunned the Germans; their fire slackened and the rest of the cutoff squad came across the road in a frantic rush. Before the last of them reached cover the automatic cannon on the German half-tracks killed Scrimpsher, tore him to pieces before he hit the ground.

"Sonsabitches!" howled someone, pounding Adam on his back. "Get a bazooka! Goddammit, Lootenant . . . get a bazooka!"

"Talcut . . ." squawked his radio. "Talcut, you there?"

"Roger! I got a hole about ten feet wide and I can't

get through it. We need mortars and more infantry
. . . for God's sake, Captain, send me some help!"

"Pull back, Talcut! Pull your people back this side
of the road and dig in so you can keep fire on it."

"Shit, Captain . . . we can cut it if you'll help us!"

"Do what I tell you, Talcut! Soon as you've got a
position, report to me for orders. . . ." The voice
drowned in the characteristic flatulence of the small
radio that died to a faint peeping.

"Batteries shot," said Ritchie. "You want me to get
some more? Weapons platoon's got some."

"If you can find 'em . . ." snarled Adam, "take this
frigging radio and stick it up their ass! Maybe that way
they'll hear me when I want mortar fire . . . an' find
us a bazooka! We can't stop those half-tracks with rifles."

Dusk was gathering; it was after four o'clock. Afraid
of bazooka fire, the German half-tracks pulled back a
little but continued to rake the forest sheltering the
Americans with fire. Beneath the racket of the automatic guns Adam heard shouting and movement in the
woods across the road: German infantry was spilling
around his roadblock, heading for Schoenberg or reaching to encircle him—no way to know which.

In the last light of day, Adam's men scratched shallow holes in the forest floor and kept up a steady rattle
of rifle fire bolstered by an automatic rifle and one
light machine gun whose crew had managed to get it
forward. Adam found Sergeant Duncker.

"I gotta go back to Company . . . Cap'n wants me. We
got to send somebody for ammo. You seen Ritchie?"

"Nosir."

"He went looking for a bazooka. I don't think they
can get a half-track or those tank guns into the woods
but sooner or later they'll get enough infantry to jump
us. Hold 'em off till I get us some help. Back as soon
as I can."

Duncker grunted. "Don't waste no time, Lieutenant. Them krauts hit us in the dark and this outfit'll
bug out. We're stuck out here like tits on a cow . . .
no way we can stop 'em without mortars."

It was bad on the edge of the forest but Adam's search into it for the company command post was a trip into hell. He stumbled into trees, fell over men hacking desperately at the frozen ground who swore at him hysterically when he stepped on them. German shells bursting in the thick branches overhead lit the ground with a stunning flash of light. The shriek of steel fragments sent Adam lunging for the earth—too late. Like a storm, he thought . . . if you heard thunder, the lightning didn't hit you.

True, but it didn't help. Each momentary explosion of light showed terrified faces and diving bodies around him and he went with them, galvanized by fear.

He found his captain finally, crouched in a shallow pit of raw earth, yelling hoarsely into a radio, Lieutenant Strahl of the weapons platoon with him. Back to back, each clutched a radio—shouting, imploring, mouthing pleas, orders—spitting into the handsets they gripped.

"Talcut, sir!" Adam yelled at Polk. "You told me to find you."

"Yeah . . . yeah . . . shut up a minute!" The captain's face, lit by shell flashes, was haggard and furious. "Litter jeep!" he shrieked into his radio. "I got wounded up here!"

The radio squealed and gargled. "Say again!" Polk slapped it violently. "Fucking Mickey Mouse gimmick . . . say again your last transmission!"

". . . Weapons company vehicles . . . on the cutoff . . . can't get by them . . ." The words came in bursts from the radio, sometimes muffled, sometimes startlingly clear.

"You want me to leave the goddamn wounded?" yelled Polk. "Get weapons company off the road and send me a litter jeep!"

There was a momentary pause in the German shelling, a brief unnatural silence, and a voice from the radio said quite clearly: "Roger your last transmission . . . leaving your wounded . . . I will relay your message."

"Shit-oh-mother!" exploded Polk, thrusting the handset at a soldier. "Here . . . try to make that shit-for-brains understand. Tell him I won't come back till I get a jeep to take the wounded out."

"Come back?" croaked Adam. Polk scrubbed his face with a filthy hand and Adam burst into protest. "Mortars, ammunition, more men . . . we can't stay on that road unless we get help."

"Too late," said Polk. "We aren't crossing the goddamn road . . . there isn't any armor on the river . . . there isn't anything this side of Saint Vith but krauts. They've got the bridge at Schoenberg and we're in the bag."

"What are we goin' to do?"

"Regiment got a new order from Saint Vith . . . link up with the 422nd, turn north and break out through Schoenberg."

"But we cut the road! We can go on if we get help!"

"We're not going to Setz, I told you! Regiment tried to help . . . they sent 1st Battalion in on our left and it got all cut up . . . never even got to the road. The armor never got to the river . . . it's trying to hold Saint Vith and Division sent us the worst piece of bullshit I ever heard. Listen to this . . ."

He thrust a rumpled page from a notebook against the faint orange glow illuminating the dial of the radio, read from it angrily: "Attack Schoenberg. Do maximum damage . . . attack toward Saint Vith. This mission"—he hawked and spat furiously—"is of gravest importance to the nation. Good luck."

Adam stared at him openmouthed. "Fuck the nation!" rasped Polk. "We're on our own and if we get out of this rat trap it'll be a goddamn miracle. Colonel Puett's right . . . only thing in that message worth a damn are the last two words—'Good luck'!" Polk spat disgustedly.

"Go on . . . do what I told you! Get your people back to Radscheid, that village across the road from where the cutoff starts. Get some chow and whatever ammo is left. We go for Schoenberg at daylight tomorrow."

The fight on the Bleialf–Schoenberg road had subsided to a sporadic exchange of fire. Nothing was visible in the forest across the road but now and again a German sergeant yelled an order and set off a burst of rifle fire from the Americans, answered by the hurried stutter of a German machine pistol.

"They're scared to move those tanks," Sergeant Duncker whispered, "but they're goin' around us on the other side."

"To hell with 'em! We got orders to pull back."

"Back? Where?"

"Village at the end of the corduroy road. Pick up ammo and attack Schoenberg at daylight."

"Thought we were goin' to the river."

"We are, but we got to take Schoenberg . . . get across there. You take the right and I'll take the left . . . make sure we don't leave anybody. Tell 'em fall back along the log road and assemble when we get to the village."

"Shit, Lieutenant! We'll never find 'em all in the dark."

"We damn sure will, Duncker . . . or you an' I'll be here till dawn lookin' for 'em. Move now!" He had never before said anything like that to Sergeant Duncker and he was pleased with himself.

Hours it took—uncounted hours. Feeling his way through the trees, Adam sought his men, whispered urgently to them. "Back . . . go back on the log road."

The German assault guns were silent but they had got artillery into position somewhere to the east and they used it logically. A battery volley would fall on the American side of the road, a pause while they adjusted the guns, and another a hundred yards forward of the last. Then they walked their fire back, shells exploding lethally in the trees.

Adam thought he found them all. Leaving a man in those woods was a crime he could not bear and he went over the ground twice despite the terror of the

German artillery pounding it. At the upper end of the corduroy road he found Ritchie and Duncker issuing ammunition, a lengthy and occasionally noisy process. When a man held out his hand Ritchie lifted a finger from the lens of a flashlight and Duncker studied the applicant in the tiny glow.

"You're not in my platoon, soldier. Go find your own." Some argued, some simply shuffled away. To his own men, Duncker doled out half a dozen clips of rifle ammunition and a single hand grenade. Adam watched Ritchie shucking clips from a dwindling pile of cloth bandoliers.

"Is that all there is?"

"Yessir," replied Duncker, "and I stole them grenades outta somebody's truck."

"Did you get a bazooka?" Adam asked Ritchie.

"I found one, sir. No use carryin' it . . . no ammo for it."

"That's a hell of a note!"

"Sure is, sir. Want some coffee?" He held out a canteen cup of bitter, lukewarm stuff. "No sugar. They put it in the kitchen truck."

"What?"

"In the gas tank. They say it screws up the motor."

"Ritchie, what the hell are you talking about?"

"We're leavin' the kitchen truck behind. Service company's doin' the same to their trucks."

The price of the fight crawled by—walking wounded —then a jeep carrying men too badly hurt to walk. Its motor growled, drowning the murmur of hurt men.

"Where they going?" asked Ritchie.

"Ratshit," replied Duncker.

"What?"

"Ratshit . . . Rotshit. Whatever they call that village across the road. There's an aid station there."

"We're supposed to attack, aren't we? What happens to them?"

"If they can walk, I guess they come with us. If they can't, they stay here . . . in a cellar with a medic."

"Christ, no!" exploded Adam. "We can't do that!"

"What else, Lieutenant? We got no ambulances. Carry 'em on a jeep and they'll freeze to death."

The jeep slipped off the logged road and its rear wheels spun helplessly.

"Give us a hand . . . push!" shouted the driver.

Adam leaned on the jeep and pushed, his feet slipping in the churned mud. The vehicle swayed, bucked, and regained its footing; inched forward. His hands found something that moved and groaned: a man faceup across the hood of the jeep.

"It's all right . . . I'm sorry. Did I hurt you?"

"Adam?"

"Yes, who's this?"

"Hyatt . . . what the hell's happening, Adam?"

"You hit bad, Shube?" Shubal Hyatt, who had told him a few nights ago he would surely have a letter from Bitsey soon. Sprawled on a jeep hood because the back of it must be full of wounded found before him. "How bad?"

"I don't know . . . legs . . . can't feel 'em."

Adam's fingers touched Hyatt's face, combed hair from it. His helmet was gone.

"Good God! What's in your hair, Shube? What happened to you?"

The driver grunted. "Just mud, leave him be, Lieutenant."

"Mud?"

"Sure . . . wheel threw it up. Gets in his hair and makes those little balls . . . they freeze."

"Adam . . . what're they goin' to do with us?"

"Take you to the aid station, Shube. Get warm and the doc'll fix you up."

"We're goin' to get out, aren't we?"

"Sure. First thing tomorrow we're goin' to Saint Vith."

Hyatt's head jerked away from his hands. "Yeah . . . what about us? You goin' to leave us behind?"

Adam gripped the face he could not see in the dark. "Easy, Shube. Take it easy. They'll fix you up in the aid station."

"Shit! You're goin' to leave us . . . the goddamn krauts'll kill us!"

How do you answer that? "No they won't, Shube. They aren't SS bastards . . . just dogfaces like us. They'll take care of you."

"Adam . . . you sonovabitch . . . don't leave me! You can find a jeep . . . take me with you."

"I can't, Shube. You'll freeze on top of a jeep."

The vehicle lurched against him, jerked away. "Adam . . . goddammit, Adam . . . don't leave me!"

Ritchie pulled him away from the spinning wheels.

Duncker's little pile of ammunition was gone and after a while someone said, "Move out . . . let's go."

"Where? Where the hell are we going?" Adam asked.

"Follow the platoon ahead of us, I reckon," said Duncker. By the time he and Adam had gathered as many of their men as they could find, there was no one to follow. They blundered through the forest, feeling their way from tree to tree, and after a while stumbled over men asleep where they sat or lay, heedless of the mud and slush beneath them.

"Who're you?" demanded Adam.

"Third Platoon . . . goddammit, watch your feet!"

"We caught up," muttered Duncker. "Lissen, Lieutenant . . . you stay here. If you get the order to move, send Ritchie back for me."

"Where you going?"

"We musta left a lot of men back there. They were asleep . . . didn't hear us go. I'll try to find 'em."

Adam was so tired he made no objection. He slumped against a tree and slept, awakened by the crash of German shells somewhere to his left. Ought to dig in, he told himself. They move that artillery and we've had it. He tried. "Dig a hole . . . get some cover," he told each man he could find in the dark. Reluctantly they hacked a little at the ground with their shovels, but as soon as he moved on they stopped. He knew that and could do nothing about it. He found Ritchie, who had a blanket, and they rolled into it, clutching each other indecently.

 4

SOMETIME DURING the night Duncker returned with a small group of soldiers, who gathered around Adam. He woke surrounded by the pale blur of their faces in the gloom of the forest.

"Shit!" said Ritchie feelingly. "We gonna have a prayer meeting?"

"How many?" Adam asked Duncker.

"Seven . . . when we started."

"What do we do now, Lootenant " someone asked plaintively.

Adam knew there was no use telling him to dig a hole. "Sack out, soldier. We won't move till daylight."

"Coffee? We got any coffee?"

"Shit-oh-dear!" That was Sergeant Duncker.

What am I supposed to do? wondered Adam. Give 'em a pep talk?

Ritchie thrashed irritably. "Lie down, Lieutenant . . . you're lettin' all the warm outta this blanket."

Dawn came with rain that turned to sleet and then snow: fat wet flakes dribbling through the branches above. Adam waked and slept and waked again to the snarl of motors. He exploded from the blanket, dragging Ritchie with him. A jeep towing a trailer bucked and lurched past, sucking Ritchie's blanket under its spinning wheels.

Shivering, trying to think what he ought to do, Adam squatted by the trail. Another jeep and trailer, then Sergeant Duncker, shaking him.

"You awake, Lieutenant?"

"Yeah . . . yeah! Who're they?"

"Weapons company, 3rd Battalion."

"Where they going?"

"Christ, I dunno. Tryin' to get close enough to back up their people, I reckon."

More jeeps and, incredibly, a three-quarter-ton truck wallowed by, then the deadly rustle of artillery shells low overhead. They burst somewhere ahead before the boom of the guns was heard. To his left Adam heard the rising growl of heavy motors and pounded Duncker's shoulder.

"Tanks! That armored outfit they promised us!"

"Aw, Lootenant, that's krauts on the road to Schoenberg. They're goin' like shit through a tin horn . . . be there before we are."

"That's our artillery. Third Battalion must have jumped off. Let's get ready to move."

He scrambled in and out of the churned mud of the trail, searched the woods on either side, shaking men awake. Since they had nowhere to go they just went back to sleep. One was awake when Adam found him, bent forward and groaning.

"What's the matter?"

"It hurts."

"What? What hurts?"

The soldier pulled his overcoat open and the pale dawn light showed his leg bare from boot-top to knee. Someone had cut off the trouser leg and wrapped a great wad of bandage around his shin and calf. He gripped it with both hands, rocking back and forth.

"You got hit?"

"Yessir . . . yesterday. Medic fixed it, but Jeez, it hurts!"

"Why didn't you go to the aid station?"

"I ain't no dummy, Lootenant. I ain't gonna stay in no cellar till the krauts find me. If we're gonna get outta here, I wanta go too."

Adam pulled the overcoat over the bandaged leg. "Can you walk?"

"Bet your ass, sir. We gonna fight now?"

"Yeah, we'll fight . . . we'll get out. You got any ammo?"

"Whole belt full."

"Good! Stick with us and we'll get out."

Adam slid into the trail and blundered along it, falling over men crouched in the muddy slot. You got to do something, he told himself. You can't just dick around these woods like this. You've got to get these people out of here. But what do I do?

"Lieutenant Talcut?" Someone was calling him.

"Here . . . I'm Talcut." Adam clutched the dim figure, peered at his face. He knew him—a sergeant from company headquarters.

"Move out in five minutes, sir. You follow 3rd Platoon."

"Where we going?"

"Lieutenant Strahl says we're goin' in on the right of 3rd Battalion. He's up front a way, he'll tell you when you get there."

"Where's Captain Polk?"

"Don't know, sir. They think maybe he got hit. Nobody's seen him since last night."

The sergeant disappeared and Adam went on until someone caught his arm and pulled. "Who's that?" he demanded.

"Ritchie, sir."

"Where's Sergeant Duncker?"

"Went back to make sure nobody gets left behind. This guy"—Ritchie put his hand on a sleeping soldier beside him—"he's last man in 3rd Platoon. Sergeant said when he goes, we go after him."

The man snored softly and Adam swore. "How's he going to know when they move out?"

"Light enough to see pretty soon now. We'll know. You goin' to stay here, Lootenant?"

"Yeah, sure."

Adam squatted, went to sleep, and Ritchie backed him against the side of the deep-cut track. He slept until the world exploded somewhere ahead of them; he and Ritchie crouched, listening in awe. Rifle fire, the crack of tank guns, and the pulsing roar of heavy automatic weapons. German—the twenty-millimeter automatic guns on their half-tracks.

"You reckon we hit that town, sir?"

Adam tried to remember what Schoenberg looked like from the east side. Third Battalion might have got to the town but there was the river to cross and the krauts must have the bridge. More artillery shells rattled overhead, adding their bursts to the cataclysm of sound ahead.

"Hope they save some for us," muttered Ritchie.

"What?" yelled Adam.

"Only one battalion," shouted Ritchie. "That's all we got left. I talked to some of 'em in Ratshit last night and they only got a couple hundred shells."

Somebody dragged the last man of the 3rd Platoon to his feet and he stumbled away. Adam stood up. "Go back down the trail," he told Ritchie, "till you find Sergeant Duncker. Wake up everybody . . . tell 'em move out . . . then come back and find me."

He ran forward, caught up with the end of the 3rd Platoon, and plodded after it. The trail dipped, rose, and he climbed, slipping and clutching at the trees beside the track. His men followed him, lurching and sweating, some of them already pulling off their overcoats. The roar of firing ahead rose and fell in surges, and something awful went overhead with a rising scream to explode only yards ahead.

Adam sprawled in the track and the screaming rush of heavy projectiles came again and again. There seemed no end to them. He looked back to see the trail jammed with soldiers hugging the ground desperately. One man came through them at a stumbling run: Duncker.

"I thought you were going to stay with the tail of the column," Adam shouted at him.

"I *am* the fuckin' tail of the column, Lootenant! We're up to our ass in krauts!"

"Where'd they come from? How'd they get behind us?"

"Down that blacktop road from up north! Tanks—biggest mothers I ever saw—and infantry all over Ratshit. They got our artillery . . . it's done . . . finished!"

"What the hell is that?" yelled Adam, jerking a thumb at the appalling noise overhead.

"Kraut . . . Screamin' Meemies! Goddamn thing shoots rockets. Lissen, Lieutenant . . ."

It was impossible to hear him. Duncker crawled closer and shouted into Adam's ear. "You get any orders yet?"

Adam shook his head and Duncker shouted again: "Maybe they forgot about us . . . let's get outta here!" Adam flinched away from him. The howl and crash of incoming rockets stopped abruptly and Duncker's urgent yelling hurt his ear. Either the krauts had run out of rockets or everybody was reloading at once.

"What do you mean, get out of here?"

"Go on . . . keep movin' till we find the rest of the company. Stay here, Lootenant, an' those krauts'll be all over us. Somebody's tryin' to get across that river an' we better go with 'em."

Adam remembered what the soldier with the bandaged leg had said: if anybody's going to get out of here, I'm going too. "All right . . . let's go."

They got the men up and moving. The forest thinned, giving way to a clearing below the crest of the hill they had been climbing. The muddy trail angled across it, and to its right, in the open, two 81-millimeter mortars were set up for firing, empty ammunition canisters scattered about them. A single crewman squatted by one of them.

"Hey!" shouted Adam. "Where is everybody?"

The soldier made a vague gesture and Adam peered over his shoulder to see what he was doing. He had tied a length of field-telephone wire to the pull-ring of a hand grenade and now he inserted the grenade in the mortar tube and suspended it there by hooking the safety lever over the lip of the tube. Standing up, he looked at Adam.

"Y'all best back off some, Lieutenant." He walked away, paying out the wire as he went.

"What the hell are you doin'?" demanded Duncker.

Adam knew. When he got far enough away, he would haul on the wire, extracting the pull-ring. The safety lever would flip off and the grenade would drop to the bottom of the mortar, exploding four seconds later. The base of the tube would probably rupture, but if it didn't it would be so badly bulged the mortar was useless.

"No more ammo, Sarge. We done bought the fuckin' farm." He reached the edge of the trail and lowered himself into the deep-cut ruts. "Y'all better get down now."

"No!" Adam yelled at him. "Don't pull that thing!"

The soldier gave him a disgusted look. "You want the mortar, Lieutenant?"

"No, but you're not goin' to blow it till I get my platoon past here. Get in the trees over there and wait till we're gone. Where's the rest of your outfit?"

"Up there somewheres, sir." He pointed vaguely westward. "Soon's I get done with this, I'll go look for 'em."

Two men, helping a third, came over the hilltop and made their way through the silent mortars. More followed, all wounded. They went past Adam without looking at him.

"Come on," he told Duncker, and climbed to the crest. The slope fell away sharply, so sharply he could not see the bottom, but a macadam road climbed a distant slope, a scattering of houses beside it. Schoenberg? Adam wondered. That must be the road to Saint Vith. He couldn't see the river and the rest of the town but they had to be there, hidden by the trees ahead. A few infantrymen were scattered along the crest, digging hard.

"Who're you?" Adam demanded of one of them, a sergeant's stripes on his sleeve.

"M Company, Lieutenant . . . what's left of it."

"Where's your battalion? What the hell are you doing here?"

"Sir, I think the krauts has got between us and the battalion. There was a bunch of 'em here a minute ago . . . we ran 'em off."

"There's another one!" yelled a rifleman, dropping his shovel and blasting off a shot from his rifle. A man came out of the trees below the ridge line, waving frantically.

"Hold it!" shouted the sergeant, "that's a G.I."

Helmetless, white-faced, gasping for breath, the soldier climbed painfully to the men, who stopped digging to watch him. When he reached them he sat down and stared numbly at his left foot. The sole of the rubberized canvas overshoe had been torn away and the heel of the boot beneath it was gone. Cautiously he poked at the damage and held up a finger smeared with blood.

"Sonovabitch!" he said. "That sonovabitch tried to kill me."

He got to his feet and started down the slope toward the mortars, but the weapons-company sergeant caught his arm.

"You're in L Company, aren't you? Where are they?"

"There ain't any L Company, Sergeant. It's gone."

"What do you mean, 'gone'? What happened?"

"We got right up to a blacktop road last night and this morning the cap'n put us straddle it and said let's go to Shoonberg. We come around a turn and there was a million krauts just standin' there waitin' for us. Trucks and tanks and them damn half-track things with machine guns all over 'em. They whipped our ass."

"Why didn't you fall back?" asked Adam.

"Hell, sir . . . we did, and here come another bunch of the bastards in trucks. We shot up the trucks but they must have been full of kraut dogfaces. Hundreds of 'em, an' every swingin' weenie had a burp gun. We took off up the hill for the holes we dug last night and they come right after us like striped-ass apes."

"You couldn't hold 'em off?"

The soldier shrugged. "Only a couple dozen of us left. No machine gun . . . radio wouldn't work . . . couldn't get any help. We ran out of ammo and all of a sudden they was all over us. Acted like they were drunk or crazy or somethin'."

"What did they do?"

"Couple of 'em grab you . . . one of 'em shucks off your watch, and his buddy shakes you down for cigarettes. They don't miss a damn thing."

"How'd you get away?"

"That bastard that got my watch, he just walked off and his buddy says to me . . ." He shook his head in wonder. "He says to me in Amurrican as good as mine, he says, 'Run, Ami.' I don't know what 'Ami' means but I got the word. I run about ten feet and he cut loose with his burp gun." He looked at Adam.

"That sonovabitch tried to kill me."

The sergeant from the weapons company snorted. "Lucky you got caught by the biggest eight ball in the kraut army . . . ten feet and he couldn't hit you with a burp gun."

Sergeant Duncker pulled at Adam's arm. "Let's go, sir . . . let's get outta here."

The mortar sergeant did not want to go with them. He wanted word from his battalion before he went anywhere.

"You know there's krauts in behind you?" Duncker asked him.

"I'm not right sure, Sarge, what is my behind and what is my front. I'll stay put till I hear from Battalion."

Adam led his platoon north along the ridge line which bent east, and he guessed it would drop down to the Our river valley a little upriver of Schoenberg. They met more walking wounded, drifting back, just back—away from the fighting. Adam told the first he encountered that the aid station in Radscheid was in German hands, there was no use trying to reach it. They listened to him, nodded, and resumed their plodding.

The roar of firing welled up from the river valley and among a cluster of bunkers along the ridge trail they found what seemed to be a command post: a couple of officers crouched over a map, messengers coming and going.

"Adam!" someone called.

"Hey, Dad!" It was Strahl, the weapons platoon commander. "What's up? Where's Captain Polk?"

Strahl shook his head. "Went off with Sears on a recon about midnight. Haven't seen him since."

"Who's running the company?"

"You're lookin' at him. How many men you got?"

"Thirty . . . maybe a few more. What are we goin' to do?"

"Hell, I don't know. First Battalion just put a company in to help the 3rd. If they get stuck, I guess we go."

A stocky red-faced man with the silver leaf of a lieutenant colonel on his helmet came up the ridge from the left at a scrambling run, followed by a major and a soldier with a radio in his arms. The major and the soldier squatted over the radio, fiddling with its antenna. The lieutenant colonel shouted at the officers gathered by a bunker and pointed down the north side of the ridge.

The group exploded, messengers scattering, and the colonel stalked off, followed by his major and his useless radio. Puett—"Ball-ammunition" Puett, they called him. He was Adam's battalion commander and all the time they were in England he had raged about their training. They turned out every day for squad and platoon exercises and sometimes even fired a few rounds of blank ammunition. Colonel Puett swore bitterly; ought to be training under live fire, he snarled— ball-ammo, not blanks.

His rage got him nothing. Even the blank cartridges made trouble. Adam remembered standing at attention before the regimental executive officer, charged with frightening sheep so badly the ewes aborted their lambs. He got out of that by buying two naked pink little dead creatures from a farmer at a ruinous price. Lieutenant Colonel Joe Puett stood up for him but nobody offered to give him back the money he paid for those aborted lambs. Now Colonel Joe Puett went down off the ridge to the north, and what was left of his battalion followed him in no recognizable formation.

Adam caught up with Lieutenant Strahl. "Where we going?"

"3rd Battalion's stuck and that company from the 1st got the hell kicked out of it. We're going to swing to the right and hit Schoenberg from the north."

"Where's the 422nd?" That was the other of the two infantry regiments that had backed out of their positions on the Schnee Eifel with orders to break out of the German trap through Schoenberg.

"Don't know. Haven't had any contact with 'em since last night. Come on . . . let's go!"

A loose mob of men—several hundred, Adam guessed—spilled down the ridge into a creek bed, jammed there for a while, and went down it in groups of a dozen or more, all organization lost.

Rifle and machine-gun fire erupted from the forest on their right. The little groups broke up, scrambling for cover, some of them returning the fire. All movement stopped, the firing slowed, and an American captain slid and rolled down the slope toward Adam, yelling insanely: "Cease fire . . . stop firing!" Adam's soldiers stared at him openmouthed.

"Where the hell did he come from?"

"Shoot the sonovabitch . . . he's a kraut."

"No he ain't! I seen him before."

The 422nd Infantry Regiment was back in contact, moving in the same direction as Adam's regiment. The two units had blundered together, each mistaking the other for Germans. The cost; a dozen men wounded in the blind aimless firing.

There was a loud, profane exchange of comment on this idiotic encounter, and after a long time Adam and his men climbed out of the streambed and worked their way, panting, to the top of the next ridge. There were men all over it, crouched, watching suspiciously. Lieutenant Strahl appeared and squatted beside Adam.

"FUBAR!" he croaked. The American army saved that epithet for conditions that defied ordinary description. "Fucked up beyond all recognition," it meant.

"Amen!" said Adam. "What now?"

"We're going with 'em . . . across the river and take that goddamn bridge."

"Who do I follow?"

"Shit, Adam! Follow what's in front of you."

There were perhaps two dozen men behind him now. Adam saw sergeant Duncker prodding a few more forward. They joined a ragged, wavering line of riflemen spilling over the nose of the ridge, the ground falling sharply to a macadam road, hugging the bank of a river. That's the Our, thought Adam. We get across that and we've got it made.

But the road was full, double-banked with vehicles, locked in a traffic jam of epic proportions.

"It's the 9th Armored . . . they made it!" All along the line men were yelling, pounding each other in glee. "Hot damn, we're gonna get out!"

Below in the stalled column of vehicles, one of a cluster of men on the rear deck of a tank pounded the shoulders of a man in the turret.

"*Amis!*" he screamed. "*Feuer frei!*"

Three hundred yards away and above the road, Adam could hear the snarl of turrets swinging to point guns—cannon and multiple machine guns. Men erupted from the trucks, scrambling and jumping into the riverbed beyond them. As if he had set off a great string of fireworks, there spread in both directions from the screaming German a flashing, roaring explosion. Everything on the vehicles that could shoot sought the crest of the hill and vomited fire.

The air around Adam cracked and burst with the flight of metal. The ground jumped, spat snow and gouts of earth, and the scrubby fir trees along the top of the ridge lit up with the cracking burst of explosive shells.

"Oh, Jesus . . . I'm hit!" howled someone.

"Get down, Lieutenant!" It was Ritchie, reaching up to pull at him. Adam sat down hard, rolled over, and crawled desperately. He reached for a tree and snatched back his hand as a close-knit seam of bullets stitched its way past him, shredded the little fir, and pounded on ahead of him. The stream of lead crossed an out-crop of rock, stinging his hands and face with flying chips.

You stay here and you're dead, Talcut. He got his feet under him and lunged upward, fell and got up again, running. The top. I got to get over the top.

Miraculously he made it. Found Ritchie, face in the muddy snow, and joined him, digging his fingers into the earth. Ritchie was babbling something and after a while he turned his head very carefully to look at him.

"What?"

"Mary, Mother of God . . ."

That won't help, thought Adam. Nobody's mother can help us now. He made his way down the reverse slope of the nose and thought: There isn't enough cover for a goddamn mouse on this hill. He couldn't find Strahl and the officers he found were no help. They only yelled at each other and hugged the ground.

You couldn't stand up. Three feet above the ground the air was half lead—howling, cracking slugs. He found a big shallow hole, an open pit full of men. Somebody had started a bunker and never finished it. There must have been a dozen men in the hole, all wounded; a single medic with big red crosses in white circles on his helmet was working on one of them.

He moved to another, then sat down, his back against the side of the pit. "I can't," he said. "I got nothin' left."

A tall slim man with a silver eagle painted on the front of his helmet, visible through the camouflage netting, came to stand, looking into the pit. He ought to get down, Adam thought. He'll get hit if he stands up like that.

A colonel—must be the commander of the 422nd.

Adam didn't know him but that wasn't strange. Second lieutenants rarely saw a full colonel unless they got into trouble. This one looked right at him and didn't see him. He was crying, tears running down his cheeks.

"Oh God!" he said softly.

Three soldiers came, carrying someone: a captain, his head rolling and bouncing as they lowered him into the pit. The captain jerked convulsively and Adam saw that one of his legs ended in a bloody jumble just below the knee. Beyond that there was nothing—no foot, no boot, nothing.

"That's enough!" said the colonel.

Adam crawled back to Ritchie, who was prizing up lumps of earth with his bayonet. "Help me dig, Lieutenant. We gotta make a hole."

"Why? We're underneath it."

"Listen!"

Adam heard the piping whistle that ended in a sharp, cracking explosion. All that infantry in those trucks, he remembered. They've got mortars. He looked back at the open pit full of wounded men. In a minute they're going to put one right in that hole. The colonel who was crying had gone away, not far, talking to some officers.

"You seen Sergeant Duncker?"

"Not for a long time. You got anything to dig with?"

"No," said Adam, watching the officers grouped around the colonel. "I better go find him. I think we're going to try again."

He crawled around the pit full of wounded and up the trail in the direction from which they had come until the ridge was too high, exposing the trail to German fire from the river road. A lot of men had discovered that and taken to the reverse slope, safe there against anything but mortars or artillery.

There was no organization that Adam could see, only men in little groups in the thick forest. Some hacked at the ground to make yet another hole, ignoring Adam; others gathered around him when they saw he was an officer.

"What're we goin' to do, Lieutenant?" was the most frequent question. Some were aggressively confident. "Why're we staying here, sir? Let's go get those kraut bastards."

Adam wondered if any of those had got close enough to the river and the road to see what was on it. He couldn't find Sergeant Duncker but he found two stragglers from his platoon who followed him when he turned back toward Ritchie. German shells began falling on the reverse slope—no more Screaming Meemies, but real artillery. That moved a lot of stragglers forward.

They must have got guns into position by Radscheid, Adam guessed. They wouldn't take a chance dumping the erratic rockets this close to their stalled vehicles on the river road, but they walked their artillery barrage across the ridge with skilled precision. They would move it closer to the road a few yards at a time until they got it squarely on the disorganized Americans milling around in the trap.

Adam ran, trying to stay ahead of the shells, but it was a losing race; stunning explosions in the trees overhead sprayed the ground with fragments. He got back to Ritchie and minutes later the shelling stopped. So did the mortars and the roar of cannon and machine guns on the river road.

"What happened? What stopped 'em?" he gasped.

"Him . . ." said Ritchie grimly, pointing at the colonel. "I think he quit."

"What? What do you mean?"

"He sent that major down there. He was wavin' a piece of white cloth."

Colonel Joe Puett was back, arguing vehemently with the colonel Adam thought was the commander of the 422nd Regiment. Puett stalked away, swearing—a stream of furious profanity. He came to peer at the road jammed with German vehicles and soldiers now, climbing out of the riverbed to stare up at the Americans. Puett's face was twisted and he was crying too.

"Colonel . . . Colonel Puett?" Adam got to his knees. "What . . . ?"

Puett spat furiously. "He quit! He surrendered! I want to hang on till dark and make a break for it but he says we can't even try. He sent out a white flag and he says we can't go." He looked down at Adam. "To hell with him . . . you want to take off, go ahead!"

Men were standing up all over the top of the ridge, some of them smashing their rifles against the nearest tree.

"Jeez," said Ritchie. "Let's get outta here, Lieutenant."

"Where? How can we?"

"Into the woods. Look . . . it's gettin' dark. We can make it." Adam stared at the mass of German vehicles on the road below. The infantry had come through them and was climbing the slope. "Come on, Lieutenant! Let's go before those bastards get here."

He pulled at Adam, and Adam followed him. There were others disappearing into the gathering gloom of the forest. He followed Ritchie, who slid from tree to tree down the hill, heading north away from the carnage on the ridgetop. After a while Ritchie sat down, breathing hard, and Adam sat by him.

"What are we going to do?"

"Cross that road . . . get over the river . . . head for Saint Vith."

"You're crazy! How're we going to get across that road? It's full of krauts."

"Be dark in a few minutes. We can slip across."

They waited. Once they heard men stumbling and scrambling through the forest behind them, calling out to each other, low-voiced and urgent.

"They're American!" whispered Adam. "We can go with them."

Ritchie pulled him back. "Better just the two of us, Lieutenant. Listen to those crazy bastards . . . they'll never make it."

He was right. The growl of motors on the road by the river never stopped, but after a long time there

was a sudden burst of firing and a distant triumphant
yelling.

"Krauts," muttered Ritchie. "They got 'em."

He's right, thought Adam. How the hell we're going
to get across that road I don't know, but maybe just
two of us can. It was wholly dark now and a harsh
wind blew down the river valley, muffling the rumble
of German vehicles in the thrashing of fir branches.

"Now!" hissed Ritchie. "They can't hear us now.
Come on!"

Carefully, testing every blind step, they inched down
the steep slope; stopped a few yards above the road.
Adam's heart sank. The clank and rumble of tracked
vehicles was so close it seemed he could reach out and
touch them, feel the heat of their flaring orange exhaust. As far as he could see to the north, the pinprick
of blacked-out headlights swam toward him. From
Andler, he thought. The column ground to a halt over
and over again, stopped sometimes for half an hour
before the motors roared and it hitched forward a
little. Andler, hell . . . they must be stacked up all the
way into Germany.

Men walked up and down the stalled vehicles. Adam
could not see them but he could hear them shouting:
officers probably, trying to do something about the
massive traffic jam. Once or twice a motorcycle came
down the road from Andler, its rider yelling for room
and getting nothing but howls of derision from the
tank crews and infantry in the trucks. Nothing moved
for hours, and Adam shivered convulsively in the cold
wind that even the thick forest did not stem.

Sometime after midnight there was an outburst of
shouted orders, motors coughed to life, and tank tracks
squealed as the drivers jockeyed for space. A few feet
at a time, the vehicles inched forward, double-banked
on the narrow road, bumper to bumper.

"How the hell are we going to get through that?"
whispered Ritchie miserably. Adam could hear his
teeth chattering with cold. We've got to do something,
he thought, or we'll freeze before daylight.

"What if we just go down and walk along the edge of the road . . . like those officers did? Slip between the trucks and get to the river. They can't tell we're American . . . not with those blackout lights."

It was incredible. Adam could not believe what he was doing. He slipped and stumbled on the broken edge of the macadam road, one hand groping along the truck or half-track beside him, sometimes clinging to it to keep from sliding into the ditch. In some of the trucks German soldiers laughed and shouted at each other; in others they sang, deep-voiced rhythmic chants of triumph. Adam and Ritchie moved faster than the vehicles, trying desperately in the dark to find a gap between one and the next wide enough to get through. It seemed hopeless. The drivers rarely let a gap develop and when it did they gunned their motors, closing up until metal squealed and clanked.

Once they met someone walking in the opposite direction and flattened themselves against the truck beside them, making room for the German to pass. He snarled something as he went; an officer perhaps? Maybe, thought Adam, fighting a lunatic impulse to laugh, I should have saluted him?

A little farther on, something clinked against his helmet, bounced into the ditch, and he flinched violently. It was an empty ration can and he looked up, frozen in terror, at a pale face in the driver's seat of the truck.

"*Verzeihung!*" said the face casually.

The growling vehicles stalled once more and when they moved again, Adam and Ritchie got lucky. A truck motor coughed and died, the vehicle stayed in place, and the one before it crept away. Adam could hear the Germans in the truck cab shouting at each other. The starter snarled repeatedly without catching.

"*Lichter aus!*" bellowed a voice, and the driver killed his blackout lights, the little blue cat's-eye lamps that threw a dim light on the macadam in front of the truck.

"Now!" hissed Adam. "Come on . . . and don't hurry!"

It was hard to heed that warning. Every nerve in his body screamed "Run!" but he managed somehow to walk casually across the front of the stalled truck. More luck—the vehicle in the adjacent lane had stopped too, its lights still burning but the driver so busy cursing the occupants of the cab of the dead truck that he paid no attention to Adam and Ritchie.

As soon as he reached the farther edge of the macadam, Adam wanted to plunge down the riverbank but he mastered that impulse too. That would surely catch the eye of the yelling driver. Turning north, Ritchie following so close he stumbled on Adam's heels, they walked the length of the truck and then left the road.

Adam almost pitched forward down the steep bank but he squatted and slid, listening to the uproar behind him, hoping desperately nobody had seen them leave the road. The near lane of vehicles rumbled and growled forward but he could still hear the futile snarl of the starter on the stalled truck.

We ought to be farther away, he thought. If he can't get it started pretty quick, he'll draw a crowd. He edged his way forward, ice crackling under his boots. There was probably ice on both banks of the river but in the middle it was open; he could hear the swift current chuckling and splashing. If only he could find a ford—a few rocks that would keep them out of the water. If they got thoroughly wet they might freeze before they could find shelter. Maybe it's so deep in the middle we'll have to swim. He put that thought away desperately.

On the road the stalled motor started. The driver raced it noisily. "Erni!" somebody yelled. "Erni, *mach schnell!*"

Looking back apprehensively, Adam walked into the man so hard their helmets clanged together. He dropped his carbine.

"*Dummer Schuft!*" growled the startled German, "*Pass mal auf!*"

Ritchie flung himself on the man, knocking him off his feet, both of them sprawling on the creaking ice rim of the Our River.

"Don't let him yell . . . stop him!" gasped Adam. He dived on the struggling figures, groping for the German's face. Ritchie was there first, one hand locked in the man's chin strap, forcing his head back, the other clamped over his mouth. The German thrashed violently but Ritchie hung on. Adam knelt astraddle the frantic German, smashing his forearm into his face.

It was impossible no one on the road heard the noise—three men kicking and flailing at each other, a terrible strangled bellowing by the terrified German. The wordless howl burst through Ritchie's hands and Adam clamped his over them.

Grunting, straining, they forced his head through the ice into water so cold it seared the flesh. Inches from his own, terrible eyes stared at Adam. Not until he saw the stream of blood snatched by the current from the man's nose did he understand why the eyes were so big and terrible—they were magnified by several inches of water.

"Leggo of him . . ." muttered Ritchie. "He's dead."

They knelt, gasping for breath, and after a while Adam asked softly, "What was he doing down here? He didn't hear us."

"Taking a leak?"

Adam shook his head. "He could pee off the back of the truck . . . or go to the edge of the road."

"Maybe he was shy," said Ritchie. "Didn't want anybody to watch him."

That was absurd but it was an absurd conversation anyway. Together they boosted the dead German into the current where he disappeared at once.

"What now?" asked Ritchie.

"We got to find a place we can cross without gettin' wet all over."

Somehow the Germans had got their traffic jam unstuck—not completely, but at least they were moving in hitches. Maybe because they don't have to worry about us anymore, thought Adam; not that we ever worried them very much. He wondered if what was left of his own regiment, the 423rd, had surrendered like the 422nd.

They must have, he decided. If they were still trying to get the bridge at Schoenberg we'd hear it. Maybe they haven't quit yet. Maybe they're still up on a hill somewhere, waiting for . . . what? There would be no help from Saint Vith—not with endless columns of krauts like this one pouring across the river.

We've got to move, he told Ritchie. Got to get to Saint Vith before the Germans sew it up in a bag. The traffic on the road above them had picked up speed, moving steadily now. Even over the wind scouring the river valley he could hear the infantrymen singing:

> . . . *Wenn wir fahren . . . wenn wir fahren . . .*
> *Wenn wir fahren gegen Eng-l-andt!*

Bastards! How can they do this to us? They're whipped—everybody said they're whipped.

"Yuch-hai-sah-sah!" The high-pitched yell rose above the roar of motors. "*Es geht ums ganze!*" Something heavy bounced down the bank, skidded onto the ice and stopped there, fizzing noisily.

"Down . . . get down!" yelled Adam.

"Wha . . .?" Ritchie's voice was lost in a twanging explosion. Shards of ice and a fan of water gouted up. The traffic on the road growled past and after a moment Adam raised his head.

"Ritchie? You all right, Ritchie?"

There was no reply. He felt his way along the bank until his hands found Ritchie, turned him over, sought his face. "You hit? Are you all right?" The young soldier made a soft noise, went limp in Adam's arms. No breath, no pulse. He was dead. How? How did they know we were here?

They didn't—the trucks rumbled on without stopping; no one came to look for them. After a while Adam knew what had happened: some comic, high on schnapps or victory, had pulled the pin of a grenade and tossed it out the back of a truck just for fun. It rolled down the bank and killed Ritchie. If it had gone into the water it would have been harmless. It hadn't.

Adam bent his head and sobbed in helpless rage. After a while he got to his feet and plodded upstream, heedless of the noise he made. He came to a rock thrusting into the river, climbed onto it on hands and knees, and peered at the swift current bubbling around it. He could see another a few feet away, the water boiling between them. He stood up and jumped. There was another rock beyond; he had found a ford. He got across with only his boots soaked.

The forest west of the river was deeper, more dense than on the hills from which he and Ritchie had escaped. He mourned for Ritchie and blundered from tree to tree for a long time before he stopped. I could be going in circles, he thought. I don't know where I am. The stuttering racket of something passing overhead made him cringe but it was no threat: a buzz bomb, a German rocket headed for Liege or a channel port—maybe even London. He could see the pulsing flare of its exhaust through the branches of the trees.

It's going west—follow it. There were more, and he guided himself on the orange track they made through the sky. No snow, no clouds, and a kraut rocket to show me the way. When he could go no farther, he sat down, his back to a tree, exhausted. There was something a little ahead that was not part of the forest—too square and regular. He crawled closer.

A bunker: plank-walled with a sandbagged roof. He found the open door and crouched by it for a long time, listening. No sound inside. Knowing it was a crazy thing to do, he crept inside, waited again. Nothing. It didn't matter what was in there with him, he was too tired to care. There was a canvas shelter half hanging on the door and he pulled it down, wrapped himself in it and was asleep before he could worry anymore.

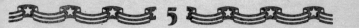

5

B ONE-CHILLING cold awakened Adam. The interior of the bunker was as silent and evil-smelling as he had found it last night: old sweat, damp charred wood, and something he could not identify.

Damnfool thing, he thought: crawling in here and going to sleep in the middle of the German army. Could have been half a dozen krauts sacked out in here. He could see nothing: the thin light of dawn reached only a little way beyond the door. He fingered the action of his carbine, found it warm and moist because he had wrapped it with him in the shelter half in which he slept.

Krauts wouldn't be dumb enough to sleep in here without a guard and they'd have made a fire to keep warm. He settled on his heels against the plank wall, trying to think what to do. His feet were so cold they ached. He tried to clench numb toes and remembered the army nurse in England.

Trench foot, she said. Infantry gets it if they don't dry their feet and change socks every day. Their toes rot and when they get to the hospital we have to cut them off. So I got to find some dry socks, Adam told himself.

That nurse—she kissed him, mouth open, tongue busy. She groaned when he sought her breasts, and then she hit him with a clenched fist.

"No! You'll be gone tomorrow and if you're lucky you'll be back in two weeks . . . flat on your ass with a godawful hole in you. Let go of me, dammit!"

He forgave her the fist because she cried and kissed

him again and said she wouldn't make love with infantry lieutenants anymore. They didn't live long enough to write and say thank you or they came back to her hospital all torn up. Ten days, she said, that's how long most of you last, and I won't sweat that out anymore.

Look for some socks, Talcut. There's nobody in here. His cigarette lighter was long out of fuel but he had a folder of K-ration matches. The third one he tried was dry enough to strike.

In its tiny glow he saw a stove and a candle in the lid of a ration tin. He lit the candle and looked around him, carbine ready. An elegant bunker: sawn planks nailed to a log frame, a triple tier of crude bunks against the far wall. Had to be American.

When the builders bugged out they took everything of value, though. Nothing left. Adam lifted the candle high and almost dropped it. There was a man in the top bunk, blanket pulled over his head, but his booted feet were exposed: American boots.

"Hey . . . hey, buddy!" whispered Adam. "Wake up!" He nudged one of the boots with the muzzle of his carbine. There was no response and he knew why. They took everything else—why didn't they take him?

They had left something he needed, though. Wadded under the head of the man on the bunk was an olive-drab cotton duck mackinaw, the kind with a wool lining and a big warm collar. Quartermaster truck drivers in England sold them for twenty-five dollars.

He pulled it out carefully and there was a canvas gas-mask cover beneath it. He took that too because it was full of something besides a gas mask: shaving gear, a towel, and two pairs of G.I. socks. A couple of candy bars were wrapped in the towel and he tore the paper from one to stuff it in his mouth.

Swallowing the stale chocolate, he put the candle on the box and reluctantly lifted the blanket, dropping it at once. There was a big field dressing bound over the face, rust-colored from the blood that had soaked it before he died.

There was something else in the bunk he had to have, though he hated the taking of it. The dead soldier wore tanker pants: heavy blanket-lined duck overalls with web suspenders to hold them up. He had to take off the man's boots to get them. I got to have 'em, he told himself, teeth clenched. I got to hide at night and if I can't keep warm I'll die.

Pulling on the tanker overalls, he carefully recovered his benefactor with the blanket. Ought to take that too, he thought, but one end was stiff with dried blood. He wolfed down the other candy bar and went to the door to study his map. It was damp and he unfolded it carefully. He had lost his compass and there was no sun to help him find direction, but the sounds of war would help.

Truck motors and the grunting roar of tanks—that would be the road from Andler to Schoenberg he crossed last night with Ritchie. He shivered, remembering the German in the river and the mindless, casually thrown grenade. All right . . . he was west of that road and the rumble of artillery fire behind him must be Saint Vith. Faint. That meant the krauts had driven all the way to the town, six or seven miles west of him.

I'll make it, Adam thought. Move at night and hide in daylight. Not in a fancy bunker like this again. Kraut patrol find a palace like this and they'll move in.

He climbed south to a wooded hill overlooking the Schoenberg-Saint Vith road and was appalled. It was jammed, double-banked with trucks, assault guns, and infantry plodding alongside. The rumble of firing to the west and the stalled German vehicles meant the Americans still held Saint Vith and pretty soon now the kraut infantry would spill off the road into the woods. Get away from it, he thought.

He moved north as fast as he dared—in that direction he would strike the woods road that went from Hochkreuz to Andler. The one Ritchie showed him. He had had trouble getting a jeep over it so the krauts wouldn't be using it for heavy vehicles.

On his map, the remembered track showed only as a dotted line—the map-makers concurred in his esti-mate of its worth—and it was less than two miles north of the Schoenberg-Saint Vith road but it took him well into the afternoon to reach it. Twice he had to hide from German patrols, thankful they were noisily in-competent. He heard them coming long before they were in sight, so he never saw them.

Burrowing into the thickest clump of firs at hand, he wormed his way up through the branches until he was clear of the ground. He was enough of a hunter to recognize a deadly peculiarity of this Belgian forest:the branches stopped a foot short of the ground and if a man lay down he could see quite a distance under them. Germans—even green soldiers—must know that trick.

Long before he reached the woods track the snarl of motors and squealing tank tracks told him the Ger-mans were using it as well as the main road. He crept close enough to see what was there and his heart sank: armored artillery, long-barreled guns reversed in travel-lock, half-tracks with antiaircraft guns, trucks, and Volkswagens.

Nobody rode the vehicles except the drivers; every other man, rifle slung, sweated and heaved at the sliding, growling armor. Even sergeants and officers helped push. These krauts were in a mortal hurry to get somewhere.

One good thing, Adam thought: they're too busy to look for Americans in the woods. He worked his way cautiously east across a series of ridges, hoping to find the tail of the column and cross behind it. Wasted hope. It was nearly four-thirty and dusk was gathering when he saw the lights of a village. Herresbach, he decided, and it was swarming with Germans, the sin-gle street jammed with trucks, headlights on and mo-tors running. More infantry, waiting for the armor to get through that ruinous track. They'll be here all night, thought Adam. What'll I do?

Find a place to hide and lie low till they get off the

trail he decided. Then I can go north and circle around Saint Vith—get in by the back door. It was snowing again, nor hard but enough for him to make tracks he didn't want to make. Best find a hidey-hole and stay put till the snow covers your trail.

He went deeper into the forest, away from the noisy village, looking for the highest hill he could find—high and hard to climb. If the Germans sent out patrols they'd not be likely to go hill-climbing in the dark. He found a straight, narrow cut through the forest—firebreak, he guessed, not a trail. There was still light enough to see that the snow-dusted carpet of pine and fir needles was undisturbed.

Cautiously he peered both ways and froze. Not a dozen yards away a man stood in the firebreak, his back to Adam. He turned and Adam edged backward into the trees. Just stay still, he told himself. Stay still and he'll never see you. The silhouette of the helmet looked American but he couldn't see the face. Moving with surprising silence, the figure drew nearer, stopping every third or fourth step to study the firebreak behind him. Must be a G.I., thought Adam. Kraut wouldn't be that careful this close to the village.

He froze against a stout pine, hardly breathing. There was a faint scrunch of boots on snow and suddenly the man crouched and pointed his rifle at Adam, who managed to let out a little breath—he was too scared to take any in.

Now he knew why he couldn't make out the man's face and knew also he had to be a G.I. He was black. Adam had seen black artillerymen in Saint Vith. Maybe their gun positions were up here.

"Don't shoot," he whispered as calmly as he could. "American . . . don't shoot!" The repetition was more urgent. The rifle moved just enough to cover him precisely.

"Yeah? Who the heavyweight champion of the worl'?"

"Boxing?"

"What else? Quick, man . . . what's his name?"

"Joe Louis!" gasped Adam.

"What color is he?"

Adam let his breath out in a rush. "Black . . . like you."

"Aawl right . . . you got it, man." The rifle lowered. "What's your name, buddy?"

"Talcut. Lieutenant, 423rd Infantry."

"Can't see no bar in this light, Lootenant. Sorry 'bout that." He put out a hand and Adam shook it. "Sergeant Julian, Triple-three Arty."

333rd Artillery Battalion, Adam dredged from memory. Corps artillery. He had seen it listed on the map of the 106th Division artillery battalion on Skyline Drive.

"How'd you get cut off? I thought corps artillery got out the first day."

"No, suh! They kept my battery other side the river to help out you folks on the line. Up to our ass in krauts 'fore we know y'all done let 'em through. Lost all our guns an' most nearly all our people. Some of 'em got across that bridge at Shaneburg an' I reckon they's a few more like me in these woods. Krauts got the rest."

"We didn't let 'em through. They came through that cavalry outfit up north."

"I reckon so. They sure enough bagged your outfit, didn't they? How'd you git away?"

"How'd you know they got my regiment?"

"I was with a bunch of your folks yesterday. Three, four hundred of 'em. They said your colonel done surrendered everbody in th' regiment."

"What was left of it," said Adam bitterly. "Where are these men you talked to?"

The sergeant shook his head. "Ain't right smart standin' here gabbin' like this, Lootenant. Krauts right over that hill."

"I saw them. I was trying to get across that trail."

"We got the same thing in mind, I reckon. How's about we find us a place to hide till they get they ass off that road. I want to get up north jus' like you.

Whut if we stick together an' try it when they ain't so damn many kraut-faces down there?"

"Good! I'm game. We ought to stay close enough to hear what's going on. Soon as it gets quiet we can slip across."

"I know a good place. Saw it this mornin'. Been up an' down this road twice today tryin' to cross over."

He led the way along the firebreak away from Herresbach, then pushed into the woods, climbing. Adam followed, sweating in spite of the cold. Trying to watch his feet, he didn't see Julian stop and ran into him.

"Right here somewhere, Lootenant. Watch where you step so you don't fall in it."

Fall in what? wondered Adam. Julian bent over, prodding cautiously at the ground with his rifle butt. It was snowing harder and Adam shivered. He was sweaty and the cold wind was refrigerating him. The black sergeant grunted softly and straightened up, raising something like a trapdoor to expose a black hole in the snow.

"Reckon it's an old machine-gun hole. Krauts musta dug it last fall when we first run 'em outta here. Get in an' I'll put this here lid on us. Time it gits snowed on awhile ain't nobody gonna find it . . . 'less he falls in it."

The cover was made of thin branches skillfully and tightly woven together. Camouflage, Adam guessed. The weather in September must have been good enough for the krauts to worry about strafing fighter planes. The woven cover was green then and light enough to throw back easily when the machine-gunner had to see out. It was a big hole, big enough for two men to sit in, legs stretched out. Long unused, the sides were cold and slimy and crumbling.

"Tell me," Adam whispered when they had settled themselves, "about those people from my regiment. Where are they?"

"Two, three miles other side the river. Big hill with

a little bitty town at the bottom. Loud-es-felt, the major called it— somethin' like that."

"What major?"

"Don' know his name but he's a doughfoot. Thought for a while I had me a fightin' cat. Got everbody dug in good, made sure we all had some ammo—even got us somethin' to eat. Had a couple of them half-tracks with quad fifties on 'em and them antiaircraft folks said they got Saint Vith on their radio. I reckoned all we had to do was sit tight an' somebody'd come get us."

"What about the krauts?"

"They tried to stomp us a couple times but they didn't have no tank an' they purely didn't like them fifties. They got a truck with a loudspeaker on it an' they played music an' said they give us hot pancakes if we'd quit." Julian chuckled.

"What's funny?"

"Big ol' doughfoot in a hole by me ever' time that loudspeaker come on, he'd yell, 'Blow it out yer ass, you kraut sonovabitch!' Me an' him, we could see that truck an' we got it. Snuck out a ways an' I give him cover with my rifle an' he lays a grenade right on 'em. We ain't heard no more about pancakes after that."

"Why didn't you stay there? Can we find that hill again?"

Julian grunted. "Not me . . . don't wanta go where them folks is goin'."

Adam considered that a moment. "They surrendered and you got away?"

"Took my foot in hand an' got the hell outta there before that major quit. I could see it comin'."

"What?"

"Kraut officer come up the road with a big white flag on his car. Talked American real good. Said all's he wanted was a truce to run his ambulances on the road but then he started talkin' about all the kraut artillery comin' along behind him."

"So the major decided to give up?"

"Not right then. Sent a lootenant with the kraut an'

told us quit shootin' till they brought him back. He come back all right an' said there was a shitpot full o' krauts with artillery an' tanks an' we was gonna catch all kinda hell pretty quick. I knew right then the rag was off the bush an' come dark I eased on off. They told us back in France krauts don't like nigger soljers an' I ain't gonna give 'em no crack at Miz Julian's boy.''

"You think they surrendered?"

"I'd lay money on it, Lootenant, had I any."

Adam sighed. "You reckon there's any more G.I.'s holding out around here?"

"Could be. There's been some shootin' behind the next village up the road with all them krauts on it."

"Where I met you?"

"Naw, other way. They ain't got a chance in hell if the krauts turn that armored artillery on 'em but if we can get across that road we'll go take us a look."

Adam shivered and buried his face in the collar of his mackinaw. He must have slept for a while because when Julian shook him awake it had stopped snowing. The sergeant was standing, his head out of the hole.

"You hear something?"

"Nope. See if you can."

The silence was complete. Either the Germans had got themselves through the forest to the west or they had quit trying. "Nothing," said Adam.

"All right . . . let's ease on back to the road an' see what's doin'."

It was not deserted. There were a few infantry stragglers and once a motorcycle, a messenger probably. He spun his wheels in the deep-churned mud and they could hear him swearing hoarsely. He disappeared and the track was empty.

"Let's go," whispered Julian.

They floundered through ruts two feet deep cut by the tracked vehicles and climbed on the north side into forest so thick they sometimes had to crawl beneath the branches. There seemed to be no other east-west trails but after a while they stumbled into a heavily used track angling northwest. Almost at once they encountered a truck, slewed across the road. Julian's hand made a faint rasp on its canvas cover.

"That's one of ours," he whispered. "Broke down or got stuck."

"You reckon there's anything to eat in it?"

"Dunno, an' I ain't goin' to look. Maybe they booby-trapped it."

About six o'clock they saw a single light, dim and unmoving. "What is it?" Adam asked softly.

"House, I reckon. Couple of 'em . . . see there. Look right close an' you can see another one. Village maybe."

"Let's wait till it gets light and if there aren't any krauts maybe we can talk the Belgians out of something to eat."

"Sheeit!" muttered Julian. "They ain't no more Beljeek than I am. These folks is kraut."

"Maybe not. We've got to be four or five miles west of the border."

They waited, shivering, for another hour until there was a pale light seeping through the dawn fog—light enough to make out a dozen stone houses clustered about a crossroad.

"Oh, yeah!" muttered Julian. "Good thing we waited."

"What do you see?"

"Look at that barn."

"I don't see anything."

"You see that big old stone barn?"

"Yeah."

"Right beside that pile o' cowshit . . . big wooden door with a little one cut in it. See him?"

Adam squinted, and not until the man moved did he see what Sergeant Julian had found: a helmeted figure barely visible in the open door of the barn. After a long while he came outside and urinated on the manure pile. Within minutes there were half a dozen more in the barnyard, each making a steamy morning contribution to the farmer's manure heap.

No word of command could be heard but one of them must have given an order. Rifles slung, they moved north through the village, a couple of men on each side of the road. They wore white snow-camouflage parkas—real ones, not stolen sheets—and their helmets were whitewashed. As soon as they left the houses they unslung their rifles, and there was still no audible command.

"Ain't no weekend soljers," breathed Julian. "What you reckon they are?"

Adam thought he knew. The battalion staff officers said the Germans who broke through the cavalry in the Losheim Gap were SS.

"That's just a patrol," said Julian. "Friggin' place is full of 'em. Look what they doin' now."

Two men pulled a tarpaulin from a strange vehicle in the barnyard—a two-wheeled trailer with a box on the axle that bore a short stovepipe. A rolling kitchen, thought Adam in wonder. He had seen pictures of them in books about the last world war and this was the same except it had rubber tires like a truck trailer. The two men carried split wood from the farmer's huge winter stack by the barn and stuffed it into the box, and the stovepipe emitted puffs of smoke.

"Chow. How many men you reckon they feed with that thing, Lootenant?"

"More'n I want to fool with." When there was light enough, Adam got out his map. "Wereth," he said.

"Wear what?"

"Name of that village . . . I think."

"You still want to go in there?"

"No thanks. Let's get out of here."

They moved southwest to a hilltop from which they could see a river running east and west and another village crossroad: Germans in the village and more on the road south of it. A battery of horse-drawn artillery was going into position in a snow-covered field and drivers led the teams back to the village. The big long-barreled guns erupted in smoke and thunder.

"One-fifties," muttered Julian. "Mediums, like my outfit."

"What do you reckon they're shooting at?"

Julian studied the map. "Could be Saint Vith but that's right far. More likely them G.I.'s that was still fightin' yesterday, poor bastards. Got no more chance than a whore's prayer."

He's right, thought Adam. No handful of Americans can hold out against all these krauts. They told us they were whipped, he thought bitterly. Where'd they get all these tanks and guns and infantry if they're whipped? Somebody sure had his head up his ass and locked. How'd they get all this stuff together without us knowing about it?

"What'll we do?" he asked bleakly.

The black sergeant folded the map carefully and shook his head. "It's goin' to be . . ." he said thoughtfully, "a while before all them generals get their shit in order an' throw these boogers outta here. Our folks'll come back all right but it ain't gonna be tomorrow. We got to find us a place to hide till they do."

"Where, for God's sake?"

"In them woods somewheres. Ain't enough krauts in the world to clean out them woods. Find us a hole an' pull it in after us."

"We've got to eat."

"You got to quit mindin' your gut, Lootenant. We'll find somethin'. That truck we saw last night ain't the only one in there. One of 'em's got to have rations on it. Come on, let's go look."

It was possible, Adam conceded. That was one hell of a cold wet hole we were in but it would do. Julian was right—the Germans would have to fall in it to find it. If we've got rations we can make out.

They went back into the forest, circling Wereth to strike the woods road south of it. The first American vehicle they found was a jeep, windshield shattered, shards of glass frozen in the ice sheeting the hood. The Germans had hit it with a machine gun, Adam guessed; head-on. There were two American soldiers in the front seat, one of them with both hands on top of the windshield, frozen there as if he were trying to hold it up. The Germans had not even come to look at their kill because there were K-ration boxes on the floor in back and half a cardboard case of canned C rations on the seat.

The floor of the jeep had a layer of sandbags on it—supposed to help if you ran over a mine, Adam knew. Julian emptied two and they filled them with cans, opening one to share the crackers and frozen jam in it.

There were more on the trail behind the jeep: a three-quarter-ton truck with a 57-millimeter antitank gun hooked to the towing pintle, then a two-and-a-half-ton truck. Must be the one we ran into last night, Adam thought.

"You think we ought to check 'em out?"

"Can't carry no more, Lootenant. Find us a place to hide an' we come back."

"What if the krauts get here first?"

"They right busy. Be a while 'fore they get in here."

They followed the track south, climbing again; passed another truck with no sign of damage.

"Cavalry," said Adam. "See the bumper marking? Must be part of that troop that was in Andler for a while."

"They hauled ass in a hurry, didn't they?"

"Sure looks like it."

"I reckon," said Julian, "you could be right about krauts smellin' around here. They ain't nothin' wrong with this deuce-and-a-half an' they could use it. They get a few of them an' they ain't goin' to be pullin' guns with horses no more. Let's get us off this road."

They climbed, sweating, a steep hill to the west, shrouded with interlocked fir and pine trees, followed an old footpath that wound to the crest, where Julian put down the sack and cradled his rifle.

"You see what I see?" he whispered.

"I sure do."

Just beyond the hilltop was the shingled roof of a

house with a fieldstone chimney rising above it. They circled cautiously until they could see more: a log house dug into the steep southern slope of the hill with a little hollow in front. Over the door were the weathered antlers of some kind of deer: twelve-pointer, Adam counted, a yard between the tips—a damn big deer.

"What do you think?"

Julian shrugged. "Sure is hid good. Ain't been nobody up that path in a long time. How 'bout that deer? Get us one like him an' we'll eat meat all winter."

Adam grinned at him. "You a hunter, Julian?"

"I done some," conceded the sergeant. "Got me a real nice mule deer one time. Nowhere near that big."

"What's a mule deer?"

"Arizona. Lots of 'em there. Reckon we better take us a look inside?"

"Why not? Beats hell out of your hole."

Adam studied the chimney of the house. Anybody in there would surely have made a fire. Julian chuckled softly.

"Ain't none, Lootenant."

"How do you know?"

"Smell it if there was a fire."

Adam studied the grinning black face and suddenly knew why Julian had whirled in the firebreak searching for somebody hidden in the trees.

"You smelled me . . . when you squatted down and pointed your gun at me. Right?"

"Sure, man. You been smokin' an' sweatin', ain't you?"

"I'll be damned!"

The door of the cabin was shut but the long iron handle turned easily under Adam's hand and the door gave to his push. Julian unhooked a fragmentation grenade from the web suspenders holding up his cartridge belt.

The door opened into a hallway floored with red tiles, another door on each side, both shut. Adam tried the one on his left. The room was cold and dark and empty. The other door was latched on the inside; the latch rattled when he pushed.

"Kick it open," whispered Julian.

Bracing his back against the opposite wall, Adam kicked hard, breaking the latch, slamming the door against the inside wall. There was light enough from a window to see the fireplace, a little pile of burned twigs on the hearth, fluffy gray ash, and the tiny glow of a live coal—not enough to make smoke. Julian grunted and Adam heard the clink of the pull-ring and safety pin of his grenade on the tiles. Somewhere in the room there began a thin terrible sound—a breathless whimper that rose to a wail, kept on rising.

"*Nicht scheissen . . . nur civilisten! Bitte . . . nicht scheissen!*" That was somebody else because the keening wail never stopped.

"Hold it!" Adam yelled at Julian. "Don't throw it!"

He jumped into the room, carbine leveled. Across the room a woman huddled against the wall, hands outstretched, an expression of wild terror on her face. The shrill awful sound was a child wedged in a corner, head down, arms wrapped about her knees, bright blond hair spilling over them.

The woman shivered convulsively. "Ah . . . ah . . ." she gasped. There was no one else in the room. Julian followed Adam, grenade ready.

"Put the pin back in that thing, for Christ's sake!" said Adam. The child raised her head, stared open-mouthed at Julian. A little girl, blue eyes white-rimmed in terror. She made a soft gulping sound and threw up.

"Jesus Christ on the mountain!" said Julian. "I ain't gonna hurt you." Adam, carbine pointed at the woman, heard him muttering as he searched the hallway for the grenade pin.

"Ami . . . you are ami?" she whispered. "Please . . ." Her English was good despite the strange way she spoke it. "No one is here but me an' the little girl. Please . . . don' shoot!"

"Move!" he said. "Move away from the wall and keep your hands out." She edged forward and there was light enough from the window to see her better: a girl; short-cropped red-brown hair, thin face with high cheekbones and metal-gray eyes. A wide mouth, extra wide, full-lipped. A tall angular girl in a green sweater and a long heavy skirt, black leather boots, the toes gray with wear. The sweater was dark German army green, but no army issued a sweater with a turtleneck like that, gathered in folds about her throat like a great untidy ruff.

Julian was back, safety pin replaced in the grenade handle. He spread the legs of the cotter key, used the angle of the door frame to wedge them wide apart. Silently, the child threw up again.

"You . . ." Julian extended the grenade toward the frightened girl. "You can talk to her?" She nodded. "Tell her I ain't gonna hurt her. Make her stop that."

Without taking her eyes from the Americans, the girl spoke: some kind of German—a slurred dialect like the farmwoman in Hochkreuz. The child whimpered.

"I think she has never see a *neger* . . . black man," said the girl desperately. "She is afraid."

"Ever'body got to see one sometime, lady. Ain't no call to take on like that."

"Please . . . ?"

"Aw, hell!" said Julian. He put his rifle against the wall and searched his pockets. The girl shut her eyes and gulped for breath.

"Now, little missy," rumbled Julian, squatting before the child. He stripped the foil from a packet of candy, separated the top piece, and held it out. She put both hands over her face and hiccuped convulsively.

"Watch it," warned Adam. Julian put the candy on the floor and got to his feet. He held out the packet to Adam, who shook his head.

Charms. Some huckster had put that name to the vile candy the U.S. Army distributed in vast quantities: half a dozen cubes stacked in a foil wrapper emblazoned "SIX DIFFERENT DELICIOUS FLAVORS!" Each cube was a different color all right but they all had the same insipid flavor.

Adam had a theory about Charms. For the first two years of the war there were enough soldiers in America to consume all the Kool-Aid some profiteering middleman sold the army. By 1944 most of them were overseas, where they could find something better to drink—in Europe anyway. The resourceful peddler turned his warehouse full of Kool-Aid powder into Charms and the army kept on buying them.

"Who are you?" he demanded of the girl.

"Anneke," she whispered.

"What?"

"Anneke . . . *Belgique*."

Sergeant Julian snorted. "That's kraut she's been talkin', ain't it?"

"If she comes from around here she has to speak German," said Adam reasonably. "They all do."

"If she's Bel-jeek she's got a I.D. card with her picture on it. Let's see it." He held out his hand.

"Please?"

"Yeah . . . I thought so."

"She doesn't understand, that's all. You have a card? It says who you are with a photograph of you."

She looked at Julian and swallowed convulsively. "It is lost."

The black sergeant picked up his rifle and the girl cringed. "I got a paper!" she said desperately. "From the police . . ." She pulled up the sweater with shaking hands and produced a folded paper. Julian took it.

"It's in frog! Can't read it."

Adam took it from him, held it to the graying light at the window: half a dozen lines of violet typescript, an ornate circular design applied with a rubber stamp, and a scrawled signature.

"*Le porteur . . .*" began the first line, with "Anneke" and an incomprehensible word written in ink in the blank that followed. "That's your name? Anneke?" Adam pointed at it.

Cautiously the girl looked. "Yess!"

"What's this?" Adam indicated the next word.

"*Familienname* . . . my family name."

"That's a name?" Adam spelled it out: " 'X-h-o-f-f-r-i-o-n.' How do you say it?"

"Hof-ree-ohn. In Sankt Vith they say 'Zhoef-ree-ohn' but that is not correct. It is Walloonie name . . . not German!"

"What the hell's she sayin'?"

"It's a pass of some kind and that must be her name . . . nobody would make up a name like that. What happened to your card with the photo?"

She shrugged. "It is lost. The police at Sankt Vith give me that paper because I don' got a card."

Julian shook his head. "She say Sank Veet jus' like a kraut. She ain't no Bel-jeek."

"I am not German!" said Anneke desperately. "Belgian police don' give me a pass if I am German."

"Maybe," said Adam.

"You stay right here, you understand?" said Julian to the girl. She nodded, eyes big and worried. "Come on, Lootenant, we got to talk."

In the entryway he looked at Adam. "What're we gonna do?"

"I don't want to go back to that hole."

"She gets away an' we'll have krauts'll all over us."

"We can watch her. Make a fire and get something hot to eat."

"Your gut's goin' to kill you, Lootenant."

"She's Belgian! She won't tell on us."

"Lootenant, you got rocks in your head!"

"What d'you want to do?"

"Get the hell outta here before she gets away or somebody comes lookin' for her an' that kid."

"She'll tell the krauts about us when they get here."

"Hell, like you said, they ain't got enough men to hunt out these woods. Lemme scare the pee outta her so's she stays put till we're gone."

The girl was where they had left her, the child curled in her corner, head on her knees. Julian pointed his rifle at the girl and she put both hands over her face. "We goin' outside now. You come outta this place an' . . ." He drew a finger across his throat. "You know what I mean?"

She watched him through her fingers, wordless.

"Get over there by the kid. You set right there till we come back."

Another nod and she slid down the wall to sit cross-legged against it.

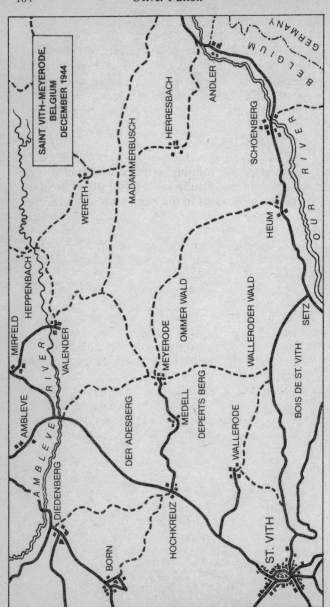

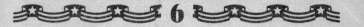

6

THE LAST trace of light in the western sky died as they left the hunting lodge or whatever it was. Adam thought regretfully of the big stone fireplace and the canned rations in the bag on his shoulder. We could have made a little fire like that girl did and got something hot to eat.

As hungry as he was, his stomach rejected the thought of half-frozen meat and beans spooned from a can in the dark. "Where we going?"

"Christ, I dunno, Lootenant! We gotta get away from this place."

"Pack this stuff all the way back across the road to your hole?"

"Too far . . . too hard to find in the dark."

"How about the truck where we got the rations? We can find that easy enough."

"So can the krauts, Lootenant, sure as hell."

"Not tonight . . . they won't go looking for it in the dark. We can get out before daylight tomorrow."

Julian muttered something and Adam wrestled with a terrible thought. What if they do? What if they find us asleep? They won't kill us. We'll just go in the bag with all the rest of the people that surrendered. We keep on running around this trap and that SS outfit will get us. They don't take prisoners.

Just like he could smell a man in the dark, Sergeant Julian knew what Adam was thinking. He stopped abruptly and put his face close to Adam's. "You wanta quit, Lootenant?"

"No . . . no!"

"Then don't think about it. You wanta quit, you go find yourself a nice pussycat kraut an' hold your hands up an' say 'Kamer-rad.' That's how you do it. You wanta fight, you stick with me."

"I won't quit," said Adam. "I'm with you."

"All right . . . let's go get us some blankets off that truck an' we'll get away from it an' sack out in the woods. Come tomorrow we'll find us a good place. These bastards ain't won no war, Lootenant . . . our folks'll come back."

They found the road, followed it north, and literally walked into the American truck skewed across it. Adam fell over Julian, who was crouched tugging at the grenade on his suspenders.

"What . . .?"

"Shoosh! Somebody in there."

Whoever was in the truck was hurt. Bad hurt. He groaned and whimpered. The door of the cab opened with a squeal and a man climbed down, slipped in the ruts, and fell to his knees. Julian was on him like a big cat, pinning him to the ground.

Whoever he had caught did not give up—he fought desperately. Adam flung himself on the dim bulk of struggling men, trying to help.

"Motherfucker . . ." said someone quite clearly, and Julian chuckled.

"Easy, buddy . . . take it easy. We American."

The struggling mass disentangled and Adam stared into a white scared face. "Who're you?" he demanded.

"Kuzyk . . . Private Kuzyk. Who the hell are you?"

They got that straightened out and knelt shivering in the frozen ruts of the road. "Who's in the truck?" asked Julian.

"My buddy, Guido . . . he's hit bad. I put him in there so he wouldn't freeze to death. He don't get someplace warm, he's goin' to die anyway."

"You're with the cavalry?" asked Adam.

"Hell, no . . . engineers. Sawmill company. Cuttin' planks for the doughs on the line."

"Ain't no line now, friend," muttered Julian. "It done gone away."

"You tellin' me? We been dodgin' krauts all day . . . where the hell did they all come from?"

That was a question that might never be answered. Kuzyk was sure of only one thing: if his buddy didn't get warm he was going to die before morning. If he lived till then and they didn't find a doctor for him, he would probably die anyway. Bleeding like a stuck pig, said Kuzyk, and I can't do anything to stop it.

"Artillery, I guess. Blew a hole in his gut you can put your fist in. He's got to have a medic . . . quick."

"Medics we ain't got," said Julian. "What d'you think, Lootenant?"

There was only one answer to that: back to the lodge on the hill. They could get him warm there anyway.

"We got to take a chance. No other way, is there?"

Julian knew what he meant. "I reckon you're right. Hate to go back to that place but ain't nowhere else we can make a fire. What about that girl?"

"She's gone by now. She wouldn't wait for us to come back."

They put the wounded soldier in a blanket, Julian carrying one end, Adam and Kuzyk the other. Julian piled the two bags of rations on the man's legs and they struggled uphill with their groaning burden. It seemed to Adam it took them hours to reach the lodge.

"Guido . . . you all right, buddy?" Kuzyk asked repeatedly. The man in the blanket grunted and muttered at first but by the time they reached the house he was ominously silent.

"Put him down," whispered Julian. "Lemme check that place out."

He came back muttering to himself, and Adam knew what was wrong.

"What's the matter?" asked Kuzyk.

"They still there." Julian peered at Adam. "That girl an' the kid."

"So what? We got to get him inside. You scared her so bad she was afraid to go."

Julian found kindling somewhere outside the lodge and cut splinters from it with his knife to make a little fire on the ashes of the tiny blaze the girl, Anneke, had made. She huddled beside the blond child, watching him fearfully. He went outside again to see if his fire showed at the chimney top, returned satisfied, and fed it wood carefully. The wounded man groaned and shivered.

"You gotta make it bigger," said Kuzyk.

"Shit!" Julian jerked a thumb at the roof. "We make sparks an' we're all dead." He fed the fire, though, and a little circle of warmth spread from it. They put Guido as close as they dared and he seemed eased a little.

"How bad is he hit?" asked Julian, lifting the blanket. "Oh, mama!" he muttered. "Anybody got a aid packet?"

"Used mine. How 'bout you, Lieutenant?" Kuzyk looked at Adam, who unsnapped the canvas pocket on his belt that held his first-aid package. He had never opened it before—the little cardboard box was worn and water-stained. He ripped it open and pulled out the gauze pad attached to a strip of olive-drab bandage. Julian shook his head. "Ain't enough."

The Belgian girl came to kneel behind him. "I help," she murmured. "I know about hurt . . . I am in school in Liege for hurt."

"Yeah?" Julian scowled at her and pulled back the blanket. "You goin' to fix that?"

Anneke's face went white. "Ooooh . . . oh, *mon Dieu!*" She put a hand over her mouth and gagged.

"You goin' to be sick," said Kuzyk, "get away from here."

They had nothing to help what was happening to Guido. Adam contributed the towel he had found under the dead soldier in the bunker and in minutes it was sodden. The warmth of the fire stopped the shivering but it probably encouraged the bleeding, thought Adam. Maybe we ought not to get him warm.

Julian must have thought the same. "Either he bleed to death or he freeze. What difference do it make?"

They decided it would be better if he stayed warm. "What's his other name?" Julian asked Kuzyk.

"Divecchio . . . Guido Divecchio. Guinea from Philadelphia. We been together ever since we went through basic in Virginia. You think he's gonna make it?"

"Maybe . . . Guineas is tough. How 'bout we eat somethin', Lootenant?"

The contents of the two burlap bags offered no surprises: olive-drab cans of C rations, all of them terribly familiar. Adam studied the cans and sighed. C rations required three things of a soldier: unquestioning hunger, a spoon, and an ingenious little device universally called a "P-38."

Why it was called that, nobody knew—except perhaps because it was as useful and prized as a captured German Army Walther pistol of that designation: a sheet-metal-and-wire-spring wonder of an automatic that rarely jammed like an American Colt and its numerous copies.

Its American namesake was an inch-and-a half-long folding can opener that was superb until the blade grew dull; then you threw it away and got another. It had a little hole in one end so it could be worn on the metal chain that held a soldier's identification tags around his neck. To keep this collection from jangling, battle-wise soldiers cut a segment from a rubber gasmask hose that fitted nicely around the edge of the dog tags. No soldier, battle-wise or green, went without dog tags and P-38 on the beaded metal chain about his neck. Only one can of army rations, the one with biscuits and jam, had a pull strip—all the rest required a can opener.

Properly, ration cans were immersed in boiling water, fished out, and opened. A less satisfactory way was to put them on or over a fire—open or punched, of course, or they might explode. You wrapped a

glove or anything else handy around the hot can to
hold it and spooned out the contents—burned at the
bottom, with a hard cold heart in the middle unreached
by heat. They used the latter means because it was
quicker.

"Try to make him soup? We can melt snow."

Julian shook his head at Kuzyk. "Not with that hole
in him."

Adam offered a warmed can to the Belgian girl but
she refused it, not even looking at the contents. Julian
spread jam on a cracker and gave it to her. "Give it to
the kid."

It took a while. Anneke coaxed and eventually the
child accepted the cracker but said nothing and would
not look at the Americans. The only sound she made
was a hoarse racking cough that became more frequent as the night wore on.

"Bring her over here . . . by the fire," urged Kuzyk,
but the child would not budge. She clung to the Belgian girl.

"Where did you come from?" Adam asked.

Anneke gestured vaguely. "Meyerode . . . the village over there."

"That's your home?"

"Please?"

"Is that where you live . . . in the village?"

"Oh, no . . . I come there from Sankt Vith when
the Germans shoot big guns into it."

"So you live in Saint Vith?"

"No, I am in Liege but the Germans drop bombs on
that town and they send many people away. I come to
Sankt Vith."

Bombs? Adam thought the German Air Force had
no more bombers. How could they bomb Liege? He
tried to get that out of the girl but she insisted the
town had been bombed and many civilians evacuated.

"Buzz bombs," muttered Julian. "You seen them
things, ain't you, Lootenant?"

That explained it: the German V-1 rockets he had
heard sputtering overhead ever since he reached the

front. By repeated questions he finally extracted from her an account of her wanderings.

Evacuated by Belgian authorities in Liege, she came to Saint Vith and stayed there for some indefinite time until the morning of the sixteenth of December when the Germans began shelling that town with long-range artillery. That made sense—when Adam had rejoined his battalion outside Auw, they said the krauts had shelled Saint Vith all day.

There had been no organized evacuation there, it seemed. The girl said she and other civilians simply took to the roads, going anywhere out of the town. She walked to Meyerode and the villagers put the people from Saint Vith in the schoolhouse.

"How come you didn't stay in the village?" Kuzyk demanded. "What the hell you want out here in these woods?"

"The Germans shoot at Meyerode too. Big guns. I am afraid and I run into the forest. I find the little girl and we hide in this house."

"Where's her mama an' papa?" asked Julian. "How come they don't keep her?"

"I do not know where is her mama and papa. She is by herself in the forest so I take her with me."

"Didn't you ask her what happened to her family?"

"Yes, I ask her but I think . . . I think something bad happen to her. She cannot speak. She cannot say what happen."

"How come those folks in the town don't keep her?" demanded Julian suspiciously. Anneke looked at Adam pleadingly.

"I do not know, sir. I find her in the forest. She can't speak—she is only crying. There is a piece of paper on her coat with a pin and it say 'Emilie.' Here . . . it is still here. You see? I think that is her name and I think something bad happen to her mama and papa and now she is so afraid she cannot speak."

Julian grunted but it sounded logical to Adam. There must be thousands of women and children like these waifs, running terrified from the German attack, hiding anywhere they could. Once again the black sergeant jerked his head at the door, summoning Adam to conference. "Gotta take a leak," he told Kuzyk.

Adam followed him and Julian was angry and frustrated. "We right back where we started! You believe what she tol' you?"

"Why not? Makes sense to me."

"Maybe so. Sure, she run from kraut artillery but I dunno about that Liege crap . . . I bet you, Lootenant, that bitch is from right aroun' here someplace an' first chance she get she gonna sneak off an' tell the krauts we is here. I been here near a month now an' I tell you all these people is kraut! Maybe they be in Belgium but they is purely kraut."

"I think she's telling the truth, Julian. Why would she want to bring the Germans here?"

"Because, dammit . . . even if she ain't a kraut-lover, what's the best way she got to get in good with 'em so's they give her somethin' to eat an' a place to stay? Give 'em three American soljers an' she's got it made!"

"Well, what do you want to do? We take Divecchio out in the snow and he'll be dead in an hour."

"I know . . . I know! But he goin' to die anyway, Lootenant."

"Well . . ." Adam shook his head stubbornly. "I won't leave him and we can't take him with us. We'll stay here till tomorrow anyway. We have to keep somebody on guard and we just make sure she doesn't get away."

Julian swore under his breath. "Yessir. You right about that guinea but we be smart to get rid o' that girl before she gets rid o' us."

"What do you mean?"

Julian grunted. "I take care of it, Lootenant. You don't even got to know."

"But, goddammit . . . I do know, and you aren't going to kill her! Not as long as I'm here and that's an order, Sergeant."

"Yessir."

Back in the lodge they found Kuzyk asleep as close to the fire as he could get. Anneke and the blond child were exactly where they had been: huddled together in the corner. Anneke watched every move Julian made and the little girl looked at no one—only coughed rackingly.

Still sullen, Julian announced he would take guard duty outside. "Only couple hours till daylight. You an' him"—he indicated Kuzyk—"can sack out awhile but Lootenant, you keep one eye on . . . you know."

"Yeah, I'll do that. Where'd you get the wood?"

"Big ol' pile right outside the door but don't put too much on."

"Right. You watch the chimney for sparks."

Adam got no sleep. He was too worried and his companions—except for the Belgian girl—were too noisy. Divecchio groaned, Kuzyk snored, and the little girl coughed relentlessly. He gave Anneke a package of the detested Charms and told her to make the child suck one, it might help the cough. Whatever else had been scared out of the child, she was still susceptible to candy. The entire package disappeared one by one and did no good at all.

Julian returned with dawn light, roused Kuzyk, and sent him outside to keep watch. "I want some coffee first," the soldier protested.

"I make you some coffee. You git on outside and watch for krauts. When it's fixed, I come get you an' you can have your coffee."

Divecchio's face was flushed and he seemed to be strangling on something. The little girl coughed, choked, and sneezed wetly, a thick discharge leaking from her nose. When she could catch her breath she cried pitifully.

"She has got fever," whispered Anneke. "She is hot."

"She's a mess," snarled Julian. "God's sake, wipe her face." He squatted to look at the miserable child, who wailed in terror. "I think," he said grimly, "she goin' die before that one." He gestured at Divecchio.

"Not here, she isn't," said Adam, zipping his mackinaw and pulling on his gloves.

"What you goin' to do?"

"We've got to find out what's in that village . . . maybe we can get help for him there. I'll take her with me and get as close as I can, then let her go. Somebody'll find her and take care of her."

"Let her go in the town?" asked Julian, appalled.

"She can't talk . . . if she could she wouldn't know where she's been. She's too little and too sick."

"Lootenant, you take that kid an' go foolin' around that place an' the krauts goin' to nab your ass. Like as not they shoot the both of you!"

Adam knew Julian's opinion of him was low, and trying to sneak up on a village full of Germans didn't improve it. Not unless he did it and got back in one piece. That would help some.

"I'm goin' anyway, and I'll be back."

"I better go with you, Lootenant."

Adam grinned at him. "No sweat, Sarge. You keep an eye on this bunch. We both go and God knows what'll happen here."

He held out his arms to the little girl. "Come on, baby. Let's go." The child shrank from him and Anneke held her tight.

"What? What do you want?"

"She needs help we can't give her. I'll take her as close to the village as I can and she must go to the houses. Someone will take care of her. Can you tell her what she has to do?"

The Belgian girl whispered to the child for a long time, using the local dialect, Adam guessed. He understood none of what he heard but it must have been persuasive. Anneke wrapped the child's shawl about her head and face, leaving only a space she could see from. The little girl came to Adam shyly.

"She knows what she must do?"

"I think so, sir."

Adam slung his carbine over his shoulder and took

the child's hand. Anneke watched wide-eyed. "I can go with you, sir? Please?"

"No," said Julian. "You stay right here."

A dozen yards beyond the door, Emilie stopped and wept. There was no use, Adam decided, trying to tow the child through the snow. She was not being obstinate, she simply couldn't make it. He picked her up, put her head over his shoulder, and hooked his left arm under her bottom, holding the carbine in his right hand.

Crazy, he thought. Talcut, you have truly got rocks in your head, and no use pretending you're doing this for the kid. You're just trying to make that black sergeant think you know whether to wind your nose or blow your watch.

He slid downhill from the lodge until he glimpsed the track from Herresbach to Meyerode, worked his way painfully west, creeping closer from time to time to make sure he did not wander from the rutted road. There seemed to be no Germans on it at all. Adam counted days and guessed it was Christmas Eve—maybe they had declared themselves a holiday.

Emilie coughed and whimpered in his ear and he put her down in the snow, moving away a little to listen for Germans. That was wasted effort. When she wasn't coughing, the child cried until he came back to her. If there were Germans anywhere around, they would hear her long before he knew they were there. He gave up trying to be cautious, picked her up, and slogged his way toward the village.

From the crest of a ridge overlooking it he could see most of the houses. Only a few Germans moving about but there were trucks, sedans, and Volkswagens parked in the street and behind the houses; smoke rising from every chimney. The only activity centered around a couple of vans in a barnyard; from time to time a German soldier shuttled between them. A command post, Adam guessed. Both vans mounted a tall radio antenna guyed to trees around them.

He might be able to get a little closer but not burdened with the coughing child. He would have to start her for the houses and as soon as he did, he ought to get away as fast as he could.

So the place is full of krauts and you didn't have to get this close to know that. You brought the kid, that's all you've done, and that won't make Julian think any better of you.

"Emilie . . ." he whispered; and she peered at him with red-rimmed eyes. He pointed at the houses. "You go . . . go there." A soldier climbed down from one of the vans and jog-trotted to the other. "See . . ." Adam whispered urgently. "Go now!"

If she went into the village they would see her. German soldiers couldn't be so different from American that they wouldn't take a little girl in. He pushed Emilie gently, pointing at the houses, and she went a little way toward them, stopped, and looked back. He waved at her but she was not watching him. She was watching something behind him.

Adam shivered, started to pick up his carbine and took his hands from it. What does she see? A German? They must have guards out. I move and he'll shoot me.

What if I just stand up slow and hold up my hands? If he doesn't shoot it's all over . . . I'm through with it. Why not? I've done all I can. I can't fight the goddamn war all by myself.

You aren't by yourself. There's Julian and Kuzyk and Divecchio. You just going to quit and to hell with them?

He picked up the carbine and made himself look over his shoulder. A man in a shabby green uniform watched him from a dozen yards away. He didn't have a rifle, he had an ax on his shoulder and he had a thick gray beard. Can't be a soldier. Adam turned on his knees, raised the carbine, and the man held out his free hand, palm open.

"Ami?" he said softly. "Don't shoot, Ami. I am friend."

"Who? Who are you?" Adam had to force the question past cold stiff lips.

"I am Johann . . . forester by Meyerode." He gestured with the ax handle toward the village. "There are many German soldiers. You want to surrender?"

"No! Will you help me?"

"What I can do?"

Adam pointed at Emilie. "I found her in the forest . . . she's sick. Will you take care of her?"

The man nodded. "Yes. I will do that. If you do not surrender, you go away quick. They see you, they kill you. They are SS."

Shit-oh-dear, thought Adam. Now you've got something to tell Julian. He pointed the carbine at the Belgian with shaking hands. "You won't tell them you saw me?"

"No. I am friend. I know the Amis who were here. I show them trees to cut and they take them away on big trucks."

Kuzyk's outfit: the engineers with the sawmill. "There is one of them in the forest there." Adam gestured vaguely. "He is hurt very badly. If I bring him here, will you take care of him too?"

"No . . . no! I cannot do that. SS shoot me. I take the little girl but I cannot help the soldier. You go away now quick. I don't tell them you are here."

He put down the ax, unslung a knapsack from his shoulders, and pulled out the knot in its drawstring. Adam raised the carbine.

"*Essen* . . . I give you something to eat, Ami." He pulled a paper-wrapped package from the knapsack and opened it. "You see . . . bread and sausage. I have no more. You take it, Ami. Take it and go away quick."

"Thank you. I will take it. There is a German headquarters in the village?"

"Please?" the old man was as nervous as Adam.

"Radio," said Adam, pointing at the vans. "A big radio. It is a command post? A German headquarters?"

The Belgian must have understood that. "There is a

general in the house of Peter Maraite . . . SS general. We have luck," he said. "They do not shoot at Meyerode with their big guns because they want the houses for their general and his soldiers. You go away now, Ami? I take the little girl and you go away?"

"Yeah . . . I'll go. Don't tell them I was here. The little girl does not speak. I think she is too afraid but don't let her tell the Germans about me. All right?"

"Yes . . . yes! You go quick now."

Adam went and in one of the houses he heard singing—German soldiers saluting a victorious Christmas, he supposed.

7

WHEN HE left Meyerode, Adam went north through the forest to get away from the Herresbach road. From the sounds of celebration in the village he doubted there would be any serious patrolling this night, but there would be stragglers on the road attracted by the noise in the village.

He got himself thoroughly lost and wandered for a long time with no more definite objective than just working uphill. The lodge was on a hill but there were lots of those in the dense woods east of the village. He finally stumbled into a narrow track and followed it away from Meyerode.

He knew he was going too far north. He could see ahead of him the lights of another village. Valender, he guessed, on the Ambleve River. I've got to go back. He found a trail leading off to the southwest and went back down that to an old roadblock he had seen before. Someone had dropped a big tree across the trail and someone else had chopped a piece from it wide enough to open the way again. The lodge is uphill from here, he thought, and climbed out of the trail.

He almost stepped on Julian, prone in the undergrowth. The black sergeant got to his feet and Adam froze in fear.

"You get lost?" demanded Julian.

Adam got his heart out of his throat and was so grateful to be back safe that he made no complaint at being surprised. "Yes, dammit. How can you see in this dark?"

119

"I hear you comin'. You get shed of that kid?"

"I left her at the village." He told Julian about the Belgian and the German general, but not what the forester said about no artillery falling on Meyerode. When he heard that, he would make another fuss about the Belgian girl and Adam wanted to talk to her first.

"That Eye-talian boy is right bad off. Don't think he goin' to make it."

"Can't we do anything for him?"

"Ain't nobody but a doctor can help him an' I wouldn't put no money on that neither."

"I asked that Belgian to help him. He's too scared of the Germans. Maybe tomorrow we can leave him where the krauts'll find him."

"If they is SS," said Julian, "they'll shoot him. Somebody else don't find him quick, he freeze to death. Best he die warm, Lootenant."

There was a pile of American equipment in the entryway to the lodge, more in the room with the fireplace. Blankets, shelter halves, and more rations. "I got it off them trucks," said Julian. "Lots more still there."

Anneke gave Adam a canteen cup of coffee and he rifled a K ration for its packet of milk powder that turned the bitter coffee a sickly gray. Kuzyk relieved Julian on guard outside the lodge, wearing everything he owned and a blanket Julian had found in a truck.

Adam drank his coffee and had a cigarette from the K ration. The packet said it was a Camel but it tasted like it had been mothproofed; maybe because it had been frozen and thawed.

Sergeant Julian did not smoke cigarettes; he split the paper and shredded them into his pipe. He used the other two Camels of Adam's three-pack and when they were consumed he knocked the ash out on the hearth.

"I'm gonna take a look aroun'," said Julian. When he opened the door, Anneke shivered.

"Cold?"

"Always I am cold."

Adam selected a small dry piece of wood from the pile by the fireplace and put it on the glowing coals. It began to pop and crackle and he moved it quickly.

"Let it burn," said Anneke. "Nobody see us. It is Christmas and they are drunk in the village. I hear them."

"You hear them what?"

"Singing. When I go out."

Julian came back and squatted by the fire. He did not have his rifle and Adam knew he left it outside so it would not sweat in the warmth of the fire and freeze up when he took it out again. He only brought it in to clean it.

At Fort Benning in the Officer Candidate School they had to take their rifles apart blindfolded and put them together again in a test to see who finished in the shortest time. He had forgotten how to do that. Not Julian. He reduced his M1 to a pile of parts in seconds, wiped and oiled them, and put them back together without ever looking at them as easily as a man uses a knife and fork to eat his dinner.

Like old Sebe, who put me on stand the first time I went deer hunting, thought Adam. On Bedford Mountain. Cap Simmons loaned me his twelve-gauge and it had dog-ear hammers and one of them was stuck. Black Sebe, who had to be sixty years old, fixed that shotgun in the dark. Then, at dawn light, a deer came and Sebe said: Spike buck—shoot 'im.

I shot him. Pulled both triggers at once and that cannon damn near tore my head off. Deer took off and I thought I missed him but Sebe said no, you hit him. He found some hair with blood on it and he said show it to Cap'n Simmons so he don't say you no good.

"See anything?" he asked Julian. The black sergeant shook his head.

"Nope. They havin' a party, I reckon."

"They're still singing?"

"They sure are—Chris'mas songs, jus' like good folks."

"You think we ought to take turns outside tonight?"

"Yessir! Don't reckon them krauts be out this night but can't take no chance. I'm goin' to get me some sack time in the other room. Kuzyk'll get me 'bout midnight an' you can take it next."

He went into the other room and Adam put another branch on the flame. Anneke held chapped hands over it and blew softly to make it catch. He watched her. Pretty girl, even in that sweater with a G.I. field jacket over it. Kuzyk must have given it to her; Julian wouldn't. The sleeves were so long she had to turn them back over her wrists.

"You lied to me about why you left Meyerode," he said. She would not look at him.

"How you know that?"

"I talked to a man there, a Belgian. Forest ranger or something like that. He says there is a German general in the village and the Germans didn't shell it because they wanted to save it for him."

" 'Shell'?"

"Artillery. They didn't shoot at Meyerode. They want it for their general."

She watched the fire, not Adam. "You say to the black man there is SS in Meyerode."

"That's what the Belgian said. Is that why you ran away from there?"

Anneke shrugged. "If there is SS maybe there is SD."

"What is that?"

"*Sicherheitsdienst*. I don't know how you say it in English. They are SS police like Gestapo only they are worse. I am afraid of them."

"Why? Are they looking for you?"

"I—I don't know."

"If they are, wouldn't the Belgians in the village hide you?"

"Maybe."

"You're afraid of the Belgians too? Why did you leave Liege? Was it buzz bombs or something else?"

"Buzz . . . ?"

Adam sketched the flight of a rocket with his finger and spread his hand to indicate the explosion at its end. She gave him a worried look.

"You make me go away?"

"And tell the Germans we're here? No," he said grimly. "We don't make you go away."

She thought about that and her eyes were big and dark and frightened. "The black man . . . he want to kill me, don't he?"

Adam shrugged.

"Yes! Oh-kay . . . I tell you. In Liege my friend Yaninka say a German soldier looks for you and the Secret Army think you are spy for Germans. It is a lie. I talk to that soldier. He is come from *Ostfront*— Russia—and he only want to say my brother August is dead."

"Your brother was in the German Army?"

"Two brothers . . . August and Peter."

"Where's Peter?"

"Italy."

"You said you are Belgian."

"My mother is come from Maspelt. It is little village by Sankt Vith. Maybe one kilometer from *Grenze* . . . the border with Germany. Every year we are with her family there in summer and when the war begin my brothers go with the German Army."

"And you . . . what did you do?"

"I go back to Liege with my father. He is Walloonie— not German. He is with the Belgian Army and when the German tanks come he goes away. I don't know where he goes."

"You stayed in Liege?"

"Yes. I have work in a store. I learn English there before the war when many English come to make a tour in the Ardennes. After the war no more but I still have work. I don't tell them about my brothers."

"So what happened after the soldier came looking for you?"

"Yaninka say I will have much trouble so . . ." She

shrugged. "I got a boyfriend in Belgian Secret Army. I stay with him. He don't let them hurt me."

Like some kind of Saturday movie, thought Adam. "You joined the resistance . . . or just lived with one of them?"

"I do some things for them. They make a little newspaper and Yaninka and me, we help. Then they catch us."

"Who? Who caught you?"

"Gestapo."

Adam looked at her in disbelief. "And they let you go?"

Anneke nodded. "That is why I am afraid. The Secret Army want to catch me and maybe the SS too."

"Because the Gestapo let you go?"

"Yes." She continued as calmly as if she were describing something perfectly ordinary. "They take Yaninka and me to the jail and they say we know you are *Widerstandskaempfer*—with the Secret Army. Now you tell us about them."

"Did you?"

"Yaninka is first. They make me look. She don't tell them and they say now, Anneke, now you—so I tell them. I don't want them do that to me."

"Do what?"

"Hurt me."

"How do they hurt you?"

She shivered and looked at the things Julian had brought from the truck, pointed at a canvas-covered box with a web carrying sling: "How you call that?"

"Telephone . . . army field telephone."

"Yes. With the Germans there is black leather on the outside, but like that—with the thing you turn to make it work. They take off Yaninka's *pulli* and they make her sit in a chair. They put a rope on her."

"What's a *pulli*?"

"Like this." She tugged at her sweater. "They got *klampfen*"—she pinched a thumb and forefinger together—"with wire to the box. They put them on her." She touched her breasts. "They turn the handle and they hurt her but she don't tell so they say, now you, Anneke."

She held out her hands to Adam. "I tell them what they want so they don't do that to me. After some days they let me go away."

"The resistance took you back?"

"Yes, until Yaninka is dead."

"Then what?"

"My boyfriend say, Anneke, you are traitor. The Gestapo kill Yaninka but they let you go." She shrugged. "I run away. I want to go to Maspelt but in Sankt Vith the Amis don't let me. I have to stay here. Then there are the big guns and nobody watch so I come to Meyerode. The people there say the SS come soon and I hide in the forest."

"Amis? That's what the Germans call us, isn't it?"

"Yes. I should not say it?"

"I don't care. Why wouldn't they let you go to Maspelt?"

Anneke hunched her shoulders. "When I come to Sankt Vith there is an Ami—American—who looks at my card. What the black man want to see. He don't like it."

"Your card was a fake . . . no good?"

"No, it is good. I got it a long time. He look at my card and he look in a big book and he say you got to stay in Sankt Vith. The Gendarmerie want you."

"Belgian police?"

"Yes."

"What do they want with you?"

"I don't know . . . maybe because what happen in Liege. I don't talk to them."

Adam was baffled. "Why not?"

She was watching him from the corner of her eyes. "I stay with the Ami and he don't tell them. After some days he say, Anneke, give me your card and I get you another one. He make a little photo for it. You want to see?"

From somewhere under the sweater she brought it

out: a blurred snapshot of a girl who did not look much like Anneke.

"Did he want money from you . . . to buy the card?"

"Oh, no! He will make it for me."

"Ah, come on! How could he do that?"

"For him it is no trouble. He is Secret Police."

"Anneke, we don't have secret police in the American army!"

"Yes! He is CIC." She spelled it phonetically and it took Adam a moment to translate. Counter-Intelligence Corps. They were soldiers who questioned line-crossers and tried to make them go back for more information. It was funny, calling them secret police. To infantrymen they were just fat cats who hung around division headquarters.

"You don't believe?" Anneke was indignant. "It is true! In the Apotheke Schiltz in Sankt Vith on the Linden Street. There is the Ami CIC." She studied the photograph regretfully. "He give me the paper from the police and say he will make a new card so I am not Anneke Xhoffrion and the Gendarmerie don't catch me. He say maybe after Christmas I take you to Paris."

What a bastard, thought Adam. A jumped-up G.I., but you can't tell because those spooks don't wear any rank insignia. He wondered why she hadn't got the ID card she had paid for in his sack.

"He didn't make the card for you?"

Anneke sighed. "The Germans come and I run away. I hope the Germans don't kill him. You think he will stay at Sankt Vith?"

I hope to God he does, thought Adam, and a lot more with him. Serve him right if he took her to Paris. He wouldn't have her long. Some French policeman would get her and pretty soon she'd have a real passport. Good enough to get her to England—maybe even the States.

"Would you like to go to America, Anneke?"

She looked at him, wide-eyed. "I don't know. It is

too far away, I think." A blast of cold air fanned the
fire and Kuzyk was back. Adam looked at his watch.
Midnight already?

"Leave your rifle outside," he said, borrowing Sergeant Julian's wisdom. "It sweats in here. It'll freeze
up when you take it out again."

"Yessir." Kuzyk made a lot of noise but Julian
moved quietly for a big man. He was there suddenly
and he scowled at the fire.

"Better get some sack, Lootenant. I come get you
in a couple hours."

He went out and Kuzyk bedded himself down in the
other room.

"The black man," said Anneke, "he don't like me."

That was a charitable view of Julian's feeling about
her. No sweat, Lieutenant, he said. I take care of her.
Anneke's eyes were frightened again.

"Please . . ." she said softly. "You are officer?"

"Yes."

"You don't let him shoot me?"

"Not unless you make trouble for us."

"How I must speak to you? I don't know your name."

"Adam. That's my name."

"Ah-dam?"

"That's right."

She took off the field jacket and sat up very straight.
She was thin but even under the sweater her breasts
commanded attention. She started to pull it off.

"What're you doing?"

"You don't want me take it off?"

"Hell, no! I'm going to sleep."

She pulled the sweater down and held her hands to
the embers on the hearth. "You are angry at me?"

"No, but don't go out, you hear?"

"Oh, no!"

She'd need more than his help if Julian found her
outside this time of night.

Adam wrapped a blanket around himself, rolled
back and forth on a folded canvas tarpaulin until he
had made a hollow for hips and shoulders, and pulled

his wool knit cap over his eyes. He could still see Anneke though. He guessed she knew, because she did not put the field jacket on and she continued to sit very erect.

Poor little slut, he thought. She's had a worse war than I have and she's still fighting. She should have stuck to that big operator in the CIC. He might have got her out of this. But she lost him and she wants me to take care of her.

He thrashed angrily over on his side so he could no longer see her outlined by the fireglow. You're a fool, Talcut, he told himself. You'd like her to take off that sweater . . . why'd you stop her? He thought of Bitsey's breasts and groaned. Never even seen them. Only once a little. Never felt 'em. Not really.

The summer they finished high school there was a party at Sue Corr's place. Marty Corr owned the Chevrolet agency in Laurel City and he was just about the richest man in town. Big house on Gallatin Street with a swimming pool in the backyard.

Must have been a dozen of us; we swam and played tag-you're-it in the pool all afternoon and then the Corrs' cook put out a picnic for us and Sue got her phonograph and we were going to dance but her mother came and raised hell.

"First y'all get dry and put on your clothes, you hear? You run aroun' like that the breeze'll get you. You'll catch polio jus' like Mr. Roosevelt."

Sue took the girls upstairs and we all used the same towel and got back in our clothes in the shower house by the pool. Marty Corr and Mrs. Corr were all dressed up and he said we're goin' to the country club for dinner; y'all be good.

Soon's they were gone, Bud Morrison got a bottle from his Model A Ford. Y'all know what I got? he said. Rum. There was lots of Coke in the icebox and he said we'll drink out some an' fill it with rum. Fat Jack Boyle said he'd rather have Dr. Pepper and everybody laughed at him. Rum and Coke, Bud said. Never heard tell of rum and Dr. Pepper.

The girls came back and Bitsey had on an old flannel shirt must have belonged to Mr. Corr. Tails hung down over her shorts almost to her knees. Looked like she didn't have anything on but that shirt. That was damn near true.

Sue played her records and we danced. T. Dorsey. Great stuff. "Two o'Clock Jump." I remember that one. I couldn't jitterbug worth a damn but Bitsey showed me. Laughed at me and teased me but she didn't really mean it. She tasted my rum and Coke and made a face but she asked for some more after we danced awhile and she got all pink in the cheeks and laughed a lot. After a while Sue put on "Honey, Please Don't Be That Way," and we danced right close. That's the nearest I ever got to Bitsey's breasts.

They weren't very big but she hadn't put on her underclothes when she went upstairs to dry off and change into Mr. Corr's shirt. She kind of bounced when she was showing me how to jitterbug and I thought something was funny and when we started dancing slow and close I knew it. Must have been the rum and Coke. Bitsey put her hands behind my neck and danced closer than she ever did before.

My God, it was wonderful. All soft and warm and I didn't have on a shirt. I guess she could tell how I felt because she put her head on my shoulder and kind of pushed away from me. I kept pulling her back and I kind of moved from one side to the other so Bitsey rubbed against my chest and she put up with it for a while, then she got red in the face and said: Adam . . . stop it.

You been goin' with Bitsey since we were fifteen and that's the most you ever saw of her—peekin' down the front of Marty Corr's old shirt. Soon's the music stopped she went upstairs and put on her underclothes. I tried to put my hand on her once but that was a long time after. In the parking lot by a motel in Columbus, Georgia. I guess it made her mad. She sure acted like it.

What the hell's the matter with you, Talcut? That girl by the fire wants to take off her sweater and let you put your hands all over her. He groaned again. Not because she's got the hots for you, old buddy.

She's scared that black sergeant's goin' to kill her and she wants you to stop him. That's all.

I bet she kisses like a fox in a forest fire. Bitsey didn't mind being kissed but you didn't know about kissing till Kelly showed you. Kellyanne Huger. Her mother said "Hugee," but my ma said she's just puttin' on airs. God knows how many Huger kids there were. They all quit school soon as they were old enough to get a job. Kelly almost made it but next-to-last year at Central High she quit too and got a job in the diner by the Trailways bus depot.

Kelly came to all the school dances though. When you brought Kelly to a dance everybody kind of winked and made fun of you but they were just jealous. Must be a lot of guys like me in Laurel City—didn't know about kissing or anything till we took Kelly to a dance. When Kelly danced she came apart in three pieces—the middle one stuck to you and the other two went in different directions at the same time. She never sat one out, though, and nice girls like Bitsey didn't like her much.

Between dances you took Kelly in the boiler room and kissed her and Kelly kept her eyes open and tongue-kissed and said that's nice, isn't it? If you had a car there was more. You drove up to the park on Lookout Point with the statue of Emma Sanson, who showed Bedford Forrest a ford across Black Creek so he could catch Straight and his Yankee raiders. Bud Morrison let me use his Model A one time and I took Kelly to the Point. He showed me how you pull the gearshift lever up on a Model A so it comes loose and you can turn it against the dash out of the way.

Still doesn't leave enough room in a Ford coupé, but Kelly didn't mind. She didn't make any fuss about you looking at her either. She'd hold 'em up and say: Kiss them . . . poor little things, they're lonesome.

The fire was almost out and Anneke was curled up as close to it as she could get. She had the field jacket on now, Adam guessed, but he couldn't tell because she was all wrapped up in a canvas shelter half, another piece of loot from the abandoned truck. He could just say, "Anneke . . . come," and she would. That's pretty low, Talcut. She's no whore. She went to bed with those men to keep somebody from killing her—or hooking her to a field telephone.

He slept then until Sergeant Julian shook him awake. It was as dark as ever and cold as a well-digger's ass, as Julian put it. He went outside and backed into a fir thicket on top of the hill above the lodge and stamped and groaned until there was a red streak of dawn in the east. Dawn brought a wind that made him shiver convulsively and when he had counted to a hundred three times—as slowly as he could make himself count— he quit and went back to the lodge to wake Kuzyk.

He woke Anneke too, trying to get the fire started again, but she stayed wrapped in her shelter half and he could hear her teeth chattering. In daylight, he knew, it would be fatal to build up the fire till it made smoke. With care, he got a few coals glowing and warmed a can from a K ration that said "EGGS AND BACON" on the lid.

"Vile" was the only word for it: a buff-colored disk of something a hell of a long way from egg with little hard flecks of stuff in it. Thawed at the edge with a frozen center he threw on the fire and was sorry. It gave off an odor as bad as its taste and he breakfasted on K-ration crackers smeared with grape jelly. When he got a canteen cup of snow melted and warm enough to dissolve a packet of powdered coffee, Anneke came out of her canvas shroud and watched hungrily. He gave her a cracker and some coffee and Kuzyk appeared, yawning and muttering to himself.

"Merry Christmas," said Adam sourly.

Julian appeared, went out, and returned, his face grim. "What's up?" Adam asked him. "You hear something?"

"Go lissen, Lootenant."

Adam went, Kuzyk and Julian close behind. The sky had cleared and there was a dribbling sound of snow melting from the trees in the early sun. Nothing more.

"I don't hear anything."

"That's right. Ain't nothin' to hear."

"That's bad?"

"Hell, Lootenant . . . means the krauts have got Saint Vith. They've pushed our people back so far we can't hear no fightin'."

"Sheeit!" said Kuzyk. "He's right. We'll never get out now!"

"Jus' gotta squeeze our balls an' hope they come back," muttered Julian.

Anneke was in the little hollow in front of the lodge, watching them fearfully, and Julian unslung his rifle from his shoulder.

"What you doin' out here?"

"I . . . I have to . . ." She gestured vaguely.

"She's gotta pee sometime, Sarge," said Kuzyk reasonably.

"G'on an' do it then," growled Julian. "You ain't back here right quick I'm comin' after you."

They went into the lodge and hugged the tiny fire, each of them wrapped in private gloom. Anneke watched Sergeant Julian, and Adam felt sorry for her.

Divecchio chose Christmas Day to die. He began to breathe in snoring groans and there was nothing they could do to help him. About noon he stopped—both groaning and breathing. Adam wrapped the torn and bloody undershirt around his head and Julian unwrapped it. He broke the chain around Divecchio's neck holding his two metal identification tags; one he put in his pocket, the other he forced into Divecchio's mouth and Anneke made a soft appalled noise.

Julian pulled the undershirt tight under the dead soldier's jaw and knotted it. "Them Graves Registration folks know to look in his mouth, they ever find him. Krauts won't look there."

"What'll we do with him?"

"Put him outside. He get good an' stiff tonight an' he's easy to tote. Take him down by the road tomorrow."

Clear weather broke the silence that afternoon. The long-absent air corps swarmed out of blue sky and fell

on the road from the Losheim Gap to Saint Vith with
a savage bedlam of noise. They were met by the
urgent hammering of German antiaircraft guns but the
rumbling thunder of their bombs continued.

"Jabos," said Julian, grinning.

"Airplanes?" asked Kuzyk.

"That's what the krauts call 'em. Lissen to that!
Man, they really got their tit in the wringer, ain't they?"

In threes and sixes and nines the sleek fighter planes
snarled over the forest to harry the German trucks on
the road. They came so low you could see the feathery
trails of their rockets when they fired them, before
they soared into the blue again. In late afternoon
when dusk fell they went home—back to warm bar-
racks in France, thought Adam bitterly. Hot showers
and a good dinner and real beds.

Their pleasure in the misery the planes had inflicted
on the Germans changed to fear. The forest below the
lodge rumbled and growled as German trucks abandoned the macadam roads and took to woods trails
where they could not be seen. The trucks were no
danger but the trails were—they required engineers
and infantry to cut trees and pile them in the mud-
holes that swallowed trucks. Their hoarse yelling came
clearly to the fugitives on the hilltop.

"You reckon we ought to go somewhere else?"
Adam whispered to Julian. They lay prone in the
thicket of firs on the knob above the log house.

"Ain't no place to go. We try to move an' we run right
into 'em. Lissen to 'em hollerin'. They all over the place."

"Just stay here?"

"What else, Lootenant? It thaw again tomorrow
like it done today, they be so busy fixin' them trails
they ain't got time to look for us. Come bad weather
again, them planes get off their ass an' they go back
on the blacktop road. Maybe then we can find us
another place to hide."

Not till after midnight did the clamor on the woods
track from Herresbach to Meyerode subside and even
then there were still a few trucks and the angry snarl

of motorcycles. It was so cold even Julian agreed they had to have a little fire. He built it carefully and when he had a bed of coals he said they ought to have something for Christmas.

They put four canteen cups of snow on the embers to melt and shaved gray, rock-hard blocks of K-ration chocolate into them. It made a thin and unpleasant brew because a lot of the chocolate simply refused to dissolve; it had to be chewed. Kuzyk spat disgustedly.

"That's awful! When're we goin' to make us a real fire an' cook up somethin' good to eat?"

"The krauts'd be here before you could finish it," said Julian.

"Okay, but—"

"No, it ain't okay. Lissen to me, Kuzyk . . . we got no more chance than a snowball in hell to make it back to our people. We might dodge krauts for a couple days but we got to find a place to get warm ever' so often. That means a barn or a shed, an' one of these damn farmers'll see us and that's all she wrote. If we lucky, we get captured—more likely the krauts just gun us down."

"So what're we goin' to do?"

"I dunno. Maybe hide in the woods daytime an' sneak back here at night. Hope to God we make out till the U.S. Army gets off its ass an' kicks the krauts outta here. Whatever we do, this place got to look like there ain't been nobody here since the war started . . . an' we ain't gonna make no big fire, you unnerstand?"

"Yeah, but—"

Julian thrust his face close to Kuzyk's. "You wanta quit, boy, you go find you some ol' daddy rabbit of a kraut that won't shoot you before you kin surrender to him. You wanta stick with me, you do what I tell you. Now, make up your mind . . . what you goin' do?"

Kuzyk stared at him, astonished; then he grinned. "Shit, Sarge, I'm stickin' with you an' the lootenant." He lifted his canteen cup.

"Merry Christmas! What the hell . . . maybe we can find us some booze before New Year's."

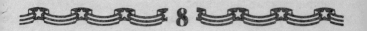

8

THREE DAYS Adam and Julian searched for a
daylight hiding place: a bunker, a cave in the rocks,
even a long-abandoned fighting hole like the one in
which they hid the night they first met. They found
many old holes, all ruinous, no bunker, and one shallow cave—the only place that could possibly accom-
modate three people.

Neither of them liked it. Sloping steeply to the
narrow entrance, the upper end was dry but the roof
so low you could not get to your knees. They would
spend the daylight hours prone, jammed together in
an airless pocket. It had only one advantage: it was in
a rock outcrop atop the highest elevation north of the
lodge before the ground fell away to the Amblève
River. From its entrance they could see both the hamlet of Wereth and the river.

Wereth was still occupied by German infantry, not
the SS that was there the first time they saw the
village, but some lesser breed of German soldier de-
tailed to labor duty. Each morning a band of them
shouldered axes and shovels and slouched off north to
a ford where the track from Wereth crossed the
Amblève to a village Adam identified from his map as
Heppenbach.

He and Julian probed cautiously closer to the river
to watch them working—not very hard—to build corduroy approaches to the ford and a makeshift log
bridge over the gap between their log-and-sandbag
abutments.

"Hope some dumb kraut tries to take a truck over

that thing," Julian commented, and Adam shook his head.

"You're right. It'll surely break down but as soon as it does some kraut engineer'll show up and that Mickey Mouse outfit will get shipped off to the war and something worse for us will come build a real bridge."

They worked their way west until they could see Valender where the German horse-drawn artillery had taken a position the morning they first crossed the Meyerode–Herresbach trail. There were still Germans in Valender, another labor unit, improving forest roads. Watching them, Adam became aware of an all-pervading rumble, growing stronger every moment. Julian nudged him, pointing up.

Two miles high a web of condensation trails marched eastward, wheeled, and swung back. The sky throbbed and muttered; even the ground seemed to tremble to the roar of heavy motors. Julian pounded him on the shoulder.

"Lookit that! Oh, man . . . loookit that!"

Hundreds of tiny black crosses spun feathery tracks across the sky. The rasping scream of falling bombs drowned all other noise and doomsday fell on something. The ground shuddered and the roar of distant explosions drew the breath from Adam's body. The apocalypse went on and on until the black specks disappeared, leaving their widened tracks behind and on the ground a sudden silence. Saint Vith or something else not far away had been wiped from the earth with unbelievable violence.

Kuzyk was a menace in the forest—he stumbled and swore and made so much noise that after the first day they left him to watch and report if Germans found the lodge. Each morning they put him in a different thicket of firs from which he could see the lodge, and gave him the additional task of watching Anneke; Julian still thought she would slip away and bring the Germans down on them as soon as she had a chance.

In the dusk of the third day they found Kuzyk gone

from the vantage point where they had left him and
Julian swore bitterly.

"Damn Polack! He an' that girl done gone off somewhere or the krauts found 'em."

"Maybe he got cold and went back to the lodge,"
whispered Adam.

They approached the house with infinite caution
and in the gathering dark Adam heard a desperate
plea: "Don't shoot . . . don't shoot!" It was Anneke,
crouched white-faced in a thicket above the lodge. She
had not heard Julian until the black sergeant was a
dozen feet from her.

"Where's Kuzyk?" demanded Adam. "What're you
doing out here by yourself?"

"He is gone," gasped Anneke, watching Julian fearfully. "He went away a long time ago. He say he is
going to a truck to look for *schnapps*."

"Dumb sonovabitch!" Julian lowered his rifle and
glared at the girl. "I done told the both of you don't
leave that place till we come back. How come you
don't stop him?"

"I cannot! I tell him don't go but he laugh at me and
say you stay here till I come back."

"Why don't you stay then?"

"Please . . . I am afraid! He go that way . . ." She
pointed east. "He is gone a long time and I hear
someone shoot. He don't come back and I am afraid. I
don't know what to do. I come here and wait for
Ah-dam." Julian grunted savagely.

"Too late to look for him now," said Adam.

The lodge was undisturbed. They made a tiny fire
and warmed canned rations, Adam and Julian taking
turn-about every two hours on guard outside. It made
a miserable night but it was too cold to stay out longer
than that. Sometime after midnight Julian shook Adam
awake, finger on his lips.

"Somethin' movin', git up!"

Shivering convulsively, Adam gathered carbine,
gloves, and helmet, Anneke watching him with white-

rimmed eyes. "Come," he whispered. "Could be a German patrol or maybe Kuzyk. Can't take a chance."

If it were Germans and they came into the lodge they would find the glowing coals of the fire but there was nothing they could do about that. If he put water on it the whole room would stink of drowned wood. He followed Julian, towing Anneke behind him.

They waited, listening with every pore of their bodies. There was movement, a rustle of branches, and the crackle of snow trod upon; then the hoarse, furious snorting of an animal.

"Damn hogs!" breathed Julian. Adam had yet to see one of them and he wondered if they looked like the mean runty little wild pigs of the Tennessee mountains. These must be bigger, they made so much noise.

At dawn they left Anneke in a clump of firs, wrapped in a blanket and a shelter half. Adam scraped snow over her until only her eyes, wide and frightened, showed, peering from the canvas.

"You'll be warm enough like that," he told her. "Don't move. Stay right here. If the Germans come, put your head down and don't move. They won't find you."

"You come back?" she whispered.

"Sure. We'll come back for you."

They found Kuzyk, kneeling with his head against a tree beside the road where the cavalry had abandoned their trucks. When Julian pushed him, he toppled over.

"Dead?" whispered Adam.

"Yeah . . . lookit that."

Kuzyk's helmet was gone. He had knelt bareheaded and they had shot him in the back of the head. Pistol, Adam guessed. The bullet had not come out through his face. An officer must have shot him. They carried little 7mm Walther pistols on their belt. He waited for Julian to repeat the obscene thing he had done with Divecchio's identity tag but the sergeant backed away, watching the trail to the north.

Of course, thought Adam. The expression of startled horror on Kuzyk's face was frozen there, his eyelashes crusted with frost. Couldn't get his mouth open unless you thawed him.

"Le's move from here, Lootenant."

They dropped down the trail, away from Wereth, though there was no way to know from which direction the Germans had come who caught Kuzyk. Julian's black face was shiny and twisted in fury.

"Pore simple Polack bastard . . . got no more sense than a jaybird an' they kill him!"

Working south of the trail they came upon an American army trailer, a big one, the kind towed by a 2½-ton truck, its canvas cover lashed down tight. It was yards off the trail; someone had unhitched it and let it roll as far into the trees as it would. Julian unbuckled the back cover and peered inside.

"Shit-oh-mary . . . lookit that!"

"What is it?"

"Mines! This mother is full o' antitank mines."

"What the hell can we do with mines?"

"Weather comes on better, the Jabos be back. Drive them krauts onto these no-good trails."

"So?"

"Gonna git me some kraut ass, Lootenant. Gonna mine me a trail from hell to breakfas' . . . blow them sonsabitches inta pig-meat!"

"You're crazy! They'll send a battalion in here after us."

Sergeant Julian laughed. "You do what you wanta do, Lootenant. Like I tol' that dumb Polack . . . you wanta quit, go find you a kraut that wants hisself a Yankee lootenant for a POW. I ain't bet no money you make it. I don't give a shit for that Polack but he musta give up to 'em an' what'd they do? Put him to a tree and shoot him in the head."

Adam stared at him. If they had a hidey-hole and stayed quiet, the Germans might not find them. They might even live until the American army came back. If they mined a trail and blew up a truck, the Germans would comb these woods for them. When they mur-

dered Kuzyk they must have known there were more
like him hiding in the forest. The only chance they had
was to make no trouble.

Julian's face twisted in anger. "You know what I
think, Lootenant? I think you got a yellow streak a
foot wide. Tell you, boy . . . you take your kraut
floozy an' get the hell outta here. I ain't gonna hide no
more. I'm gonna kill me some krauts."

Adam pushed both hands into the frost-stiffened
canvas cover of the trailer and it creaked. Black
sonovabitch. He's crazy. I don't want to be shot like
Kuzyk. But I can't let this black bastard call me yellow. He pushed away from the trailer and Julian put a
hand on his shoulder.

"I don't mean that, Lieutenant. You all right?"

"Yeah. You know how to make these things work?"

"Bet your ass I do."

"Where we going to put 'em?"

"Road we crossed first night I saw you. That's what
they gonna use when them Jabos come back."

They got burlap sandbags from a jeep and loaded
mines into them. A dozen was all a man could carry.
They made three trips from the trailer to the Herresbach–Meyerode trail, sweating despite the bitter cold.
Seventy mines plus a few. One watched the trail and
the other scooped snow from the rutted tracks till he
reached frozen earth. No way to dig into that, and no
need.

Just get 'em on hard ground, said Julian, and showed
Adam how to pull the safety collar from the fuse and
arm the mine to explode when something crushed
through the snow and reached the metal spider on top
of it.

"Tip that mother an' she go up," he chortled.

By four-thirty in the afternoon dusk was falling and
they had to stop. "Make too many tracks an' they
know somebody been at they road," said Julian. "Le's
go git us some coffee."

"Got to find Anneke," muttered Adam.

"Leave that bitch freeze, Lootenant. She only make us trouble."

"No," said Adam. "She won't. The Germans are looking for her and so are the Belgians. She can't go anywhere."

"What you mean?"

Adam told him Anneke's story. When he finished Julian chuckled. "She as bad off as we are. Howcome she didn't find her a G.I. to look after her 'fore the krauts got here?"

"She did. When she got to Saint Vith one of those CIC spooks took her ID card away. Told her he'd get her another one if she'd climb in his sack."

"Pore little hoor. All right . . . le's go find her."

It was New Year's Eve but they had no celebration. They made coffee of melted snow over a little fire in the lodge and half-warmed canned rations on the coals. Julian held out a can of ham chunks and lima beans to Anneke and she shook her head. "No . . . no, I thank you."

He smiled at her, his big white teeth gleaming in the firelight. "Don't be 'fraid, little missy. I ain't goin' hurt you. Ain't much good, but you better eat some."

New Year's Day, the first of January 1945, dawned cold as ever but clear, and the air corps came—British or American, they could not tell, but the fighter-bombers snarled down the macadam roads bombing and machine-gunning everything that moved on them. Julian was right. By noon the Germans abandoned the blacktop roads and took to the forest. From their vantage point on top of the ridge, he and Adam watched the trail they had mined and Adam was sorry they had done it.

Horse-drawn artillery spilled off the macadam at Andler and plodded over the track to Meyerode. Horses could not detonate a mine but a gun or a loaded caisson cut through the snow to the violent death beneath it. When they did, the iron-wheeled gun or limber was blown into the air and the wheel team of horses butchered.

If they had been killed when the mine went off it would have been better, but they were not—only mortally hurt and they died screaming in their harness. Julian exulted over the gun crews killed; Adam mourned for the horses. Most of Tennessee was still farmed by mules and horses.

In the night they took more mines from the trailer and buried them in the snow on the trail from Meyerode south to the Schoenberg–Saint Vith road. In the dawn they stopped, made for the lodge, and were caught. A canny German sent a patrol of infantry down the trail from Meyerode, probing in the half-light with their bayonets for mines. Plodding up the trail, exhausted, Adam and Julian ran squarely into this unexpected reaction.

In the dawn fog Adam saw shadowy figures lunging off the trail into the trees. The forest exploded with the flickering orange glare of rifles and machine pistols and he ran for the shelter of the trees, fell, got to his knees, and reached for Julian, prone beside him.

"Git, Lootenant . . . git outta here!" groaned the black sergeant.

"Come on! Run!"

"I'm hit . . . git the hell outta here."

Adam stood to pull him upright and something struck his right hand a stunning blow, spinning him away from Julian.

"Run, boy!" panted Julian. Laboriously he worked his rifle into position and began firing.

Adam ran, blood from his hand spattering the snow around him. The Germans sifted out of the forest, closed around Julian, and took his rifle. Adam saw that over his shoulder. He did not see what happened next. He was running again but he heard the pistol shot and knew what it meant.

Like Kuzyk. They would kill any American they caught in the forest whether he tried to surrender or not.

Adam ran, fought his way through the trees, staying off the trail which was certain death. He could hear the Germans shouting behind him. He reached the crest of the hill, saw Meyerode below him, and turned into the dense forest to the east.

You can't get away, he told himself. They'll catch you and kill you just like Julian. The money, he thought, crouching in the scrub trees bordering a bare field—they won't have that. He pulled the bandolier from his waist and searched for a place to hide it. Beside him a weather-blackened stone cross rose from a slab of concrete.

"Heinrich Gerhardt von und zu Ahrens," said the legend cut into the crossarm; if there was more, it was covered by snow blown across the field, layered on the exposed face of the monument. Behind the cross under the concrete slab he found a hole—a badger den, he guessed.

The bare knob was strewn with abandoned American equipment—helmets, packs, and boxes of machine-gun ammunition. Somebody had come to the end of his war here. He dumped belted ammunition from its steel box, stuffed the bandolier of money into it. Panting, he scooped snow from the hole, hoping the badger was gone, and pushed the olive-drab box as far under the slab as he could reach.

With his good hand he stopped the mouth of the den with snow, brushing away spots of blood; then he ran again. The shouting of the Germans grew fainter. They must be searching for his trail. Whenever he stopped to gasp for breath, he scooped up with his right hand the telltale spots that fell from the left, held high to slow its bleeding. When he could run no more, he wrapped his hurt hand in his scarf. He was afraid to pull off the torn glove and look at the wound.

His back against a tree, he waited, eyes shut and shivering. If they found my trail they'll be here soon. Nothing I can do . . . dropped the carbine somewhere.

What would you do if you had it? You wouldn't even use it to help Julian. He groaned and pounded his leg with his good hand. He was right, Talcut . . . you're a goddamn coward. Krauts'll kill you sooner or later. Why didn't you stay with him? They'd have killed us both but maybe we'd have got some of them. But you ran. That black man had more guts than you'll ever have and you ran off and left him.

No use telling himself he couldn't have done Julian any good. That didn't make him feel any better about what he did. He put the hurt hand on his leg and it throbbed painfully. You can just sit here, you gutless jerk, till the krauts find you or you bleed to death. I won't do that, he told himself. I got to get away. He hauled himself to his feet and pushed away from the tree.

Where? Where can I go? Not the lodge—it won't be dark for hours. The cave . . . they had left Anneke in the cave. She'll help me do something about my hand. He worked his way along the ridgetop, climbing until he could see the roof of the lodge below him. It seemed deserted but if the Germans had found it they'd be waiting inside. They'd know somebody had been there and they'd just wait for him to come back.

He found the cave, crawled to the low entrance, and whispered urgently, "Anneke . . . Anneke?"

"It is you, Ah-dam?" Her voice was soft and frightened.

He squirmed into the dark hole, groped until he found her, and sobbed with relief and exhaustion.

"Ah-dam, what has happen? Where is the black man?"

"He's dead. They caught us."

"Oooh . . . they are coming after you?"

"I don't think so. I got away from them."

Anneke found his hands, gripped hard, and he gasped, snatching away the hurt one.

"What is the matter? You are hurt?"

"My hand," he groaned.

"They shoot you?"

"Yeah."

"We must go outside so I can see. Maybe I can help it."

"No! They're looking for me . . . we go outside and they'll see us."

"You got to do something. Does it bleed?"

"Yes, but I wrapped the scarf around it so it wouldn't make spots on the snow."

"Oh . . . poor Ah-dam! What can you do?"

Wait, he told himself. Wait right here till dark, then see if they're in the lodge. If they aren't, we can make a light and fix my hand. He explained that to Anneke and she put her arms around him.

"Come close, Ah-dam. I make you warm."

He must have slept a little, he was so tired. Anneke woke him, tugging at his jacket, and he gasped, struggling to sit up.

"Shh," she whispered. "It is all right. It is dark outside. Can we go now to the house?"

Lights marked Wereth. Adam looked up. No stars, no air corps—the Germans felt safe. He felt his way down the cruel rock ledges, Anneke clinging to his belt. A bitter wind threshed the topmost branches of the firs. If there were Germans still searching for him he could not hear them but they couldn't hear him either.

"The house, Ah-dam . . . we got to find the house," whispered Anneke.

"It's right here. Has to be." He slid down the last outcrop of rock into the snow-covered cushion of pine and fir needles.

"I cannot see," whimpered Anneke.

It had to be here. Adam crawled back uphill into a wall—a wall of logs above a stone foundation. They had gone past the lodge and the obstruction was its downhill side.

"You stay here," he told her.

"Where you go?"

"Look in the window . . . see if there's anybody inside." He felt his way along the logs, reached their end, and climbed again. With his good hand he found shutters—the window of the room with the fireplace.

He knelt and eased a shutter open an inch, praying the hinges would not squeak.

The interior was absolutely black, no hint of light. You think they'd make a fire to wait for you? They're sitting there in the dark. Not even SS were that good. They'd talk to each other. He waited—ten, fifteen minutes? It seemed an hour. There was no sound in the lodge. He climbed as carefully as he could to the front, slid into the hollow where the front door ought to be. It was ajar. Did we leave it like that? He couldn't remember.

He pushed it open, felt the cold tiles of the entryway. The door to the room where Julian had slept was open, silent cold darkness beyond it. He found the door to the other room—shut. Got to his knees and turned the iron lock handle a millimeter at a time. The minute sound it made was thunderous to him. Again he waited, minutes. The silence was absolute. They couldn't be that quiet. There's nobody in there.

He went back to the door, called softly, and Anneke came. He was so cold now he was careless. His lighter was in the right-hand pocket of his jacket and he could not reach it with his good hand.

"Anneke?"

"Yes?"

"Get my lighter . . . in my pocket." He guided her hand. She found it and he coached her in a hoarse whisper: "Flip it open and spin the little wheel."

She fired the Zippo after several attempts and Adam cringed. Mercifully the room was as they had left it—no Germans. She held up the lighter and by its dim light he made sure the window was still covered by canvas; then he found a box of K rations in the pile of stuff Julian and Kuzyk had brought from the trucks.

With Anneke's help he tore it open and set the carton alight on the hearth. She fed the quick flare of waxed paper with splinters from Julian's kindling until she had a small fire going, then took an empty can outside to fill with snow. She put it by her fire and added more wood around it.

"I make you coffee, Ah-dam. It is here?" She poked at the contents of the K ration box. He showed her the little packet.

"Tear it open and put it in the water."

They shared the weak brew, sipping in turn from the hot can, and Adam crouched by the tiny blaze. "Find something to eat, Anneke . . . one of those cans." He pointed at the pile of rations in the corner.

"Your hand, Ah-dam . . . let me look."

He held it out and she unwrapped the scarf, made a small noise when she saw the glove. Carefully she pulled it off and Adam held his hand to the light of the fire. The bullet had entered from the outside between his second and third fingers and torn out through his palm. Between the knuckles was only a little dark puncture, in his palm a hole the size of a half-dollar rimmed with congealed blood.

"Jesu!" whispered Anneke.

Adam studied the palm in wonder. Pistol—had to be a pistol. A Mauser rifle slug would have torn his hand apart. An officer with a pistol? Same one who killed Julian probably. Bastard got lucky with this shot. In the pile of equipment he found a medical aid-man's belt, in one of the pockets a little glass tube of brown liquid. Iodine, said the label. He broke off the tip, spilled the liquid into the hole in his palm and groaned.

"It hurt?"

"Unnh!"

"You must cover it up." She broke open a package containing bandage and wrapped it about his hand.

Adam grunted. The iodine burned and kept on burning incredibly. Anything burns like that, he thought, has got to be doing some good. He knelt by the fire and Anneke selected a can of food from the pile.

"Is good?" She held it to him.

"Doesn't matter . . . open it." He pulled his dog tag chain from his shirt, showed her the can opener. She could not get it off the chain and had to open the can holding it under his chin. Beans and frankfurters: he knew as soon as she cut into it. When the contents bubbled and popped on the fire, Anneke found a plastic spoon and dipped them out—a spoonful for each of them in turn.

"Is okay?"

"It's awful . . . but we've got to eat."

"I think it is good. What are these things in it?"

"Sausage," said Adam. "German sausage."

"Americans put German sausage in their food?"

"Anneke, nobody in America would eat this crap. It's only for soldiers."

"What you going to do, Ah-dam? Where do you go?"

"There's no place to go. They're looking for me now. If I try to get away, they'll catch me."

"You stay here?"

"Hell! They'll find this place. Nothing to do but give up."

"Give up?"

"Surrender . . . quit!"

"Oooh . . . no! They kill you, Ah-dam."

"And you?"

"They take me away. Then they kill me. Ah-dam . . . ?"

"Yeah?"

"Don't surrender, Ah-dam! You can get away . . . hide in the forest. Please, Ah-dam."

"Take you with me?"

"Oh, yes . . . please! I help you."

Her eyes, big and dark and pleading, searched his face. That was funny. She thought he could save her. Julian knew you haven't got the guts to fight but this girl thinks you will.

Not fight. Mess with their road anymore and they'll get you. There's a hell of a lot of woods around here, though. Maybe you can hide. Can't stay here. They'll find this place. Find the cave too. Got to have a lot of places to hide. Move every day.

"Ah-dam . . . you don't surrender?"

"I guess not."

"You stay here tonight?"

Good as anything, he decided. Go looking for something else in the dark, you'll make a lot of noise. Maybe they've got an ambush set up waiting for you.

"Yeah. Let that fire go out."

He sat staring at the dying coals and mourned for Sergeant Julian. He'd have got us both killed but maybe that's better than running like a rabbit till they find you.

Anneke spread a blanket on the floor as close to the tiny fire as she could, put another on it, and tucked a shelter-half around them. She took off the field jacket Kuzyk had given her, put that on top, and sat cross-legged to pull off her sweater. Shivering, she wrapped her arms about her and Adam stared fascinated at her breasts, nipples big and dark in the last glow of the coals.

"Come," she said simply. "It is more warm."

He blamed his awkwardness on his bandaged hand but that was not his only problem. He had never been in bed with a woman—had dreamed of it lustfully for years but had no real understanding of the mechanics of the thing. He got himself into Anneke's bed without removing anything but his boots and jacket. She squirmed busily, taking off her skirt and whatever she wore under it, he supposed. After a while she tugged at his trousers, complained softly.

"Take them off, Ah-dam . . . you be more warm."

She pushed and tugged gently and skillfully, peeling him down layer by layer. "Put it on top," she murmured. "Put it all on top of us." It took a while but she reduced his protection to shirt and long johns and went to work on them.

"Hey!" he protested. She unbuttoned the shirt and started on the underwear.

"I make you warm, Ah-dam." She pulled him to her, cushioned her breasts against him, and her legs sought his. Her body moving against him generated more than warmth and he sought her face in the darkness. He found it, and her mouth welcomed him.

Her tongue was not bold like Kelly's, it explored timidly, touching and retreating, returning cautiously.

Fake, he told himself. She just wants you to help her . . . that's all it is. But she made room enough between them to move her breasts against him and he didn't care what she wanted.

"Come . . . come here, Ah-dam!" she whispered, hands moving, coaching him. Complying eagerly, he scattered the clothing piled on them and she freed a hand to fetch it back. He applied himself more diligently and Anneke moaned, clinging to him, moving beneath him.

"Aaa . . . nh!" he groaned, and forgot everything except the explosion building within him.

"No . . . no," gasped Anneke, "not so quick!" But her own small movement negated that plea. Adam stiffened and drowned in a storm of physical excitement beyond anything he could do to check it. He subsided, gasping, and she made a soft deprecating sound.

"Oh, Ah-dam . . . you are too quick! Come, I show you."

He was warm, his hand hurt no longer. Anneke fitted herself against him, boneless, infinitely soft and warm and close. Gently, carefully, she moved beneath him, brought him again to mindless pleasure, held him there for a splendid moment, and tipped him over the edge, exploding with him, crying out triumphantly.

When he could breathe he would have tried again but she laughed and kissed him, put a finger on his lips.

"Stop, Ah-dam," she murmured. "Is enough . . . please!"

Light seeping through the shuttered window awoke him, but he was not cold. Anneke moved against him, murmuring, and he hated leaving their shared warmth. Daylight would bring the Germans out though—even soft fat ones left behind to guard Belgian villages. He extracted himself from the bed, teeth chattering, and peeled his clothes from it.

She sat up, turned from him with an engaging modesty, and pulled the sweater over her tousled head. While he was gone for more wood from the pile outside, she put on her skirt and boots.

He knelt by the hearth, blew on a last coal, still alive, fed it shavings split from a log with his knife. By the time he had a little flame, Anneke brought snow in a can to make coffee. He stood up and she leaned against him, offering her mouth.

"Is okay, Ah-dam?"

His hand behind her head pulled her close and he kissed her, tugging gently at a little gold earring. "Ooh!" murmured Anneke. "Don't pull it!" He ruffled her dark red hair with his fingers.

"Why did you cut it so short?"

"What? What do you say?"

"Your hair . . . why did you cut it off?"

"The Gestapo do that. It is long now, Ah-dam, see?" She reached up to make a little twist of hair behind her head. "If I got a ribbon it don't look so funny."

Her lips were cold and stiff but that made no difference. What a way to lose a war, Talcut, he thought. He did something he had never dared do with any girl before—pushed a hand beneath her sweater, cupped her breast, and squeezed gently. They cut her hair— shaved it, probably. She told them what they wanted so they wouldn't hurt her but they didn't just turn her loose for nothing. She paid for that—just like she paid you last night. So what? She's got nothing else to give and she gave it to you. She watched him with worried eyes.

"You are angry?"

He smiled at her. "No . . . how could I be angry?"

She put her arms around his waist, her head under his chin. "Please, Ah-dam . . . you don't make me go away?"

"No, we'll stick together."

"Please?"

He kissed her again. "You stay with me. We'll hide till the Americans come back."

Easy to say—hard to do. It was a waking nightmare—the kind where you run and hide and run again and what hunts you comes so close you hear it sniff and breathe. They hid in the cave and a German patrol found it. Afterward Adam guessed they were from the eight balls left to guard Meyerode and Herresbach.

They stood about the mouth of the cave and talked loudly and one of them threw a stick grenade into it that struck the roof and fell between Anneke's feet. "Kick it!" hissed Adam desperately and she did, whimpering in terror.

The hissing grenade rolled and bounced back to the entrance and exploded with a deafening roar. The Germans simply went away without even looking to see if they had killed anyone.

Driven by cold and hunger, they went back to the lodge after dark and Adam sat against the wall by the hearth all night, holding a grenade. If the Germans continued to search the forest they would surely find the lodge. He must have slept in snatches when exhaustion overcame him, but his luck held: no Germans appeared. Real second-stringers, he decided. They hunted only by daylight.

He returned to the trail from Herresbach to Wereth, Anneke clinging to him, and searched the abandoned American trucks until he found a rifle and some ammunition for it. He was afraid to go back to the cave and they hid in a dense thicket of firs, watching in frozen terror a German patrol thrash through the forest below them. Sadsacks they were, head and face muffled in scarves, strips of blanket wrapped around their boots. They lumbered and shouted through the forest and they must have found another cave to toss grenades into. The muffled explosions reverberated through the trees.

That's what they'll do if they find the lodge, thought Adam. They haven't the guts to search the place—they'll just chuck grenades in. That night they stayed in the forest and learned it was impossible. They grew so cold they had to move, blundering and stamping through the firs.

"Oh, Ah-dam," whispered Anneke when dawn drove them back to their thicket, "I am so cold! We got to make a fire."

"Not here. Even those dumb bastards'll find us if we make a fire."

They had nothing to eat. Anneke had saved a narrow cardboard packet of cigarettes from a K ration and they shared them. "TWENTY GRAND" said the label. Anneke's long lips, gray and stiff, cupped her cigarette, clung to it until it was too short to hold any longer. She drew the smoke into her lungs with long gasps, coveting the momentary warmth, and Adam broke the third cigarette of the packet in half, gave her a part to light from the butt of her first.

"We go back to the house tonight, please, Ah-dam. We stay here and we are dead. We are freeze with cold."

She was right. They could not live through another night in the forest. Before darkness fell, he crawled within sight of the lodge and watched it. Incredibly the Germans had not yet found it.

It was heaven: coffee and a can of stew warmed on a little fire, a nest of blankets and canvas on the stone floor by the hearth. Anneke took off her jacket and sweater, helped Adam remove his clothing, and made love to him again.

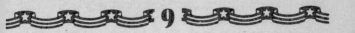

9

IF I ever get home, Adam told himself, I'll never go hunting again. You live like a rabbit and you know how he feels—afraid to hide and scared to run. The German soldiers from Meyerode were hopeless hunters but they thrashed and shouted through the forest every day. Not eagerly. Someone must have decided there was at least one American left to search for, and he made these clods do it. They were easy to evade, you could hear them coming a mile away, but sooner or later, whoever made them hunt would teach them how—put a dozen men on stand and drive the forest with the rest, just like back home.

When they figure that out, thought Adam grimly, you're a goner. You've got to stop trying to dodge them—got to hide and stay hidden all day. And that damn lodge. It was incredible they had not found it, yet every night he and Anneke returned to it—they had to.

He found half a jerrican of gasoline on a wrecked American jeep, and after that the only fire they made on the hearth was in an empty ration can with a little earth in the bottom soaked with gasoline. It would heat coffee and something to eat but it gave little warmth. Anneke murmured in protest but Adam thought it safer than a real fire. It could be smothered instantly, leaving a telltale stench of gasoline, but that disappeared quickly in the drafty old building.

They just might have made it if it hadn't been for his hand. He tried to keep it clean and bandaged but inevitably he used it and it became infected. It swelled and the torn palm hurt all the time—worse, it began to drain, a thick discharge that smelled horrible, and he knew he had a fever. Anneke's willing body was no help. Some nights he could not sleep at all, his hand throbbed so badly. He packed it in snow but that was little help; as soon as the snow melted the pain came back worse than ever.

He tried to reckon how long this nightmare had lasted and gave up. It had to be January 1945, but neither he nor Anneke could figure out what day it was. Doesn't matter, he thought. If the American army doesn't come back mighty quick, the Germans won't have to hunt you much longer. How long, he wondered, do you live if you've got gangrene?

Anneke choked when she tried to replace the noisome bandages, and he pulled his hand away. She was crying.

"You know, don't you?" he asked her hoarsely.

"What I know?"

"If I don't get this to a doctor it's going to kill me."

"Oh, Ah-dam! They don't help you . . . they will shoot you!"

"Can't be worse than dying of gangrene!"

"Please?"

"Rot! My hand's rotting, Anneke . . . you know what that is! I don't think those Germans will shoot me. I don't know what they are but they aren't real soldiers. If I don't scare 'em, they won't kill me. I'll just sit in the trail till they find me."

She put her hand over her mouth and whimpered. "And me? They catch me and the Gestapo find out. They kill me."

"You've got to get away, Anneke . . . to a town. Saint Vith, maybe. You're Belgian and you speak their language. Somebody will help you."

"The *Gendarmerie* look for me too!"

"Dammit, there aren't any Belgian policemen left in Saint Vith! If you can get there, the people will help you and the Germans won't know the difference. Listen . . . listen to me carefully. . . ."

"Yes? I listen."

He told her about the bandolier of money hidden in the field above Meyerode. "You can find it . . . under a stone cross at the edge of the field." He shut his eyes and remembered the name on the cross, made her repeat it until he was sure she would not forget.

"Heinrich Gerhardt von und zu Ahrens . . . say it again." She repeated it once more, like a frightened child whispering a lesson. "You get that money and you can pay somebody to help you. There's American and British money too, and it's got to be worth a lot here."

She put her arms around him and sobbed forlornly. "You are good to me, Ah-dam. Please . . . you don't surrender to the Germans. We find your money and we both go to Saint Vith."

"If we could get there," he said grimly, "what good would it be? You're just one more Belgian—the Germans couldn't tell you from the rest of the people. What could they do with an American soldier? I got to find a doctor, and I'd be like a skunk at a lawn party . . . the krauts'll smell me."

"Oooh, I am so afraid!" She pointed at the jumble of American equipment in the corner of the room. "You got everything, Ah-dam . . . your army got everything! You must got something to help your hand. Why you don't find it?"

Adam stared at her and she cried again. "I am sorry, Ah-dam . . . don't be mad at me."

"I'm not mad at you, Anneke." He kissed her gently. "You're right! I didn't think of it."

"What? What you don't think?"

"Sulfa powder!"

"What is that?"

"Just what I need! It's stuff you put in a wound that gets infected and it works like a charm. They told us about it in England."

"It is here?" She pointed again at the equipment.

"No, ordinary medics don't carry it but I saw an

ambulance on the trail with those trucks. If the krauts haven't cleaned it out, there might be some there."

"Oh, Ah-dam . . . we go look for it now?"

"No, I'll go tomorrow early . . . soon's it's light enough."

"I don't go with you?"

"You hide in the forest. Stay close to the lodge so I can find you when I come back."

"You find it, Adam . . . I know you find it. Then you are all well again and you don't go to the Germans. Come, I make you warm."

"No, I smell too bad." That was only an excuse. He was so dizzy and feverish he couldn't make love.

The stench of his hand was frightening. Even in the freezing wind it was sickening. Twice he had to sit down and slide over a particularly steep outcropping of rock. Ought to get a branch and wipe out his tracks in the snow but he would do it when he came back. No use doing it twice. That was funny when he concentrated on it. If he had this much trouble getting down, how would he ever get back?

When there was no more hill to slide down, he rested against a tree and stared at the glade before him. Like a lobby. A hole in the forest all roofed over with trees. Somewhere a faint snoring sound grew to a roar and faded, accompanied by a pulsing rattle. He could hear the sizzling rush of rockets and their thumping explosions.

Some fool kraut on the Schoenberg road and the Jabos caught him. Adam let his head fall back against the tree, shut his eyes, and thought of the man driving that airplane. Children—they were all children, those pilots, but maybe they knew there were still Americans in these woods. You might be the only one left, he thought.

By Meyeroder stream at the bottom of the Adesberg there was a long meadow, tilted but smooth and frozen hard. Go when the Germans in Meyerode are all asleep and tromp out a big "SOS" in the snow. The

Jabos would see it next day. Stay there and wave when they come back.

Hide in the woods and get a lot of dry branches. After dark there'd be a little plane like the Brits used to bring stuff to the French underground or one of our artillery observation planes—"Maytag Messerschmitts," the pilots called them. There's a good moon now. He can find the meadow. Light a fire . . . two fires . . . one at each end. Anneke can do one.

The plane would land. He could see it bouncing and swaying up the slope in the snow. It would spin around and the door would open and the pilot would yell: Get in quick. Then he'd say: Jeez, there's two of you, and I'd say: No sweat . . . he's real light. Boy, are we ever glad to see you! Anneke could sit on my knees or maybe there's a place in the back of those things. She'd fit in a little place. What about when he sees it's a girl? I'll say she's a Belgian resistance fighter. That's what I'll say when we get to France or wherever he came from.

There was a harsh squealing in the woods and the crackle of frozen snow. Damn wild pigs. He hoped it was a dead kraut they were fighting over—not an American. He wanted to think about the airplane, not pigs.

Pipe dream, Talcut, he told himself. No airplane's going to land in the dark in the middle of the German Army to haul your ass out of here. Cut it out. If you don't find something for this stinking hand, it won't matter anyway. The hogs'll get you like whatever they've got down there in the woods.

He shook his head to clear it and studied the cavernous lobby. Three rutted tracks fanning out from a frozen sump hole with logs and branches sticking out where somebody tried to fix it so he could get a truck or a wagon across. He could see where the horses had thrashed and fought the mud before it froze hard.

Madammerbusch. That's what Anneke called this place. That track there, it goes from Herresbach to Wereth. The cavalry tried to get out that way. The worst one goes to Valender and that's a good way to get to the meadow by the Adesberg.

Maybe there won't be room for three people in the plane. Leave Anneke? No . . . I'll say take her and come back for me tomorrow night. But you'll never get out then. Krauts all over that field when they hear the plane land.

She'll tell what happened, though, and so will the pilot, and they'll send Ma a medal and Mr. Parkinson'll write a big long editorial in *The Messenger* about Adam Talcut, Laurel City's hero lieutenant.

Be all right to give up then. Krauts'll fix my hand and when the war's over I'll get out of prison camp and go home and man, will they ever make a fuss about me. Bitsey too. Ah . . . Bitsey. What the hell will you do with two women, Talcut?

He was jarred out of that happy problem by the howl of more fighter planes and the rumbling thud of bombs. Must be a lot of trucks on the Schoenberg road. That first one went back and got his buddies. Give 'em hell, flyboys. Way up, a mile up, somebody began ripping a huge piece of paper and tore it right down to the ground. The sound drove Adam scrambling for shelter in the rocks but before he got there a stunning blast shook the branches of the firs.

Close . . . too close. Damn fool dropped his bomb way short. Or maybe just had one left over and didn't want to lug it home. It was warmer in the rocks. Wind couldn't get at him. Either that or he had fever again. He put a hand on his face and it was all sweaty. Just scared sweat, he told himself. He shut his eyes and waited and after a while his hand didn't hurt so much.

What if they don't believe me about Anneke? What if the Belgians get her when we land in France? She's as scared of them as she is of the krauts. Would they do what the Gestapo did to her friend in Liege, or just shoot her? Probably hurt her till she says what they want to hear and then kill her. Not if I'm there, they won't. But you won't be there. You're going to give her your place in the plane so you can quit and be safe in a POW camp till the war's over.

Come off it, Talcut. Get your head out and go look for that sulfa powder. Where does that other trail go? He knew he had followed it before but he couldn't remember where it went. Ah, yes. To the road south from Meyerode and you know about that. After we killed all those horses we were going to put mines in that one too but they caught us and killed Julian. Poor goddamn horses. How come the blitzkrieg kraut army has so many horses?

All right. Let's go up the Wereth track. Must be some medic's stuff in one of those trucks. On his feet he felt better. He wasn't so dizzy. Stay out of the road, Talcut, he told himself. Harder walking, but if you meet somebody you're in no shape to chase rabbits. Run like a rabbit, you mean.

He climbed laboriously into and out of a couple of big 2 ½-ton American trucks and found nothing. Half a pack of cigarettes in the dash compartment of one. Anneke would like them. Chesterfields. Even frozen she'd like them. Then he struck gold. A ¾-ton truck squatting like it was gut-shot. Back wheels gone so it must have hit a mine. Funny the front wheels didn't set it off.

There was a terrible mess in the back of the truck but it was medical supplies: pasteboard boxes of plastic bottles all bulged and split. Plasma? What good if it was? He didn't know how to use it. He found a wooden chest, olive drab with names and numbers stenciled on it in white. A tray of instruments—scissors and knives and what looked like nickel-plated pliers. Beneath that a lot of little brown packages in wax paper. The first one he tore open was full of little glass Syrettes. Morphine? It didn't seem to be frozen, so he put some in his pocket. More brown boxes with cellophane packets in them.

"SULFANILAMIDE POWDER" it said on the packets, with a whole sermon of tiny fine print beneath. You got it, Talcut, he chuckled, and stuffed the box into his pocket with the Syrettes.

Now there was something more than pigs squabbling over frozen meat in the forest: a grumble of motors. Jabos must have run 'em off the road and they're back in the woods again, on the trail from Herresbach to Meyerode. If Julian was here we'd find some more mines and drive those bastards out where the planes could get them.

Julian's dead, Talcut. Nobody left to put mines on the trail but you, and you haven't got the guts to do it. He let himself down carefully from the back of the ruined truck and clung to it dizzily.

Man, you are in a bad way, he thought. He pushed off from the truck and went back to the trail junction someone had called Madammerbusch. Anneke? How would she know what they called it? Probably Julian. That black bastard knew everything. Squinting, he selected the trail leading up by the lodge and set off, panting. It was hard going and he was sweating and that made his hand smell worse. He held it up so it wouldn't throb so painfully and almost missed the spine of rock that led off to the lodge.

He went up it on hands and knees, stopping frequently to brush out his tracks in the snow with his scarf-wrapped hand. When he saw the log house he stopped to rest. No smoke from the chimney—no krauts. He would have to rest again before he looked for Anneke. He slid down into the hollow in front of the lodge.

"*Wilkommen!*" said a man by the door and pointed his rifle at Adam. He wore the long green coat of a Volksgrenadier. No helmet—a long-billed green cloth cap with the earflaps buttoned under his chin and a black-and-white-checkered scarf wrapped around his throat and over the cap. Adam held up his hurt hand, not in surrender but just to stop it throbbing.

"*Nun . . . verwundet, ja?*" said the German, grinning. He lowered the rifle and banged the butt against the door of the lodge, calling out something. A whole crowd of people spilled out.

One was an officer—he had shoulder straps of worn silver braid on his long coat with two little metal bottle caps on them. Adam tried to remember if that made him a first lieutenant or a captain. Three more soldiers in the shoddy ankle-length coats and a man in a brown-and-green-mottled camouflage smock. He wore a gray billed cap with the top all squashed down.

Another just like him appeared, pushing Anneke before him. Shit, thought Adam. They caught her. When she saw him she shut her eyes like she was going to cry. Last to appear was a little girl with long blond hair spilling from under a knit cap. I remember that cap, Adam thought. Emilie. They got her too?

Had to be Emilie. Kid I took to Meyerode because she was sick. Belgian woodcutter said he'd look after her. The officer and one of the men in a camouflage smock were arguing about something. The officer looked at Adam.

"You are officer or soldier?" he demanded in labored English.

"Lieutenant," said Adam, unbuttoning his coat and pulling out the collar of his shirt to show the single gold bar of his rank. The German pointed at the brass crossed rifles on the other side of the collar.

"What is that?"

"Infantry."

"Ah! You are wounded?"

Dumb question, thought Adam. He can smell it from here. The camouflage smock started shouting again and Adam studied the child, wondering how in the world they had found her. She wiped her nose with a mittened hand and pointed at him, saying something. Funny. She never said anything when she was here.

"*Verdammte Freischuetz!*" said the man in the camouflage smock.

"You . . ." said the officer to Adam, "you have kill German soldiers?"

I could tell him there's a war, thought Adam, but that won't help. I know what he means. He unwrapped the scarf from his bandaged hand.

"No, I am wounded."

"Why you do not surrender?"

"I am waiting," said Adam, "for my army to come back."

The German officer made a scornful noise. "Your army is run away. It does not come back."

He had to translate that exchange into German for the two in camouflage jackets and they exploded in noisy protest. When the shouting stopped, Adam asked mildly, "Who are they?"

"*Belgier*," said the officer disgustedly. "*Walloonie SS.*" The way he said it, Adam knew what he thought about them.

"You are SS?"

"No, thanks God! I am captain, *Heeresflak. Berufsoffizier.*"

Adam understood he was a captain in something that wasn't SS. That was all that mattered.

"What's he yelling about?" he asked, indicating the Belgian SS man. The captain looked puzzled and Adam tried again. "What does he want?"

"He want to shoot you. The little girl say you are *Freischuetze.*"

Adam stared in wonder at Emilie. "What is that?"

"*Guerillakaempfer . . .* partisan."

Adam understood. "No," he said, "I am a lieutenant in the infantry. I wear my uniform and I am no partisan." That was all he could think of to say but the captain seemed to accept it.

"Yes, I see. I tell him it is not correct to shoot you."

That's good, thought Adam. He tried to give the captain a correct military look but he was having trouble again making his eyes stay in focus. Whatever was wrong with his hand had a strange effect on his eyes. Like an electrical short circuit. When it happened he could neither see nor think clearly. He scooped a handful of snow to rub on his face.

The Belgian was shouting again, his face red and angry. He can't do anything, Adam told himself. There's only two of them and the captain has four. The officer snapped an order and two of his soldiers pulled Adam to his feet.

"They take you to Herresbach," he said. "You can walk?"

"Yeah . . . sure."

"They put you on a truck there. If there is a medical officer he look at your hand."

"Ah-dam," said Anneke, "please, Ah-dam . . ."

The little girl, Emilie, was speaking again, pulling at the coat of one of the Belgian SS men. The soldiers boosted Adam out of the hollow.

"Ah-dam . . ." Anneke's cry was desperate. "Help me, Ah-dam!"

He looked back. The Belgian twisted her arm and she cried out again.

"Son of a bitch!" said Adam, struggling dizzily.

"Go!" said the officer. "In the village are more of them. Go now or they come and shoot you. I cannot stop it."

Three of the soldiers went with Adam. He tried to go back but they would not let him. "*Komm*," they said. Out of sight of the lodge, they took his wallet and wristwatch, grinning at him cheerfully. "*Alles aus, Ami. Fuer du, der Krieg ist fertig.*"

They came to the intersection of trails at Madammerbusch and took the one toward Herresbach. A little way along it one of them pointed at something in the forest: an American half-track. He made his way to it, climbed on the track, and peered inside. He found something and held it up.

"*Wass ist'n dass?*" he asked Adam.

"K ration."

"*Ration . . . Essen?*"

"*Ja,*" said Adam. He was not looking at the German. He was looking at the impenetrable wall of fir trees through which he could not see the lodge. They'll

kill her just like they wanted to kill me. That little
devil told them where we were.

The soldier in the half-track tore the waxed paper
from the box and beamed. "*Cigaretten*," he said, holding up a packet of Wings. Tough, thought Adam.
Sometimes you get Camels but Wings are better than
Twenty Grands.

There was a dead American by the half-track, on his
back, one hand held up as if reaching for something, a
gesture that would last until he thawed or somebody
buried him. Someone—a German with a macabre sense
of humor probably—had put the upthrust hand to
work. A strand of field-telephone wire rose from the
snow on one side of the body, took a turn around the
hand, and sagged back into the snow on the other
side.

There was something else partly covered by snow:
an American submachine gun—not a gangster tommy
gun but the stamped metal kind everybody called a
grease gun. So simple even an American G.I. couldn't
screw it up. Magazine's still in it but it's probably
empty, thought Adam. And for sure it's frozen.

So what? You wouldn't take a chance on it. You
just walked off and left her and you know what they'll
do to her. Laurel City's boy hero. When Julian got hit
you ran. Ran off and they killed him. If it hadn't been
for Ritchie you'd have surrendered on that hill, and
then they killed Ritchie. The only damn thing you've
done to the Germans since then, Julian made you do.
You, Talcut, you're a gutless wonder.

All three of his guards were at the half-track now
and one of them held out something to him. "Hey,
Ami . . . *Schokolade*?"

Adam shook his head. Real Boy Scouts, aren't they?
If they hadn't got you off, those SS bastards would
have shot you. It simmered up slowly inside him, a
cold grim anger. I'm not going to run anymore and
I'm not going to any damn kraut POW camp either.
He got his jacket open with his good hand and pulled

down the zipper of his tanker pants. The Germans watched curiously as he groped inside them.

"*Wass denn?*" demanded one.

"Gotta piss," muttered Adam.

"*Pissen* . . . Oh-kay," said one, grinning.

Adam concentrated on the grease gun, trying not to urinate on the dead American. He got his hurt hand out of the scarf and bit his lip till his mouth filled with the salt-sweet taste of blood. The agony demanded noise he couldn't afford. He picked up the wet gun and tried to make the bandaged hand hold it but the fat black fingers wouldn't close. He could clamp it against his thigh, though, and pull back the cocking lever with his good hand.

The hinged cover over the ejection port popped halfway open. Got to drink more water, thought Adam. Didn't get it thawed out. He forced the cover all the way open with the forefinger of his left hand, slapped his palm on the bottom of the magazine to make sure it was seated and worked the cocking lever again. A fat, shiny .45-caliber cartridge popped out.

"*Mensch!*" yelled the German in the half-track. "*Pass mal auf*, Dieter!"

Adam shot him first. The grease gun fired twice, jammed, and when he worked the lever, began firing again. It didn't make the breathless ripping "bur-rup" of a Schmeisser—more deliberate, as if measuring out the big .45-caliber slugs.

Adam was careful. After each burst he let up on the trigger and pointed the gun at the next German. When the magazine was empty all three were down but one of them was groaning, trying to get up, groping for his rifle.

He found it but he couldn't pick it up and Adam kicked it away. The German stared at him, mouth open in accusation. Go on, Adam told himself. Get it over with . . . mash his head with the goddamn grease gun. He couldn't do it and he almost cried in relief when he saw there was no need.

"*Mutti . . .*" said the German hoarsely, and folded

up, his head on his outstretched legs. After a moment he sagged over in the snow and was silent.

Adam ran, stumbling, not in fear but with a fierce, proud joy. I wish Julian could have seen me. He ran because they must have heard the shooting at the lodge and somebody would come to see what had happened and they were not going to catch him again. He got into the Herresbach trail and followed it until exhaustion stopped him and made him think. Got to find a place to hide, and don't leave tracks.

He went on, panting, until he encountered an old roadblock, a tall pine felled across the road, enough of it cut away to let vehicles pass. He climbed onto it and worked his way along the trunk till he was stopped by thick branches. Do what you did when you saw the German patrol the day you found Julian.

It was hard with his useless hand but he did it. He lunged off the downed pine into a stout fir, flailed his way through its branches to the trunk and climbed as high as he could. Wait till dark, he thought. Then what? Try to find that Belgian woodcutter at Meyerode?

That's crazy. It's full of those SS bastards and when he finds his dead Boy Scouts that Wehrmacht captain will be worse than they are. You got to get the hell out of here, Talcut. He tried to see the sky through the fir branches, to see how much light was left, but he couldn't.

It was snowing again: the silent snow of the Ardennes, sifting through the trees soundlessly, clinging to their branches, covering the earth beneath them. For the first time, Adam welcomed it—whatever trail he left in his stumbling flight from the half-track would disappear in minutes as would the dead men he left there.

He wedged himself into the branches of the fir and something teased his face—a long shiny strip of silver foil. Christmas trimming courtesy of the U.S. Army Air Corps: something they threw out of their airplanes so the Germans couldn't find them with their radar.

Adam held his face up to the snow, relished its cool

touch; wedged his hurt hand in the branches above his head and waited for its throbbing to quiet. The branches moved, stirred by a wind that was strangely warm, the snowflakes no longer silent but clicking minutely as they fell—sleet, then rain.

You can't stay here, he knew. You'll get wet and when the wind changes you'll freeze. Laboriously he calculated what he needed: something to eat, but first a place to get dry and make a light so you can put that sulfa stuff on your hand. And a weapon—what happened to the grease gun?

Dropped it when you ran from the half-track. Go back and get it? He thought about that carefully. They must have heard the shooting. They must have found those Boy Scouts you killed and tried to find you. They didn't look very hard—not on the trail to Herresbach. They took them back to Meyerode.

All right. Maybe they found the grease gun and took it with them but there's food in that half-track. He worked his way down the trunk of the fir tree, reached the ground and waited, straining to hear movement in the wet forest. He moved a yard at a time, one tree to the next, waiting at each, mouth open and listening.

It was easier in the trail, but twice he had to sit down and rest and it took him a long time to find the half-track. He found it with his hand in the dark, stumbled over something and recoiled: the dead cavalryman, but he couldn't find the upthrust hand holding the wire. Crouching, he searched. Couldn't be the cavalryman; this one was facedown and there was another beside him.

He knelt, holding up his hurt hand, and wondered if he had found another truck and more dead Americans. No truck—he could feel the cold wet steel of the track links and he found yet another body; long sodden overcoat with a big collar. Germans: the three he had killed.

Nobody had found them. Either they didn't hear the shooting or they paid no attention to it. He sat down against the track, too tired and dizzy to do anything else.

You can't stay here, he thought. They might not come till daylight but they'll come as soon as they miss these poor bastards. He tried to think what he ought to do but it was too complicated. Divecchio and Kuzyk dead. Julian dead and they've got Anneke. Julian was smarter than all of us but they killed him. They'll kill you too unless you run.

He couldn't find the grease gun. He thought for a moment of taking a rifle from one of the Germans but that was sure death when they caught him. The wind scrubbed the clouds from a few stars so he could see the bulk of the half-track and the dark smudge on the melting snow of the bodies. He blundered west along the trail until he fell into the sump hole marking the junction at Madammerbusch.

Back to the lodge? Crazy . . . every patrol they send out will stop there now. Meyerode? That Belgian wood-cutter? If you can find him, maybe he'll help you. He climbed dizzily out of the trail and made his way through the forest south of it. A long time later he sat against a tree and cried with exhaustion and the pain in his hand.

He won't help you. That goddamn kid told him about the lodge and he told the krauts. You're screwed, Talcut. He must have slept because the snarling buzz of a motorcycle on the trail woke him and there was light enough to see for a few yards around him. The motorcycle went away and there was no more traffic and after a while he knew why. The clouds had closed in again and that meant no American planes, so the Germans were back on the macadam roads.

Adam studied his wounded hand. If he took the bandage off he was so cold he might never get it on again. He tore open a packet of sulfa powder with his teeth and tried to sift some under the bandage. He doubted it would do much good that way.

It took him until noon to get close enough to Meyerode to see the village, not clearly, because some combination of rain and frozen ground had raised a ground mist. He was too far away to see much but the radio vans were gone. That meant the Germans had driven so far west their command post had to move after them but there were still soldiers in Meyerode. He couldn't tell if they were SS but it didn't matter now. When that Wehrmacht captain found his three men he'd be worse than SS.

Wind thrashed the branches overhead, cold wind again, and Adam shivered. He got to his feet and looked longingly at the village. Wind blew the mist away and he could see it better, red tile roofs, smoke blowing from a chimney, and something strange on a leaning concrete telephone pole. He crept a little closer and a terrible cold certainty gripped him.

Short hair, but a skirt: a woman. They didn't shoot Anneke, they hanged her. Put a rope around her throat and hanged her on the telephone pole. Left her there for the soldiers and the villagers to stare at. Murdering sons of bitches. His anger exhausted him and he cried again. After a while he turned south, found the track to Wallerode, and plodded along it, oblivious of danger.

Somewhere here was where they killed Julian. All dead now—everybody but you, Talcut. Doesn't matter anymore. First kraut I see I'm going to sit down and wait for him. He came to a hamlet he thought must be Wallerode and reneged on that promise. The soldiers in Wallerode had brown-and-green camouflage smocks and he wouldn't give those bastards the pleasure of killing him.

Circling the edge of a clearing, he found the wreck of a two-wheel cart, dead horse still in the shafts, driver dead beside it. The clearing killed them. American fighter-bombers working the macadam road must have seen them when they came out of the trees. Some hotshot pilot sprayed cart, horse, and driver with his machine guns and tore them apart.

Two things Adam found and took: a blanket dragged with difficulty from the dead horse and a chunk of stale dark bread in the pocket of the driver's coat. He wrapped the blanket around him, sat on the horse, and ate the bread, gathering up the crumbs that fell to the ground.

In the last light of evening he scrambled down a steep slope to a creek, crossed it dry-foot jumping from rock to rock, and climbed the western bank to a field of old furrows, untilled. It took him a long minute to realize that beyond the field there was no forest. Houses—dead houses like everything else in this corner of hell. Not a light anywhere in more houses than he could count.

Saint Vith, he thought. I finally got back to Saint Vith. What good is that? Looks like the krauts took the civilians away.

I'll find a dry place in one of those houses. Wait for somebody to find me. This town is so far behind the front, all the combat soldiers are gone. Must be full of quartermaster people and truck drivers. Just what I need—the kind Julian called an old daddy-rabbit of a kraut that wants to capture a real live Ami.

The first house had no roof, something had blown it away, but he was too tired to search for something better. Behind the house he found a shed, a stall where they must have kept a horse or a cow. There was a big pile of wet straw and he burrowed into it gratefully.

10

ADAM WAS hungry, cold, and exhausted. As soon as the damp straw warmed him a little, he slept—no gift, because he wandered from one terrible nightmare to another. He fled again with Julian from the German patrol but when Julian was hit he did not say, "Run, boy!" He said, "Help me!" He didn't help him; he ran away and woke sweating, trying to remember what Julian really said.

He slept again and Anneke called him: "Ah-dam . . . help me, Ah-dam!" He didn't help—he just went away with the Volksgrenadiers, glad it was over. He stood under the leaning concrete pole in Meyerode, looking up at her face, twisted in agony, and woke himself by his anguished shouted denial. I couldn't help it . . . they wouldn't let me come back.

Then he was back on the forested hill above Schoenberg, what was left of his platoon watching him accusingly. Do something, they said. Get us out of here. He implored his radio to send him help but it only muttered and squealed. That woke him again, hating himself, and the radio continued to squeal.

You're off your rocker, he thought, frightened. He held his breath, listening. The damned thing squeaked but there was more: the scrape and clink of someone digging. Carefully he pushed away the straw. There was a hole in the roof of the stall, and incredibly enough starlight to see there was nothing—no one besides himself in the shed. The noise was outside and on hands and knees, a cautious inch at a time, he crept to the door.

The digger worked at a mound of frozen earth. What he wanted was beyond Adam but there he was, crouched, working hard. "*Dreck!*" he muttered, and flung something away.

He was in the shadow of the mound but Adam could see his feet: heavy shoes, thick socks, above them bare legs. He puzzled over that until he saw the skirt. A woman? Adam watched her, baffled. Not a soldier—a woman. Maybe she'll help me. He reached through the door and put his hand on her shoe.

"*Herr Gott!*" she gasped. After a moment she turned her head very slowly, held out something to him.

"*Bitte . . . nur eine Kartoffel!*"

He knew that word. She was digging potatoes buried for the winter behind the stall. Not her potatoes, or she wouldn't be digging in the dark. He didn't know how to ask for help so he held out his bandaged hand.

She sat on her heels to look at it. The thin light showed him big frightened eyes and little more. He moved a little, out of the shadow of the door, and she sucked in her breath.

"*Ami? Du bist Ami?*"

"Yes."

She touched the bandaged hand with a finger and Adam snatched it back. "*Tut weh . . .* hurt?"

"You speak English?"

"*Nein.*"

She said "hurt," she must understand a little. He held up his hand again. "Will you help me?"

She watched him intently. "*Soldat?*"

"Lieutenant. I need help . . . for my hand."

"*Bitte?*"

Either she knew little English or she was playing dumb. He remembered three American five-dollar bills in his shirt pocket; the Volksgrenadiers hadn't found those. He showed them to her but she couldn't see what they were. She had a flashlight, the kind the German Army used, recognizable by a continuous squeaking when it was in use. It had no batteries and a

vigorous pumping of some part of it generated a dim
wavering light.

"*Amerikanisches Geld!*" She touched the bills and
Adam pulled them away.

"You help me?"

After a brief silence she found another English word.
"Oh-kay. *Moment mal.*" She grubbed more frozen
potatoes from the mound, threw them into a small
wooden wagon, and got to her feet. "*Komm!*" she
said.

The wagon squealed piercingly and Adam realized
that was what he had thought was a radio. There were a
lot of potatoes in it; she must have raided other places
before she came here. When the wagon stuck, he
pushed it, helped her get it into the street. He wondered if he could trust her.

"*Belge?*" he asked.

"*Aber ja.*"

Maybe. Saint Vith was six or seven miles west of the
German border but that didn't mean anything. He
stopped abruptly and she turned to peer at him.
"*Komm,*" she said again. "*Kein Angst.*"

Yeah. No sweat, G.I. Got to take a chance, Adam
told himself, and hope to God if she calls the krauts
they aren't SS.

The last time he had seen Saint Vith it was a shabby-
looking town with no class. Now it was not even a
town. Even before the moonlight showed its ruin he
could smell burnt wood, wet plaster, and the acrid
stench of explosives. What had been houses were
mounds of rubble, the street reduced to a narrow path
at the bottom of a trough of junk.

"Good God!" he muttered.

"*Ja! Alles kaputt.*"

"The Americans did this?"

"*Ami oder Tommi . . . machts nicht aus!*"

Here and there a house still stood but there were
few of those. Somebody's airplanes had flattened the
place. Adam wondered if there had been any warning
of the devastating raid. Probably not. If it was full of

German soldiers, nobody worried about the civilians. Come spring, he thought, and it'll smell a lot worse. Must be a lot of people under this mess.

If anyone still lived in the ruins they were careful to show no light. Where the rubble stood high enough to block the moonlight, it was so dark Adam had to feel his way, following the squeaking wagon. Only once was there any sign of German soldiers: a sliver of light at the window of a standing house and the soft music of a harmonica to which men sang a plaintive song. He caught a few words:

> . . . *ein ganzen jahr und noch viel mehr,*
> *Er liebt eine madel, kein endes mehr.*

Funny. Why a sad song? They whipped our ass, didn't they? The woman stopped before a row of houses which seemed to be in total ruin. She was trying to get the wagon out of the trough in the rubble and he helped her boost it into what he guessed had been the kitchen garden of a house reduced to a pile of brick and charred wood. At the edge of that monument she pulled up a trapdoor and disappeared into total darkness. After a moment she called out to him.

"*Hast du streicholzen?*"

"What?"

"*Feuer!*"

A match she wanted, he guessed. He gave her his cigarette lighter and heard her fumble with a lantern, muttering at the balky Zippo, but she got it going. There was not much in the cellar room: a bed, a table, some chairs, and a small stove; a recent addition, he guessed. Two pieces of stovepipe connected by an American army ration can rose to what had been the floor of the house. She was prepared to last out the winter, though. The back wall of the cellar was lined with neatly stacked billets of wood and several sacks of charcoal briquets.

She elbowed him out of the way and went back up the steps, for her potatoes he hoped. She backed down, skirt lifted and bulging with her loot. That practical expedient revealed nothing because she wore another skirt beneath the outer one. Adam went up and scraped the remaining potatoes from the wagon, brought them to the cellar, and dumped them in the basket in which she had emptied her skirt.

The lantern gave enough light to tell a little about his dubious protector. She was young, with dark hair under her shawl, a small round face with determined mouth and watchful eyes. She moved a sack of charcoal, exposing planks shoring up a collapsed section of stone wall, and pulled away a neatly fitted section to reveal an opening into darkness exuding a strong odor of burnt wood.

"*Schnell*," she snapped, but when he put his head into the odorous darkness she tugged at his arm. "*Erstens Geld!*"

"What?"

She rubbed thumb and forefinger together in a gesture that was unmistakable and Adam handed over his greenbacks.

"*Gut!*" she said, and he crawled through the opening. He had a moment of panic when she replaced the plank door behind him, thinking of all the things she could do now she had him locked in this hole. The least of them was simply to go away and leave him until he made enough noise to attract unwelcome attention.

She had returned his lighter but it was nearly dry and made only a flickering that revealed two things at once: he was in a sort of stone-walled cave and most of it was occupied by the most incredible machine he had ever seen: a steel box squatting on miniature tank tracks with the front wheel and handlebars of a motorcycle projecting from one end of it. He looked at the thing in baffled wonder.

The end with the wheel and handlebars must be the front because there was a sort of cockpit on top of the box behind them. The driver inserted himself in that, Adam supposed. The back end was open with a seat facing to the rear.

An armored half-track motorcycle? Only the krauts could make a thing like that. He wondered if the driver made it go with pedals or the sprocket wheels of the track were driven by some kind of motor inside the armored body. His lighter faded but before he snapped it shut he saw something more alarming: the jacket and trousers of a black uniform thrown on the rear seat.

Panzer or SS? Both German armored troops and the SS wore black uniforms. Maybe there were insignia that would tell him which, but the lighter was finished. Adam shivered and sat on the rubble heaped against the wall, wondering if he had just made the worst and last mistake of his life.

Even if she doesn't tell him about her Ami prize, the kraut who owns this monstrosity will come back for it sooner or later. Adam sighed; the sooner the better, I reckon. Hardly room for me and this Rube Goldberg machine in here. He propped his feet on the thing and it squeaked protestingly.

How the hell did they get it in here? His brief examination had revealed no other entrance than the hole through which he had climbed. Must have been on the ground floor, he decided, and it fell into the cellar when the house was bombed. Someone had dug away the rubble around it and patched up the ceiling with planks. They'll need a crane to get it out. Damn thing must weigh a ton.

There was noise in the cellar room behind the plank wall: the thump of the trapdoor and a man's voice. Panzer or SS? That would take a little time because whoever it was had something to settle with his woman.

They were arguing; even in German Adam could tell that. "*Dummling!*" she exploded, but they lowered their voices and he understood nothing more. The argument ended and someone pulled the panel from the plank wall, admitting a dim light into Adam's cave.

"*Heraus, Ami!*"

Now we find out, thought Adam. He squeezed through the narrow opening and blinked in the lantern light. The woman worked at the stove and a man in greasy black coveralls grinned at him.

"*Grüss Gott*, Yankee."

"Yeah . . ." said Adam. "Hello."

"Oh-kay."

"You speak English?"

"Sure."

Seating himself on the bed, the man opened a bulging rucksack, took out half a dozen cans of American rations which he put on the floor by the kneeling girl. She stopped puffing into the stove to examine them curiously.

"*Ami Ration . . . schmeckt gut*," he told her, "*und noch mair.*" Beaming, he produced an unopened pack of Camel cigarettes.

"*Du . . . Josef!*" she chortled. He opened the pack, took three cigarettes from it; one for himself, one for the girl, and—astonishingly—one for Adam. She fished a burning splinter from the stove, lit her Camel, and passed the light to her benefactor, who shared it with Adam. "*Aber gut!*" she murmured happily.

"*Natuerlich!*" said the man, winking at Adam. "Good ration, good cigarette . . . you got everything good, Ami."

"Yeah, thanks." What the hell goes on here? wondered Adam. Is he just fooling with me?

"How you are called? Your name?" asked the man on the bed.

"Talcut. Lieutenant Adam Talcut."

"*Leutnant! Herr Gott*, Virginie, *du hast ein Bonze gefangen!*"

"Hah!" muttered the girl, studying the ration cans.

The man thrust out his hand. "I am Josef and she is Virginie."

Adam took the hand in wonder. "I'm Adam. Pleased to meet you." Crazy. We're both crazy, I reckon. What's he up to?

The girl giggled. "Ah-dam," she said, just like Anneke. Josef slapped her bottom lightly.

"*Pass mal auf, Kätzchen!*" He squinted at Adam. "So, Ami . . . you think your army comes back?"

"Sure."

"We got many tanks. You see the big one . . . *Koenig Tiger*?"

Adam jerked a thumb upward. "The Jabos take care of that."

"*Du lieber Gott!* Goddamn Jabos!" Virginie hissed something at him and he grinned again. "Oh-kay. She say the war is finish . . . *Alles aus.* You think she is right?"

"Sure. No way you can stop us. Are you a soldier?"

"*Natuerlich . . . Panzergrenadier. Nord Afrika, Russland, Frankreich.* I fight all those places."

"Then you know it's over. You can't win."

"*Nu ja.* Maybe Virginie is right." He pointed at Adam's hand. "You are wounded?"

Adam held out the hand and Josef studied it for a moment. "*Ach!*" he muttered. He looked at the girl, who was watching them, and said something in rapid German. She shook her head and Josef pushed her. There was another noisy discussion but at the end she got to her feet and went out.

"She goes to bring Luzie," said Josef.

"Luzie?"

"*Ja*, she is *Schwester* in Sankt Josef hospital. Very good. She will make your hand oh-kay and she don't tell nobody."

"Then what?"

"Please?"

"What," asked Adam, speaking slowly and clearly, "do you do with me?"

Josef smiled. "Virginie say we must keep you . . . don't tell nobody. When Amis come you say to them what we do and they don't make me go to *Gefangenenlager* . . . prison camp for German soldiers. Oh-kay?"

It is, thought Adam, just possible this crazy kraut is telling the truth. Why not? He's not wearing his uniform . . . maybe he's a deserter. Even the krauts must have deserters. He wants to make a deal and that's great. That girl of his is pretty smart. She told him to do it. He held out his good hand.

"I give you my word of honor . . . you don't tell the soldiers I am here and I will tell the American army you have been good to me."

"*Gut!*" Josef shook his hand.

Virginie returned with the nurse, Luzie, a slim pale woman who cut the bandage from Adam's hand with practiced skill. It was black and swollen with an angry red hole in the palm. Virginie made an appalled sound but Luzie paid her no attention. She demanded water in a cup, added something from a bottle she took from her bag, and scrubbed painfully at the wound with a wad of paper bandage.

She had scissors too and she used them to cut away parts of Adam's palm she apparently considered no longer useful. She must be right, he thought, because the removal didn't hurt. He pulled the sulfa powder from his pocket and showed her the two cellophane packets. For the first time her expression changed.

"You have more?" she asked eagerly.

Adam shook his head and she opened one, sifted a little of its contents into the torn hand and carefully rolled the packet tight. "This one for you," she said. "I take the other one."

Her English was crude but very exact. Adam's hand hurt badly now but he decided he was in no position to be greedy.

"All right . . . sure."

"Good! I come tomorrow night if it is possible," she said, and left.

Virginie attacked a ration can with a knife, swore bitterly, and Adam grinned at her. "Here . . . give it to me."

Just one of the family, he thought as he worked on the can with his P-38. Virginie was fascinated and he showed her how to use it. "*Herr Gott!*" she murmured. She opened the can: ham and lima beans—a repellant mess, thought Adam, but when Virginie warmed them, she and Josef found them delicious. They examined and rejected a can of ration crackers. "*Kommissbisquit*," Josef said scornfully, and brought from his rucksack a round loaf of heavy dark bread from which he cut a piece for each of them. When they had finished the ham and lima beans he pushed more cans at Virginie.

"*Noch wass*?" She shrugged and Adam put a finger on one.

"This is good." He opened it and Virginie tasted with a finger.

"*Unglaublich*!" It was canned fruit, orange and grapefruit with chopped cherries, and she sucked her finger in delight. Josef hooked out a taste and groaned.

"Goddamn Amis," he muttered. "This is for soldiers?"

"Sure," said Adam. "Look at this." He opened a small round tin and pried from it a disk of dry fruitcake. His hosts tried it and sighed.

"*Donnerwetter*!" said Josef, his mouth full. "Where is the cognac?"

"No cognac," Adam told him, "but coffee." The tin with the biscuits had several packets of Nescafé— instant coffee—and he showed Virginie how to make it in a can of water, laying out the packets of sugar and powdered milk that came with it.

"Is only for officers?" asked Josef suspiciously.

Adam shook his head. "For everyone . . . officers and soldiers."

"How can you lose a war when you eat like this?"

Virginie added a final touch: a bottle of colorless liquor from which she poured a little for each of them. Adam gasped when he tasted it, and they laughed.

"*Schnapps*," said Josef. "*Mirabel Schnapps*. Is good, no?"

"What is it?" Adam managed.

"*Pflaumen* . . . plums. You know what is that?"

The stove glowed and so did Adam. The plum whiskey helped. He pulled off his jacket and Josef peered at the embroidered cloth insignia sewn on the left sleeve of his shirt: the shoulder patch of the 106th Division.

It was circular: the golden head of a lion, full face, on a blue background with a red-and-white border. Not an impressive lion, he seemed to have a worried look, and Adam remembered back in Indiana an argument among the company officers about whether his tongue hung out or he carried something in his mouth. Shubal Hyatt said it was a brown paper bag with a bologna sandwich in it—that was why the soldiers said they belonged to the Bag Lunch Division. Josef put a finger on it.

"*Der armer alte Loewe.*" Virginie leaned to look, and giggled.

"What do you call it?" asked Adam.

Josef grinned. "You don't get mad?"

"No . . . tell me."

"German soldiers come here from the Schnee Eifel say they catch many Amis with that sign. They call it 'the poor old lion.' "

They both watched Adam, expecting, he guessed, an explosion of anger at that scornful view of his division. He mastered it and Virginie understood. She touched his arm. "*Es macht nicht aus*, Ah-dam . . . *Krieg ist Krieg*," she murmured softly.

Adam wanted to change the subject. "You speak English very well," he told Josef, who responded happily.

"Good, hey? I learn before the war. I fix automobile for British in Stavelot. They come in the summer to make a tour and when their automobile is broke I fix it."

"Stavelot? You are Belgian then?" Virginie understood that and made a scornful sound.

"*Ganz Deutsch*," she said.

Josef shrugged. "We are . . . how you say? We live on the border. Before twenty years this is Germany, then they say it is Belgium." He winked at Adam. "So now we are Belgian? Virginie say she is Belgian but she is smart girl." He put a finger on Virginie's snub nose and pushed gently.

"Smart . . . *schlau vie eine Fuchse.*" Virginie pushed the finger away but she smiled at him. "*Ja* . . . Oh-kay, Amis win the war and I am Belgian like Virginie."

Adam chuckled. Looks better all the time, he thought. This operator won't send for the military police. "The Belgians will come back with my army. They won't put you in jail?"

"Nah! Everybody know Josef. They got to make something to eat on the farm, don't they? Got to fix the tractor. I do that. They don't got a tractor, I got one. You see him?" He gestured toward the hidden cave.

"What is that thing?"

Josef grinned. "*Kettenkrad. Ein tolles Ding, ja?* Opel Olympia motor . . . four cylinder, one and a half liter . . . very strong. Pull four hundred fifty kilogram. Good tractor. When the Amis come I take it out and the farmer give me bread and eggs and everything good to eat when I pull his wagon for him. He got no horses now. My army take them to pull artillery."

"You found it here?"

"Ah, no! I am by Bastogne with my Panzegrenadier company and my company chief say to me, Josef, the *Kettenkrad* is broke and we leave it at Beho—that is little village not far from here. He say you go and fix it, Josef, bring it to Bastogne."

He shook his head. "I fix it but I don't go to Bastogne. There is big fight there . . . Ami *Fallschirm-jaeger.* Parachutist, eh?"

Adam nodded. "Bad," said Josef. "They are bad like SS. And there is no snow . . . the sky is clear—*Jabowetter.*"

"What is that?"

"You know what is Jabo? When is good weather they are like flies. They catch me on the road with my *Kettenkrad* and they eat me up so I don't go. I stay with Virginie. I put the *Kettenkrad* in her house so nobody see it."

"How did you get it in there?" asked Adam curiously.

Josef snorted. "I put it up there"—he jerked a thumb at the ceiling—"but the Ami comes with big bombs and Virginie's house is finish. Sankt Vith is finish. It fall down here but is not hurt."

"Can you get it out of there?"

"Sure. I get it out oh-kay. But hear me, Ami . . ." He pointed a finger at Adam. "We keep you here with my *Kettenkrad* and we give you something to eat and we bring Luzie to fix your hand. Oh-kay? When your army comes to Sankt Vith you tell them what we do . . . Virginie and me. You don't let them put me in a camp for German soldiers."

"On my honor," said Adam solemnly, "I will do that." Might not be all that easy, he thought, but no use telling him that. "Can you get a paper so they think you are Belgian?"

Josef and Virginie discussed that at length and she nodded. "Good," said Adam. "It is better that way."

Virginie gave him a blanket and a shabby Wehrmacht overcoat to make a bed in the cave and woke him the next morning, demanding by signs his can opener. He found more coffee among Josef's loot and a tin of jam for the dark moist bread. The can containing the jam had a new can opener in a little paper folder and he gave it to Virginie.

Josef went off on some business of his own, seemingly unconcerned about the German soldiers in Saint Vith. Maybe he had another uniform hidden somewhere to wear when he went out. Adam made more coffee, shared it with Virginie, and watched her curiously. Unopened tins of American rations she hid in the cave with Josef's prized tractor, empty ones she scrubbed clean and put on a shelf. Adam supposed the krauts demanded that women save cans and tinfoil just like the American government did.

There was a clatter of disturbed rubble above and someone rapped on the trapdoor. "Virginie?" said a man's voice.

She gasped and pushed Adam into the cave. "*Sei

ruhig!" she hissed. "*Ganz ruhig!"* She slammed the plank door into place and Adam heard the bag of charcoal thump against it.

"*Moment mal!"* he heard her call. He crouched in pitch darkness, afraid to move a muscle. He crouched until his legs ached but he dared not move to ease them. In the cellar a man's voice rumbled and Virginie protested something, but then she laughed and they spoke so softly Adam could only imagine what was happening.

His imagination was lively. Maybe Josef wasn't the only soldier who brought Virginie presents of American rations. Did this one know about Josef? What if Josef returned and found him with Virginie? If they got into a fight the German military police might show up. They would make a magnificent catch—an American lieutenant, a German deserter, and a stolen half-track motorcycle. That thought made unpleasant waiting.

After an eternity there was silence in the cellar; Virginie's visitor must have gone. Adam waited a little longer, then scratched cautiously with a finger on the planks. Virginie shifted charcoal and opened the panel a little.

"*Was dann?"*

He tried to put his head out but she pushed it back. "*Nein! Bleibt ruhig!"*

"Who was that?"

She understood the question and wrinkled her nose in distaste. "Rudi. *Deutsche Soldat. Verdammt Bayerische Schuft!"* There was more, hissed at him urgently and he understood she did not want him in the cellar. Adam settled himself against the plank wall, the German overcoat and the blanket wrapped around him against the cold.

Rudi, eh? Sounded as though she didn't like Rudi but if he hadn't got what he came for he would probably be back. It was not a happy prospect but he surprised himself by falling asleep. Virginie awoke him, reaching through the opening to shake him.

"*Komm!"*

Luzie was back, her pale thin face worried, but she cleaned his hand and sniffed it. "Is good," she said. "*Kein Wundbrand.*"

"What is that?"

She thought a moment. "Gahn-gren-e? That is correct?"

Adam nodded. Proud flesh, they called it in Tennessee. He was pleased she found none in his wound. "This . . ." said Luzie, opening the packet of sulfa powder, "it is very good. You can find more?"

"No, I gave you all I have."

While she wrapped his hand in a paper bandage, Josef reappeared, making a tremendous noise, and Virginie kissed him even before looking at what he brought. Either she's feeling guilty, Adam thought, or she's really fond of him.

She helped Josef slide a heavy slatted wooden box bound with wire down the steep stairs and Adam stared in astonishment. A whole Ten-in-One Ration, food for ten men for an entire day. "You hit the jackpot," he told Josef, who peered at him curiously.

"Break it open," Adam told him and Josef found pliers to cut the wire and something to pry the box apart. The women gasped at the wonders spilling out as Adam held up cans and packages.

"Breakfast rations, canned bacon, box of biscuits, jam, salmon, dry cereal, canned milk, canned corn . . ." he cataloged the cornucopia of food. "Hamburger, pork and apple . . . paper towels, matches, soap, five packs of Chesterfields, and"—he shook his head in disgust—"five packages of Charms!"

"*Du lieber Gott!*" said Josef in a hushed voice. Virginie snatched up a little waxed-paper packet and sniffed it.

"*Seife!*" She had found the soap.

"It is like Christmas!" murmured Luzie.

Adam's hosts were generous with their treasure. They filled Luzie's bag with tins, added a pack of cigarettes and one of the little bars of soap.

"*Danke . . .*" said Luzie, "*Vielen danke!*" She

looked hopefully at Virginie and put a finger on something more. "*Du hast so viel. Darf Ich, bitte?*"

Matches she wanted, and Josef put two folders in her bulging bag. There was something more Luzie wanted that Virginie had not yet identified because she could not read the label but Luzie seemed reluctant to speak. Adam silently put a packet of olive-drab toilet paper in her bag and she blushed.

She fled, clutching her booty, and supper was a feast. Josef had a little schnapps to celebrate his marvelous find or theft while Adam opened cans and Virginie stuffed charcoal briquets recklessly into her stove. She reached blindly for an unopened can and Adam took it away from her.

"No, that's for breakfast."

"What is that?" demanded Josef.

"Canned Australian bacon."

"*Wass?*" asked Virginie suspiciously.

"*Speck!*" Josef told her, beaming.

They ate until they could hold no more and Adam sought through the cans until he found one labelled "PUDDING." It was a glutinous mess but sweet, and he topped it with apple jelly from a breakfast ration. Virginie sighed and licked her fingers, pulled Adam's head down to kiss him on the cheek, saying something he did not understand.

"What did she say?" asked Adam.

Josef laughed. "She say *der Fuehrer* don't eat so good."

That was the night of January 17 and the next day brought an alarming rumble of tanks and other heavy vehicles. It began early in the morning and continued till dusk. Adam couldn't tell if they were going east or west and Virginie was no help. She went up to peer from her trapdoor and came down in haste to hustle Adam into his cave. "*Panzerfahrzeuge,*" was all he could get out of her. "*Viele . . . gar viele. Bleibt ganz still, Ah-dam!*"

In his cave he could hear the motors and sometimes even the squeal of tracks. Either the krauts were call-

ing off their attack or reinforcing it mightily. Not till
Josef appeared in his black Panzergrenadier uniform
did he learn what was happening, and Josef's worried
face boded ill.

"SS Panzer Korps. Two . . . maybe three Panzer
Divisionen. They say they get more tanks, more men.
Damn Jabos kill many tanks."

Good, thought Adam. Funny how Josef blamed all
German losses on the fighter-bombers. They were great
tank-killers but the armor and infantry must have got
their share. Then an awful thought occurred to him.

"They bring new tanks here from Germany?" If
Saint Vith became a resupply depot for an SS armored
corps, the life expectancy of Lieutenant Adam Talcut
was considerably shortened. Josef shook his head.

"I think no. They go to Germany now. There is
much trouble on the East Front . . . maybe Russkis
make a big attack to help the Amis."

Bravely, Luzie came again to rebandage his hand. It
was truly beginning to heal now. There would be a
hell of a dimple in his palm and a ropy scar on the
back of his hand, but that didn't matter. His fingers
were stiff and hurt when he used them, but that didn't
worry him either. They would get better and he was
sure there was no infection now. Sulfa powder had
worked a miracle.

Next day the weather must have cleared because
morning brought the snarl of fighter planes rising repeatedly to a swelling roar as they dived on something. Kraut antiaircraft guns crackled defiance but
Adam could hear the hiss and heart-stopping crash of
rockets. The Jabos had caught the SS tanks pulling out
of the ruined town.

Josef went out for a little while but he was back
quickly, looking even more worried. Virginie demanded
something and she must have won for he left the cellar
grumbling. He returned with two heavy containers,
the kind Americans copied from the Germans and
both armies used for gasoline or water. G.I.'s called
them jerrycans no matter what was in them.

"*Wasser*," said Josef. "Come . . . help me."

He used Virginie's hatchet to pry a step from the stairs close below the entrance and wrestled with a stout wooden beam stored beneath them. Adam helped him set it up, one end on the floor, the other through the gap made by the missing step to bolster the trap-door. They must have used it before, as it was cut to fit exactly.

"You think they'll bomb the town again?" Adam asked him.

"Listen, Ami."

Adam listened. "Goddamn!" he muttered. There were not only fighter planes, there was artillery, distant but audible. The Americans had come back sooner than anybody thought. That was why Virginie wanted water—no one would leave the cellar now.

They sat around the stove and said nothing. Virginie was restless and Adam helped her move the remaining tins and packets into the cave. She fed the wooden slats of the ration crate into the stove and Josef coiled the wire that had bound it. Like Virginie, he saved anything that might prove useful. That night the American guns moved closer and their shells rustled over-head, exploding east of Saint Vith.

Next day was worse. Josef went out and came back at once, and while the trapdoor was open the noise of American artillery was appalling. They still did not seem to be shooting into the town but they were coming a lot closer.

"Ami infantry," said Josef. "They are in Hunningen and soon they are here. There are tanks too." Virginie moaned and he scowled at Adam.

"You tell them, Ami, what we do? You tell them we keep you here?"

"Sure, I'll tell them. You got some Belgian papers?"

Josef shrugged and showed him a tattered identity card with a photograph so bad any of a dozen men could use it. "Not German," he said vaguely.

On the twenty-first of January the artillery ran out of targets to the east and hammered the ruined town.

It was worse than bombing, Adam decided. Airplanes couldn't hang around and they ran out of bombs. The pile of tumbled brick above the cellar was a help but when a shell burst on it a powder of mortar and dust sifted into the cellar and Virginie's cans rattled on the shelf. The guns were relentless, pounding the remnants of Saint Vith until she cried and clung to Josef.

"*Herr Gott!*" he shouted. "They got to stop. How they got so much?"

Adam shivered and shook his head. They would never run out of shells. In his mind's eye he saw them coming: pouring off ships on the coast of France into an endless snake of trucks that rolled, never stopping, into Belgium. At the guns they dropped their load and went back for more—a mindless invincible power pounded Saint Vith and it would never stop—only move on into Germany.

He waited grimly for the cellar to collapse on them, but despite his fear he was proud of that awesome power. Bastards ran over us but they got their ass in a sling now. Why don't they quit and run?

Something must have run. The American artillery followed it but what came after the artillery was even more deadly—a rising roar of rifle and machine-gun fire punctuated by the blast of mortar shells. Infantry, thought Adam. They don't kill you by accident like bombs and artillery. Some scared bastard kills you with a rifle.

Above the sound of aimed fire rose the grumble of tank motors and the squeal and clatter of their tracks. That's all she wrote, thought Adam. He climbed the stairs despite Virginie's plaintive objection, to push up the trapdoor a little and peer out.

In the narrow path marking where the street had been, a soldier crouched and pointed his rifle at Adam. "Outta there, you goddamn kraut!" he yelled. "Handy-hoke!"

He was draped in a dirty sheet, a hole cut in it for his head, and his helmet was smeared with some white substance. He was filthy, bearded, and lethally dangerous, and Adam thought he was beautiful.

They're here . . . they came back. "Blow it out your ass, dogface!" he said happily, "and put that goddamn rifle down. Don't you know an American when you see one?"

11

ADAM SQUATTED beside the soldier. "What outfit?"

"Seventh Armored. . . ." The infantryman shifted his rifle cautiously, studying Adam's strange mix of uniforms. "Who're you? What you doin' in that basement?"

"Lieutenant Talcut, 106th Division. I been waitin' for you."

The soldier looked doubtful. Never heard of the 106th, Adam guessed. He pulled his dog tags from his collar and the infantryman examined them carefully.

"Yeah . . . Talcut, all right." Somewhere in the gathering dusk a rifle barked, answered by a nervous burst of fire. The infantryman hunched his shoulders. "Fuckers don't know when they're whipped."

He seemed satisfied about Adam, though. He shifted his crouch to watch the darkening street and after a moment he sighed. "You got a cigarette to spare, Lieutenant?"

Adam felt guilty. It was wrong that he had cigarettes and this G.I. had to cadge one. He pushed a half-pack at the soldier. "Keep 'em, you need 'em more than I do."

He went back to the cellar and Josef let him in. The only light was a candle flickering in the draft that came with him.

"I told you they'd come back," he said triumphantly.

Josef shrugged. "I don't think they come"—he looked at Virginie—"but she is right. You are going now?"

"Sure. I have to tell them who I am . . . find out what happens to me now."

Outside, another muffled shot, another nervous response. "*Ja*," said Josef. "*Scharfschuetze . . . verfluchten jungen!*"

"What?"

"*Kinder* . . . children! Now we got little boys in the army . . . they don' know the war is finish. Somebody got to kill them."

Virginie caught Adam's sleeve, pulled hard. "*Bitte . . . bitte*, Ah-dam . . ." She looked at Josef and spoke urgently.

"What is it? What does she want?" asked Adam.

"She is afraid if you go away. Ami soldiers don' know we help you. Maybe they do something bad."

Possible, thought Adam. Until the town was cleared of German snipers, army or civilian, the 7th Armored Division could be hard on its people. The firing continued, rose to a roar, and died away slowly. They must have got that one, thought Adam. He could wait. A man could get shot out there in the dark. Anything moving was a target. He grinned at Virginie. "I'll stay till tomorrow."

She understood. "*Gott sei dank!*" she whispered.

In the morning, she gave him coffee and he took off the Wehrmacht overcoat he had worn since he came to her cellar, folded it, and put it on the bed.

"You don't forget what you say to me?" asked Josef.

"I don't forget. I'll be back."

He made his way out of the rubble-choked alley into a wider street with a cleared way, to an intersection where an American military policeman directed a flow of jeeps and trucks moving briskly.

"Where's the command post?"

"Which one? There's a dozen of 'em." The M.P. stared at him. "Where's your helmet, soldier?"

Adam sighed and produced his dog tags. "You're an officer?" said the M.P. doubtfully.

"That's right. Is the 7th Armored C.P. here?"

"Yes, sir. Right down there." The soldier pointed at a cluster of vehicles before a big stone building set back from the road, its front scarred by bomb fragments. Adam remembered it. Once a long time ago he had gone there to try to give a bandolier full of money to somebody in his division headquarters.

Avoiding the jeeps and their waiting drivers, he cut through an old cemetery and wished he hadn't. It held a huge bomb crater with a rim of shattered monuments and uprooted coffins. The remaining monuments leaned away from the crater as if repelled by it. By a battered church there was a crowd of small crude wooden crosses and Adam stopped to brush the snow from one and puzzle out the letters painted on it black.

"Fu. Otto Heim. V.G.R. 294. gef. 20.12.44," it said. The 294th Volksgrenadier Regiment. They came through Auw, he thought. Maybe Otto helped run us out of our outpost by the old mill. He didn't last long. "gef. 20.12.44." Must be the day he was killed. They put the day first and then the month, he decided.

The next one had fallen over and Adam straightened it. "Fdw. Emil Proschke. V.A.K. 978." The date was illegible. The cross beside it was upright. It said, "Am. Samuel Moore. 0-2355207. T44. gef. 21.12.44."

A German named Samuel Moore? Couldn't be. The "Am." must mean American. They had copied his dog tags meticulously, even the "T44" that meant his antitetanus inoculation was current. "O" could be his blood type, but right before the serial number it meant he was an officer. Lieutenant Sam Moore, I bet, thought Adam.

He was surprised the Germans took so much trouble with a dead American. Do we do that for them? Maybe just because he was an officer. The Germans made more fuss about officers than the American army. But there were American G.I.'s there too. "Harris, William T." had "Amerik soldat" above his name, and before his serial number, "E.M." Germans and Americans mixed together and that seemed strange to

Adam but the krauts were funny about rules. He remembered the Wehrmacht captain at the lodge in the forest who said, "He want to shoot you but I tell him that is not correct."

The Sankt Josef's Kloster was swarming with Americans who paid him no attention, and the G-1 of the 7th Armored Division was in the same room in which the 106th Division personnel officer had once told Adam he had no business collecting money from soldiers without giving them proper receipts. Adam was not surprised; this was the fourth American division to use Sankt Josef's for its headquarters and maybe the Germans just left the American room-assignment plan on the walls.

He found a major in a tanker jacket with a Colt .45 in a shoulder holster who looked up, frowning.

"Yes . . . what is it?" He studied Adam for a moment and looked puzzled. "Who are you?"

Adam held out his dog tags for inspection. "Second Lieutenant Adam Talcut, sir, 423rd Infantry, 106th Division."

The major stared at him. "Where the hell did you come from?"

"I've been here since we got overrun, sir."

"Here? In Saint Vith?"

"No, sir. I was in the woods until I got wounded, then some people here in town hid me from the Germans."

"I'll be goddamned! You telling me the truth, Lieutenant?"

"I didn't make it up, sir. I'll bring the people if you want to ask them."

"Sonovabitch! Hey, Allen . . ." He beckoned a captain. "This man says he's a lieutenant in the 106th and he's been here ever since the krauts got here."

The captain looked at Adam and nodded. "It's possible, Major. Corps said we might find some of them. I'll take care of it, sir."

He was doubtful of Adam's story. He rechecked the dog tags, asked for an army identity card. Adam told him he had been captured once and the Germans took his wallet with all his identification. The staff captain searched at length through a bulging loose-leaf notebook.

"Here it is . . . Talcut, Adam, 423rd Infantry. MIA—missing in action, 16 December 1944."

"How did they get that date, sir? I was with my company till the nineteenth."

The captain shrugged. "Just means they don't know what happened to you. Must be seven or eight thousand of your division nobody knows anything about after December 16." He gave Adam a cold look. "Most of them were captured. They say two of your regiments surrendered."

"Yes, sir," said Adam grimly. "What was left of them." He pointed eastward. "About seven miles from here. We thought we were going to get some help but it never got there."

The captain's eyes glittered and Adam was pleased. *He knows his division was supposed to counterattack and help us get out—and he knows they never did.* The staff officer slammed his doomsday book shut.

"You," he said carefully, "were there when they surrendered?"

"Yes, sir."

"How did you get away?"

"Private Ritchie and I slipped into the woods. It was almost dark."

"Ritchie? Where is he?"

"Dead, Captain." Adam took a deep breath and held it until his anger subsided. "There were three more for a while—two engineers and a sergeant from corps artillery—they're all dead . . . sir."

The captain held up his hands defensively. "Take it easy, Lieutenant. I know you're probably telling the truth but you know I have to check it out." He pointed at a chair. "Sit down and cool off. You want a cigarette?"

He scribbled on a series of message blanks, pausing once to look at Adam. "You know the names of the men who were with you?"

"Sergeant Julian, Corps Artillery; Corporal Kuzyk and Divecchio. I don't know if Divecchio had any rank. Kuzyk said they were both engineers."

"This . . . whatsisname . . . Di-vetchio? He said he was an engineer too?"

"Divecchio never said anything, Captain. He was wounded when I found him and he died the next day."

"All right . . . all right! That's enough for now. When you get to Army they'll sort it out. Now, here's what I want you to do. . . ."

Two hours later, Adam had a complete uniform, blankets and a poncho, and a temporary identity card. He also had a throbbing arm. When the medics found he had no shot record, they cheerfully inoculated him against everything that threatened a soldier.

"Lose your shot record, you get 'em all," said the aid-man, grinning wickedly. "Here's a new card . . . hang on to it."

He spent a long time with a sergeant in the quarter-master graves-registration section doing his best to mark on a map where the bodies of Ritchie, Julian, Kuzyk, and Divecchio might be. He was not very precise about that but the sergeant seemed to understand. That finished, he went back to the suspicious staff captain.

"All finished? Got everything you need?"

"Yes, sir. What do I do now?"

"Tomorrow we'll send you to army headquarters. They'll finish processing you and decide what to do with you."

Adam considered the thought of more "processing" with distaste. "Can you tell me, sir," he asked after a moment, "what will happen . . . where I'll wind up?"

"Hard to tell, Talcut. If Army is hard up for infantry lieutenants—and I don't see how they can be anything else—they might assign you to a combat unit right away. If you're lucky you might get all the way to France and a replacement depot. They'll probably ship you to a combat unit but you might get a couple days' leave before you go." He looked at Adam. "Paris, maybe. Think you can hack that?"

"Yes, sir."

"There's one other thing . . . I saw a message on it the other day but it's got away from me. I think they're sending some of the MIA's we've recovered all the way to the States. You get ninety days Triple-R and a job at a training center."

"Triple-R?"

"Rest, recuperation, and rehabilitation leave."

"How do you get it?" asked Adam cautiously.

"Pure triple-distilled, ninety-proof luck, Talcut. Go see the headquarters commandant now, he'll find you a place to sleep. You eat in the officers' mess. Be back here at 0700 in the morning."

"Yes, sir." Adam saluted and hesitated.

"What?"

"The people who hid me here in town, Captain. I want to do something for them."

The staff officer shook his head. "Can't help you. See the civil-affairs officer . . . we just got one. I think he's with the headquarters commandant."

Adam found the civil-affairs officer, a first lieutenant no older than himself, lecturing an elderly Belgian wearing a police uniform. The lieutenant's French was so bad even Adam could understand it. The Belgian stalked away after a while and the lieutenant swore explosively.

"That's the highest-ranking gendarme in Saint Vith and he thinks he ought to be chief of police."

"What's the matter with him?" asked Adam.

"He's been here all the time and the krauts didn't shoot him, that's what! He's a goddamn collaborator . . . I can't run this town with that kind of people."

"You're supposed to run the town?"

"Police, waterworks, gasworks, garbage . . . clear the streets, bury the dead . . . and feed the civilians. I've got a six-man detachment and no money. Do you want something?"

"You need a good auto mechanic?"

"Godalmighty, yes! You got one?"

"I'll go get him." Adam had told his story so many times he had it reduced to bare essentials. The civil-affairs lieutenant listened in awe. He wore crossed rifles on his collar but he was a highly specialized breed of infantryman who had obviously never served in a combat unit.

"That's the damndest story I ever heard! The Belgians said there were Americans in the woods killing krauts but I didn't believe it."

"Well, there were some. Can you take care of my friend?"

"Sure, bring your Belgian . . . I've got work for him."

"There's just one thing," said Adam. "He may be Belgian but he's also a deserter from the German Army."

"Oh, hell! Why did he help you?"

"Because he's a deserter . . . and he wants to stay in Saint Vith. I think he comes from somewhere around here. He was in a panzer division that went to Bastogne and they sent him back to get some kind of armored motorcycle. That's when he deserted. He hid the thing in his girl's cellar and stayed with her. The people in the town know him."

"His girl? Is she German too?"

"Lieutenant, until after the First World War this town was German. They gave it to the Belgians then but a lot of these people are still German. His girl is Belgian by the book but she doesn't even speak French. So what? She hid me in her cellar and he found us something to eat . . . kept the krauts from finding me. All they want is out of this war . . . they've had it."

"Well . . . if he can fix dead trucks, I can use him."

"Can you keep the CIC from sending him to a POW camp?"

"Sure, unless his outfit was at Malmedy or something like that. I won't hide a war criminal. Is he SS?"

"No, I think he was in the 116th Panzer Division."

"They've got a clean record. I can fix him up. If he's

any good I'll give him some kind of papers. If he's from around here I'll make him a Belgian . . . no sweat."

"Can I bring him now?"

"Sure. You think he knows anything about the waterworks?"

Adam chuckled. If he didn't, Josef would figure it out pretty quick.

Josef's astonishing command of English won his case. He received a typewritten certificate that he was employed by the 1205th Military Government Detachment, U.S. Army—with an impressive rubber-stamped authentication. It said his nationality was "Stateless" but the civil-affairs officer promised an improvement in that if he could really repair battered vehicles, even more if he could get the power plant at the city waterworks to run.

"Can you do it?" Adam asked when they left the 7th Armored Division headquarters.

"He is only *leutnant* . . . lieutenant, like you?"

"He's a first lieutenant."

"*Ja, Oberleutnant.*" Josef grinned. "I am good with lieutenants. Sometime I got trouble with captain but not lieutenant."

Virginie dealt with their return in accord with her upbringing. She asked no questions, found a cup and two glasses at Josef's command, and waited, big-eyed, while he poured schnapps into them. Not until he touched her cup with his glass and said gravely, *"Ganz gut, Kätzchen,"* did she squeal in delight.

She kissed Josef and then Adam, eyes sparkling. *"Ich danke Ihnen,* Ah-dam. *Ich danke Ihnen viel mal!"*

Adam looked at Josef, who shook his head. "Virginie has make you captain. She don't speak so to a lieutenant."

She would not let him go back to Sankt Josef's Kloster for supper. She lifted the lid of a pot on her stove and Josef groaned ecstatically. *"Hasenpfeffer! Um Gott es Willen . . . wo kommt dass?"*

"*Das geht sich nicht an!*"

"*Haben wir auch nudeln?*"

"*Ja doch!*"

It was better than anything the officers' mess could make from army rations. By the time they finished Virginie's stewed hare and noodles and the bottle of schnapps, it was too late to tempt nervous sentries guarding the armored division headquarters. Adam slept by the stove.

In the chill gloom of dawn, Virginie woke him in a startling way—her cold chapped lips moving against his. He tried to sit up and she put both hands on his chest, kissed him again, her lips warmer now. Her tongue flickered momentarily against his and she shook him lightly.

"*Aufstehen*, Ah-dam. *Es ist schoen sechs Uhr.*"

When he left the cellar for the last time, Josef gripped his hand, grinning. "You are good man, Ah-dam. You keep your word. I hope you get a place where nobody shoots you no more."

Virginie kissed him demurely on his cheek. "*Lebe wohl*, Ah-dam," she murmured. "*Komm gut nach hause!*"

At the G-1 office in the Kloster he could not find the captain who had told him to be there at seven o'clock. A sergeant took him to the major with the shoulder-holstered pistol; again Adam waited until the officer finished leafing through a stack of messages before looking up.

"Well, Talcut, where the hell have you been?"

"Sir, the captain said I was to report here before seven o'clock and he would send me to army headquarters."

"Don't bullshit me, Lieutenant. We've been looking for you since five o'clock this morning. That truck got off early . . . it's been gone for an hour. Where were you?"

"Sir, I stayed with the people in town who kept the Germans from finding me."

"Yeah! Well, if you'd stayed where you were told

to, you'd be on that truck now." He glared at Adam. "There's a convoy going back for rations at five o'clock this afternoon. You be on it, Talcut, or I'll send you back under guard. You got that?"

"Yes, sir."

"All right. You fool around anymore, Lieutenant, and I'll report you absent without leave."

Adam departed, shaken. He had somehow expected he would be welcomed back to the American army with pride in his lonely fight behind German lines. Far from it. They didn't believe him. *That major thinks I've been shacked up with some girl in a cellar the whole damn time.*

Maybe I can catch a ride out of here before that convoy leaves—the sooner the better. If I do, he thought grimly, *I better tell that major what I'm doing or he'll have the M.P's looking for me all over Belgium.*

He started for the office of the headquarters commandant, head down, in bitter thought, and collided with someone in the hall: a big man, broad-shouldered, his chest straining his short uniform jacket. Over the left pocket was a double row of medal ribbons, on the shoulder straps the big silver star of a brigadier general. Adam backed away, stammering apologies. He had never seen a general this close, much less tried to run over one.

The general was as deep in thought as Adam had been, whistling tunelessly to himself. He stopped whistling and looked at Adam with tired eyes.

"Who are you, Lieutenant? You just get here?"

"I'm sorry, sir . . . I beg the general's pardon . . . I wasn't . . ."

The big officer waved away the apology. "Forget it, son. Are you a replacement? When did you get here?"

Adam swallowed hard, launched once more into his story, and the general listened attentively. When Adam finished, he clapped him on the shoulder.

"Good man! We had some of your people with us here. They got away when your regiment surrendered and went right back into the line. Good soldiers! You're going back to your outfit now?"

"Sir . . . I don't know where it is . . . if there's anything left of it. The G-1 here is sending me back to Army for reassignment."

"That's damn foolishness! One of your regiments got out . . . they're attached to us." He turned on a sergeant who had been following him.

"Where is that outfit, Hansen?"

"424th Infantry, sir, at Diedenberg, about six miles north of here on our left flank."

"The 424th? Ah, yes . . . Colonel Reid?"

"No, sir. Colonel Jeter is regimental commander now. Colonel Reid was wounded a few days ago."

The big general patted Adam's shoulder companionably. "Come in here, son." He strode into a room occupied by some staff section of the 7th Armored and all activity ceased in a respectful silence. "Carry on, men," said the general cheerfully. "Just want to use your phone."

Adam listened awestruck. In minutes, the general had his connection. "Clarke here," he said gruffly. "Put Colonel Jeter on." There was a moment's silence and the big officer sighed. "General Clarke," he said gently. Another silence, very short.

"Well, who's the exec? Put him on." The conversation was brief and one-sided. Not really a conversation, more an announcement. Sometime that afternoon the 424th would receive a second lieutenant named Talcut who wanted to rejoin his division. They would find a job for him. The general put down the phone, rubbed his hands, and beamed at Adam.

"How's that, son? They're short of platoon leaders. They'll take care of you and you don't have to go through some damn depot to get there."

"Ah . . ." said Adam.

The general gave him a puzzled look. "That's what you want, isn't it?"

What would happen if he told this general he would rather go to a replacement depot was unthinkable, so

Adam didn't think about it. He shut his eyes and nodded and in a moment had enough sense to say, "Yes, sir." After another moment he said faintly, "Thank you, sir."

"Don't mention it." The general looked immensely pleased. "Hansen?"

"Yes, General?"

"See that Lieutenant Talcut has everything he needs and get him a ride to the 424th command post. I'll be with the G-1." He grinned at Adam. "Need a few lieutenants myself, son. I'd take you but I always like to get a man back to his own outfit if I can."

When he was gone, Adam looked at Sergeant Hansen. "Who is that?"

Hansen looked disgusted. "General Bruce Clarke, Lieutenant, who else?"

"Is he the division commander?"

"Hell no, sir, Combat Command B. He held this town for five days last month. Took the krauts two more to push him back to the Salm River. All that hooraw about them novelty troops in Bastogne . . . they wouldn't had a chance if he hadn't stopped a whole friggin' kraut corps dead in its tracks for a week."

CCB, 7th Armored Division—that's the outfit that was supposed to break through to us, thought Adam. Well, if they had a whole German corps on their back I reckon they had all they could handle.

Paris? Triple-R leave in the States? Talcut, you damn fool—you just blew that away. All you can hope for now is a million-dollar wound, so bad they'll ship you home to get well. Unless you get dead first.

And that general. He never even thought I might want to go home. He honest to God thought all I want is to get back to the 106th Division and fight some more. Well, he's wrong but he sure hasn't got any doubt about it and I'd sooner go than argue with him.

Sergeant Hansen found him a carbine, wasting no time haggling over its issue by a supply office. He took

Adam back to the quartermaster graves-registration section and selected one from a pile of weapons there.

"You wouldn't rather have a rifle, Lieutenant?"

Adam shook his head. Despite its short range and chronic inaccuracy, he was used to a carbine now. The corporal who seemed in charge of the roomful of dead men's arms and equipment made an additional offer.

"You got a watch, Lieutenant?"

Again Adam shook his head. He would need one where he was going. The Volksgrenadiers at the lodge in the forest had taken his along with his wallet. The corporal opened an ammunition box on a table and took out a wristwatch, a big round nickel-plated one, gave it to Adam. He looked at it, bemused. Its dial bore a beaming Mickey Mouse whose gloved hands told the time.

"All we got, sir. Good ones don't make it to us."

Hansen also found him a ride north in a jeep belonging to the 517th Parachute Infantry Regiment, another of the disparate units attached to the 7th Armored Division. It was loaded with bags of mail for the paratroopers and the 424th, and the driver seemed knowledgeable about the situation north of Saint Vith. Establishing that Adam belonged now to the 424th, he added one more to Adam's collection of reasons why he wished he had not encountered General Bruce Clarke.

"We're on the left of the 7th Armored and your outfit is on our left. We'll attack tomorrow."

"Attack what?"

"Hell, Lieutenant . . . the krauts is all I know. Push those bastards back to Germany, I guess."

The driver took his jeep west and north from Saint Vith, complaining bitterly that he had to go so far to get to Diedenberg. His own paratroop regiment was not far from Saint Vith. In the gathering dusk of late afternoon he unloaded Adam and some bags of mail at a half-ruined building in a village. It had been a shop once—"*Metzgerei*" said the sign hanging crazily over a gaping hole that must have been a show window. The hole was closed now by canvas, with a little yellow light leaking around its edges.

The soldiers inside were more interested in the mail than Adam. "C.P. is up the road in the schoolhouse, Lieutenant," they told him. Adam found it and eventually a captain at a field table festooned with telephone wires and a stenciled tin sign, "S-1."

"I'm Lieutenant Talcut," he told the captain, who looked blank for a moment. A soldier with corporal's stripes on his field jacket leaned over the table to point at a message form.

"Uh-oh!" muttered the captain. "You're General Clarke's Lieutenant Talcut?"

"Yes, sir."

"You were in the 423rd?"

"Yes, sir." Adam was sick of going through a story no one believed. He said nothing more and the captain asked no questions. General Clarke hadn't been on the phone long enough to explain Adam's history but maybe these people had other sources. One way or another they would have found out where Lieutenant Adam Talcut came from.

"Second Battalion," said the captain. "Colonel Jeter assigned you when General Clarke called."

"Should I report to the colonel?"

"He's gone to 1st Division to talk boundary and artillery." The captain pointed at a big wall map, its acetate cover cluttered with blue and red grease-pencil lines. "We're left flank unit of 7th Armored and 1st Division is on our left but they're 5th Corps and we're in 18th Airborne. Corps boundary runs between us and that's always a bitch."

The captain pointed at a soldier crouched over a typewriter on an upended box. "Give him your name, serial number, and home address. The regimental exec isn't here either and there's no use your hanging around till he gets back. We jump off at daylight tomorrow and you've got a lot of homework to do before then. Your battalion's at Lommerscheid about a mile south of here. I'll get a jeep to take you."

He frowned at Adam. "We need platoon leaders but we never got one this way before. I hope you and that general know what you're doing."

Lommerscheid had only half a dozen houses, all of them, Adam could see in the dusk, shattered by artillery fire. The cellar of one had been reinforced with timbers to make a sturdy bunker occupied by the battalion command post.

The battalion commander had gone somewhere and Adam saw the executive officer, a major who was not surprised at his appearance. "Talcut, eh? We've been expecting you."

A captain working at a map board gave Adam a sour look. "You want me to brief him on the attack order, Major?"

"No, George, his company commander can do that. The more time he has with his company, the better. He hasn't got enough anyhow."

"That's for damn sure," muttered the captain. "I think he ought to stay with the company C.P. and let Sergeant Talley take the platoon."

"I know what you think, George, and you heard the colonel when you said it the first time." He got to his feet and winked at Adam, holding out his hand. "George is our S-3, Talcut. Good ops officer but he gets notional sometimes. We're glad to have you. Check out with the headquarters company commander, pick up any equipment you need—if he's got it—and report to your company. He'll show you where to go. Good luck, Lieutenant."

From the battalion headquarters company Adam received a compass, a flashlight, and a half-sheet of paper with radio and telephone call signs mimeographed on it. His company was only a hundred yards away, the clerk told him; only house in the village still standing. "Too good a target for the krauts," he added. "I guess that's why battalion didn't take it."

A second lieutenant stopped, looked at Adam in surprise, and put out his hand. "Where the hell did you come from? Barriger, motor officer. Remember that weekend pass we had in Indianapolis?"

Adam dug up that memory with difficulty. A couple of weeks before the division left for England . . . four lieutenants in a ratty motel . . . chased girls, drank too much cheap whiskey, and went back to Camp Atterbury to learn they had orders to go to the war. He had not seen Barriger since.

"We heard the 423rd got wiped out. How'd you get away?"

"Hid out in the woods till I got wounded and the krauts caught me. Got away again and some people in Saint Vith hid me in a cellar till the 7th Armored came back."

"Jeez! What're you doin' here? I thought they shipped people like you back to France for a while." Adam shrugged and Barriger stared at him in astonishment. "You volunteered for this?"

"I reckon so."

"Goddamn, Talcut . . . you got gold-plated rocks in your head!"

Adam found the farmhouse and his company commander, a young captain so exhausted he went to sleep while he was talking. When he did, a soldier minding the telephone took the cigarette from his fingers and put it carefully in a can lid on the table.

It was unnerving. When the captain woke he picked up the cigarette and continued talking as if he had never stopped. "Attack at first light tomorrow . . . column of platoons, your platoon leads. Line of departure right in front of this farmhouse. Axis of advance: Hochkreuz, Medell, Depertsberg ridge. Sieze the crest of Depertsberg and dig in before dark. No artillery prep. Company mortars support you, battalion mortars on call. Any questions?"

"Yes, sir," said Adam desperately. "I don't know where those places are. I just got here."

"Talley will show you. He's had the platoon since Lieutenant Longino got hit." He turned to the soldier at the telephone. "Get Sergeant Talley."

Someone brought Adam a canteen cup of coffee so hot he was still waiting for the lip of the aluminum cup to cool when a short, thick-set soldier wearing the stripes of a technical sergeant appeared, stood his rifle by the door, and saluted the captain.

"Talley, this is Lieutenant Talcut. He takes over your platoon as of now. I've given him the attack order for tomorrow but he's never seen the ground. Walk him through it on your map."

"Yes, sir." The sergeant's face was expressionless. The captain lit another cigarette from the minute stub he held in his fingers and looked at Adam.

"This regiment is all that's left of the division, Talcut. We've taken a lot of shit about what happened to the 106th and we don't want any more. Don't screw up tomorrow, you hear?"

"Yes, sir."

"All right . . . you're on top of that ridge by tomorrow night or you don't command anything in my company. You understand?"

"Yes, sir."

Adam followed Sergeant Talley from the farmhouse to a roofless barn where it was too dark to see anything, but Talley whispered to him, "Watch your feet, Lieutenant."

The warning was explained by the snoring of men, rolled into their blankets and sleeping on the floor. A stall in one corner had been covered with shelter halves to make a narrow cubicle in which a Coleman lantern gasped out a dim light.

"Pump that thing up, Wetzel," said Talley. He gave Adam another cup of coffee and spread a tattered map sheet on the stone floor, pointed out where they were, and traced with his finger the axis of the attack in the morning.

Hochkreuz Adam knew. His battalion had been billeted there until the Germans attacked and they went forward to help the artillery. He had driven through Medell with Ritchie when they went to the outpost at the ruined mill and he had seen the Depertsberg ridge from the other side, from the woods track where the

Germans killed Sergeant Julian. He tried hard to remember the ground he would have to cross in the
morning.

"How come we don't have any artillery support?"

"They said all the artillery is concentrated on a
place called Amblève in the 1st Division sector on our
left. Supposed to be SS there."

"That's bad. Can we get some if we get in trouble?"

Talley gave him a hard look. "Not supposed to get
in trouble, Lieutenant."

Adam considered that reply for a moment and
decided there was nothing he could do about it. Not
now. If he did all right tomorrow he could straighten
Talley out.

He finished his coffee, felt his way inside the barn to
take a leak, and returned to the shrouded stall. Private
Wetzel had scraped up a heap of moldy straw for him
to sleep on. He took off his boots, tucked his socks
under his shirt, and pulled on a dry pair, rolled himself
into his blankets, and nodded at Wetzel. The soldier
pulled the field telephone into his own blankets and
reached to turn the Coleman lantern as low as it would
go without dying.

Adam ached for sleep. A year ago Virginie had
waked him with her lips and since then he had wandered from one jolting screw-up to another. But as
soon as he lay down, watching the flickering orange
glow of the lantern on the canvas above, his head went
into high gear.

How could I have got myself in this mess? How in
the name of God am I going to lead a platoon of
soldiers I never saw before in an attack tomorrow?
They won't even know they've got a new platoon
leader. That damned general—if I hadn't run into him
I'd be halfway to France by now.

He groped in his shirt pocket for cigarettes, found
his lighter—refilled with gasoline from the paratroop-
er's jeep—and spun the flint wheel. A jet of flame
erupted that awoke Wetzel with a snort.

"You want a smoke?" Adam asked him softly.

"Nunh!" said Wetzel, and was instantly asleep again.

Don't think about tomorrow, Adam told himself. Won't do you any good. Sergeant Talley thinks you're a dumb horse's ass but he'll see you don't screw it up. I hope he will. Think about Bitsey.

At least she finally wrote you a letter. Sent you a bottle of whiskey for Christmas. I ought to have written to her today. If she wrote again she's probably got her letter back by now. I suppose they just write "Missing" on the envelope and send it back to whoever wrote it. Should have written Ma too.

Talcut, he told himself, this has got to be the worst day of your life. You haven't done anything right all day. But thinking of Bitsey provoked memory of another bad day.

In the month before his division left Camp Atterbury he was given five days' leave to visit his home. Two of those the Greyhound bus company required to get from Indiana to Tennessee and back. The other three he had in Laurel City. About noon on the first of those he walked to Bitsey's house.

"Why, Adam!" said Mrs. Payne when he knocked on the door. "Where did you spring from?"

"I have a couple of days' leave, ma'am."

"That's fine, Adam, I know how pleased your mother must be."

"Is . . . is Bitsey home, ma'am?"

"I'm sorry, Adam. Bitsey went to Memphis to see your cousin Raiford. He's in the hospital there. You know he was hurt real bad?"

"I knew he was hurt, ma'am. Ma didn't know how bad."

"It must be right bad, Adam. Bitsey asked the Red Cross people but they wouldn't tell her, so she took the bus and went to find out."

"Oh . . . I see. When will she be back, Mrs. Payne?"

"Not till Friday, Adam. You can see her then."

"No, ma'am, I reckon not. I've got to be back at camp before then."

"Oh, Adam, I'm so sorry. Come in, son, and have some dinner with me. I hate to eat alone."

Ma would be mad, but he went in anyway. He wanted to know how Mrs. Payne felt about him and Bitsey. She said he looked real nice in his uniform and gave him a little glass of scuppernong wine. He hated scuppernong wine but he pretended to like it.

Old Mattie, the black woman who had cooked for the Paynes as long as Adam could remember, called them to the dining room for chicken hash and little flat crisp corn dodgers.

"I'm sorry there's no dessert, Adam," Mrs. Payne told him. "We don't get enough sugar now to make anything good."

He made conversation for a little while, then said he had better get back to his ma. Mrs. Payne had said nothing about him and Bitsey and it didn't look like she was going to.

"I'm surely glad you stopped by, Adam," she said. "When you go by the bank, say hello to Mr. Payne. If he'd known you were coming he'd have been here for dinner."

"I will, ma'am. Please tell Bitsey I'm sorry I missed her."

"Of course I will." She paused for a long moment. "Does she write to you, Adam?"

"No, ma'am."

"Oh, that's too bad!" She regarded him gravely. "I reckon," she said finally, "you tried to hurry her, didn't you, Adam?"

"Yes, ma'am . . . I reckon I did."

She patted his arm. "It'll be all right, she'll get over it. Sometimes . . ." She paused again. "Sometimes I think Bitsey is a little too strict. I can't change that but I'll see if I can't get her to write to you. You be careful now, Adam, you hear?"

Whether it was my ma or Mrs. Payne . . . one of 'em got her to write to me. Maybe that letter is still in the house in Hochkreuz where I got it. The whiskey is surely gone but who'd want the letter? And my picture of Bitsey. Maybe when we go through Hochkreuz tomorrow I'll have a chance to look for them.

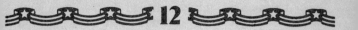

12

FIRST LIGHT. Attack at first light, he said. There isn't going to be any light, thought Adam— first or any other kind. There was a ribbon of luminescent gray in the eastern sky but it was already disappearing behind a bank of clouds, big black ones full of snow. The farmhouse a dozen feet away was just a darker bulk in the gloom. It suddenly emitted a slit of light and someone rasped a warning.

"Get outta the friggin' door!"

Adam recognized Talley's voice. There were two doors at the back of the farmhouse; soldiers went in one and out the other and one of them had held open the blanket screening the exit, sending a bar of orange light across the muddy farmyard.

Wonder what he thinks about me? He's had this platoon almost two weeks and now they tell him: Step down, Sergeant, you got another lieutenant. Nobody explained where the new lieutenant came from but Adam suspected Talley knew. To hell with it, he thought, but he was worried. A month of combat had made a mile of difference between this platoon and the one he had lost in December.

These men didn't bunch up around the farmhouse like his platoon would have. They stayed off in the dark and went in one at a time, a dozen yards apart, and only one of them screwed up coming out. What was going on inside was another proof how much this outfit had learned in a month.

Sweating over a gasoline stove that filled the room with a harsh gasping noise, a cook poured batter from an aluminum pitcher onto his griddle and shoveled a six-inch pancake off it for each man who stopped before him. There was a stockpot of coffee on the second burner and the men dipped their canteen cups in it. On a chair by the exit door were sugar, canned milk, and two big tins, one of peanut butter and the other of grape jelly to smear on the pancake.

A stove and a company cook to make sure every man got a hot breakfast and no messkit to wash. The 424th had learned a lot since the Germans chased it across the Our River.

"That's all of 'em, Lieutenant," said someone in the dark. "Frenchy brought you a pancake. Give him your cup an' he'll get you some coffee."

Talley again. Adam gave his canteen cup to a shadowy figure and peered at his platoon sergeant. "Who's Frenchy?"

"Beljeek, sir. We call him Frenchy. He'll stick with you an' you use him for a runner."

"Where'd he come from?"

"Some kind of policeman, Lieutenant. Picked him up when we left Saint Vith an' he's been with us ever since. Good man. Knows this country real good."

The thick layer of peanut butter on his pancake choked Adam. He scraped it off with a finger, knowing it would make him fiercely thirsty if he ate it.

"He's a civilian?"

"We're short, sir. No replacements for a week. He took out a kraut machine gun in the fight at Ennal and the company commander made him a corporal. We all chip in to give him some pay. You don't have to worry about Frenchy, sir."

Adam swallowed with difficulty. "He's the platoon runner now?"

"Yes, sir. Best we ever had."

The strangling noise of the stove in the farmhouse stopped and the platoon of infantrymen Adam had inherited was gone into the night. An occasional mutter of voices or a clink of equipment told him they were still near but he could see none of them.

"Get in line," Talley told them. "Single file an' keep your distance. Third squad lead off. Where's the machine-gun squad?"

"Here, Sergeant."

"You got a radio to talk to the mortars?"

"No, Sergeant. We'll string a wire."

"Good. Stay where you are. I'll pick you up before we move out, an' you go with me. You run short of ammo, you holler. Every rifleman's carryin' a spare belt for you."

Smart idea, thought Adam. I wonder if Talley came up with that one.

"Come on, Lieutenant, let's get 'em on line." Talley plucked a rifleman from the gloom and splashed through the muck of the farmyard, followed at careful intervals by the rest of the platoon. Adam went too, around the farmhouse into a rutted track, and Talley gripped his arm.

"You stay here, sir. I'll string 'em out an' be right back. Hold the last man right here."

"Yeah," muttered Adam. I may be in command but Talley's running this show. I got to do something about that today. The men plodded past him, following Talley along the track. When the last one lumbered out of the gloom, Adam issued his first order.

"Stop," he muttered. "Stop here."

Surprisingly, the farmhouse was taking visible shape though there was no dawn light, only a cold wet lessening of darkness. Talley came back and questioned the machine-gunner with the field telephone.

"Go now?" Adam asked.

"Not yet." After a moment the man with the phone raised his hand.

"Now we go," said Talley. "Where you want me, Lieutenant?"

All right, now you earn your pay, Talcut. "With the machine-gun squad, Sergeant. I'll send Frenchy back if we get stuck. Let me know if they break some artillery support loose for us."

"Don't hold your breath, sir. Whoever's got the artillery won't let go of it."

"All right . . . where's Frenchy?"

"I am here, sir."

"Stick with me."

Adam felt his way along the farm track to what he thought was the center of his line of riflemen; there was light enough now to see them watching him. Ahead was a dense thicket of snow-crusted firs planted in neat rows. Adam cursed them. A murmur came down the line of soldiers: "Go! Sergeant says tell the lieutenant, go!"

What do I say? wondered Adam. He could think of nothing but what the instructors had dinned into his sun-baked head at Fort Benning. Like a line from an Errol Flynn movie. "Follow me!" he croaked.

There was no telling in the trees who was with him. He stumbled and fell and scrambled to his feet, heard someone thrashing in the thicket behind him and was grateful for that. God, get us out of here, he prayed, and was rewarded by dim light and no more trees. They ended in a straight line at the bottom of a snow-covered field rising to the east.

Wind had scoured off enough snow to show the tops of old furrows looping across the slope. Whatever had been planted there was gone, nothing left but a few ratty shocks of stubble, and beyond the distant crest a glimpse of red-tiled roofs: Hochkreuz, that would be.

Where I was when this mess started, Adam thought, gasping for breath. Maybe I'll find my footlocker and Bitsey's picture if the krauts haven't bagged it. On either side of him, his men appeared from the fir trees in a ragged line, not looking at him but studying the crest above. Their concentrated attention got immediate response.

A German machine gun shattered the dawn with a long burst of fire and the line of riflemen dropped as if pulled by a string. Bullets cracked overhead—too high. Either the gunner didn't know his business or he couldn't depress his gun enough to hit the slope. Doesn't matter, Adam realized. He knows we're here and now he'll get mortars on us.

Never stop under mortar fire, they said at Fort Benning. Keep moving, because a mortar gunner hates to shorten his range. Adam got to his feet, wondering if he looked as big as he felt: a great stumbling target.

"Go, dammit!" he yelled. "Keep moving!"

Might be good advice for mortars but not for a machine gun on top of a great slow swell of ground. Adam climbed into the German's line of sight and the slugs sounded like a string of firecrackers inches above his head. He dropped like his riflemen, making love to the frozen ground, and again he was under the German fire—not much, but enough.

He remembered all the things you were supposed to do when that happened and did the one thing they said you never do—nothing.

"You see him, Lieutenant?" That had to be Talley, yelling from down the slope.

"No! He's over the crest."

"Go on! We got to find him!"

Stand up and when he blows you away maybe somebody will see him? He's right, Talcut . . . and if you don't get this show on the road, Talley will do it for you. Numbly he levered himself to a crouching run and stumbled forward. "Come on . . . keep movin'!" he gasped.

Some of them did. From the corner of his eye he saw them. The need to find that machine gun kept him from looking behind him. The kraut gunner, distracted by so many targets, emptied a whole belt of ammunition in a single long burst and Adam found him: a winking orange flash at the bottom of a stone barn. He pointed, yelling, but there was no response from his men.

They might have learned how to get a hot breakfast, he thought, but they're still green . . . they won't shoot. None of them wanted the attention of that kraut gunner and none of them, Adam knew, would move until he did.

Talley got the light machine gun going and a stream of orange tracer bullets arched up the hill, rousing the German gun to stuttering fury. Adam and his riflemen went down again.

"You dumb shit . . ." Talley brawled. "Cut the tracers! You're just showin' him where you are!"

There was an angry exchange of shouted insults and Adam heard Talley bellow at someone to bring another belt of ammunition. With or without tracers, the American machine gun stirred up more trouble—not mortars, but *Panzerfaust*, an antitank rocket launcher. Adam heard a rocket sizzle overhead and explode behind him. Another caromed off the frozen ground ahead of him and spun away with a ripping noise. He never heard it go off but the German must have seen it hit. He had a bracket now and lobbed in more rockets. He seemed to have an endless supply.

"Medic!" someone was bawling. "Get a medic . . . Gulick's hit!"

I ought to go help, Adam told himself, but his motor wouldn't work. He was in a broad furrow where the machine gun couldn't reach him and he stayed there, frozen. His riflemen copied him and he heard the thud of entrenching shovels hacking at the ground. Like sand crabs they were gouging shallow holes beneath them in which to hide.

They'll never go unless I do, Adam knew, but he had only two choices: stand up and let the kraut machine-gunner cut him in two or stay flat till his buddy with the *Panzerfaust* improved his accuracy. Instant or delayed suicide, and no matter what his head knew, the rest of him opted for delay. Only Talley moved, crawling forward till Adam could hear him yelling.

"We got to move, Lieutenant!"

"I know . . . can't we get some artillery?"

Talley swore explosively and crawled back to the field telephone the machine-gunners had brought with them, spinning out wire behind. He got no artillery help but the company commander took a hand. He sideslipped a platoon to the left, rammed it up the hill supported by the 81-millimeter mortars of the battalion heavy-weapons company.

That attack gained some ground and the company commander poured in his reserve platoon with two tanks someone had given him. Adam heard the snarl and squeal of their tracks bucketing uphill but before they could reach the crest they provoked their own special kind of terror: an antitank gun somewhere in the village, firing with a flat lethal blast of sound.

"An 88!" shouted someone. "Sonsovbitches got an 88!"

The big 88-millimeter gun was supposed to be an antiaircraft weapon but the Germans had found good work for it on the ground. No American armor could stand up to it. Adam saw one of the Shermans take a hit and the tank didn't just stop—it bounced backward. The turret hatch popped open, expelling smoke and two men—no more. Maybe the others got out the bottom, Adam thought; there's an escape hole somewhere on the bottom of that thing. He hoped they found it. The tank sounded like a pan of popcorn, ammunition exploding inside it. Every time one of its 75-millimeter shells went off it jerked and squeaked on its tracks like a great stricken bug.

The other tank darted to and fro, churning up snow and earth in great furrows, stopping momentarily to fire, then moving again—but not toward the deadly antitank gun. Even that disaster brought no artillery support but the heavy-weapons company did its best: their mortars dumped high-explosive shells on Hochkreuz and their heavy machine guns lashed the village with tracer fire. The measured pounding of the 1917-model guns was an antique response to the breathless rattle of German weapons, but they had a singular virtue: long after the Germans had burned out every spare barrel they had, the old water-cooled Brownings would still be firing.

The remaining tank pulled back and the attack stalled again, but unlike Adam's platoon it did not stay frozen. A few men went scrambling up the hill, more followed, and above the roar of rifle and machine-gun fire Adam heard a thin triumphant yelling and the twanging bark of hand grenades. They killed the crew of the antitank gun, or the Germans got it away, for it fired no more and the lone American tank came forward, pulling more riflemen with it. The firing in the village slowed to occasional shots, there were a few more grenades, then silence.

They've got it, Adam knew—they're just cleaning up now—and something else he knew: they took that village because some lieutenant got off his ass and led them in.

"Pack it up," he heard Talley shout at the machine-gunners. "Let's go!"

Adam got to his feet and watched the sergeant climb toward him. Talley didn't look at him. He watched the machine-gun crew and spat scornfully.

"Anytime now, Lieutenant."

Adam looked at the ridiculous watch they had given him in Saint Vith. Three hours on this goddamn hill, he thought. Stuck to the ground. He avoided Talley's eyes and waved his platoon forward. Cautiously the riflemen left their shallow holes to follow him.

More tanks hobbyhorsed into Hochkruez, crossed a shell-pocked macadam road, and sought cover among the houses east of it. Adam stared appalled at what lay beyond: another bare slope, longer than the one he had just surmounted, on top another village, bigger than Hochkreuz, with a steep forested ridge behind it. Medell, he guessed, and at once the Germans announced they held it with the shocking blast of a heavy antitank gun. They had got their 88 out of Hochkreuz or they had another one. Its armor-piercing shell did not explode; it ricocheted off the frozen ground and screamed over Hochkreuz.

Adam called Frenchy and they poked cautiously forward until they found infantrymen crouched among the houses. A lieutenant sat on the stoop of one, morosely studying his hand. When he let the fingers dangle, blood dripped from them and a soldier trying to tear open a paper-wrapped bandage swore at him.

"Gahdammit, Lootenant . . . hold it up!"

The lieutenant looked at Adam. "You're Talcut?" he demanded hoarsely.

"That's right."

"Where's your platoon?"

"They're here. Who're you?"

"I'm your company commander . . . I guess. Captain's dead and Lieutenant Beech got hit soon's he took over. Where the hell have you been?"

Before Adam could think of a reasonable answer, another officer appeared. This one had a white bar painted on his helmet; a first lieutenant who had been too close to an exploding shell or had run into something. His nose was bleeding.

"Who's this?"

"Talcut," said the second lieutenant. "He just got here."

"Ah! How's your platoon, Talcut? How many'd you lose?"

"We're not bad hurt."

"Good! What's left of your company is attached to mine and we're goin' for Medell . . . right now." He jerked out an arm. "You take the right an' my company'll be on your left. Griff," he told the other lieutenant, "whatever you can find of the rest of your company is the reserve. Stick with the tanks and keep 'em moving. We get hung up and I'll call for you. Got it?"

"Yessir."

"All right, Talcut, move out . . . and keep moving, you hear?" He wiped his nose on his sleeve and went back to the road.

"Who is he?" asked Adam.

The lieutenant who thought he might be Adam's company commander shook his head disgustedly. "F Company. Isn't enough left of us to cut the mustard so Battalion put them in." He scowled at Adam. "You been about as much good as tits on a boar hog, Talcut."

"Yeah . . . I know."

Talley helped him root out the riflemen and they got them up and moving with the men of the company on their left. At once the German defense of Medell shifted into high gear. They had at least four machine guns firing now and some light mortars—a fiendish little weapon because you could hear the piping whistle of its shell before it hit the ground and burst.

The reserve company with the tanks slipped left again, looking for a soft spot, and Adam shared with his riflemen a feeling of keen loneliness. One by one they dropped to the ground and Adam heard again the clang of shovels clawing at the ground. I got to have help, he thought. I can't get 'em going without help. He rolled downhill to the light machine crew, who watched him apprehensively.

"Where's Talley?"

"Don't know, sir."

"You still got a phone line to Battalion?"

"Yessir."

"Lemme have it . . . and get that gun goin'!"

"What am I goin' to shoot at, Lieutenant?"

"See that town?"

"Yessir."

"Try to hit it."

He spun the handle on the field telephone, it clicked, and a voice said with startling clarity: "This is Taxi Switch." That was Battalion, Adam remembered, but to get artillery support he had to begin with his own company . . . or maybe the company he was attached to now. Better try his own first.

"Taxi, give me Packard . . . Packard!"

Squatting, he waited, flinching as the German mortar shells dropped from the top of their arc with an obscene wheezing chuckle. They struck with a crashing roar no light mortar could achieve and Adam stared, horrified, at Hochkreuz. He had his artillery, all right, but it was falling a hundred yards behind him.

"Lift it . . . they're behind us!" he screamed at the phone. "Operator . . . Goddamn . . . Operator!"

Sergeant Talley was pulling at his shoulder. "Get down, Lieutenant! That's incoming . . . it's kraut!" Adam stared in disbelief at the orange-and-black explosions pounding the village.

"Taxi . . ." he howled into the phone, and someone responded in a quiet measured voice.

"This is Taxi Three. Who are you?"

Taxi Three? That had to be the battalion operations officer, the captain who thought Talley ought to be leading Adam's platoon.

"We got to have artillery, sir! Can you get us some fire?"

"Who is this?"

"Talcut! We need artillery . . . quick!"

"What's the matter? What's going on?"

"We're pinned down . . . machine gun . . . and artillery."

"You're getting kraut artillery?"

"Behind us . . . on the road in Hochkreuz."

There was a long silence. Adam thought the line had been cut but the captain was still there.

"Talcut . . ." There was a cold edge to the voice, audible even through the field telephone. "I can't get you any artillery. Third Battalion's got priority. How many kraut machine guns?"

"One . . . maybe more. Can't tell."

"Batshit!" said the phone explosively. "One machine gun and you're pinned down? F Company's catching hell and one kraut's got you stopped? Listen, Lieutenant . . . get off your ass and get that platoon moving! You hear me?"

"Yessir."

"Then get going! If you can't do anything else, get some of those machine guns off F Company's back."

Adam gave the phone to the machine-gunner and stared hopelessly at the village on the crest of the slope.

"Talcut . . . Talcut!" the phone squawked.

"Yessir?"

"Have you moved out?"

"Nosir. . . ."

"Goddammit! If you can't hack it, put Sergeant Talley on the phone."

Adam lowered the phone and it squealed incoherently; the captain was yelling so loud he locked the sound mechanism.

"Talcut?" He must have eased off a little. "Dammit, Talcut, stay on the phone! Did you hear what I said?"

"Yessir."

"Is Sergeant Talley there?"

Adam knew what that meant and rebelled. He jerked a wire from a terminal on the phone and handed it to the machine-gunner.

"Don't put it back till I tell you."

A little less noise, he thought, and I bet I could hear him without the phone. I got to do something and they won't even give me mortar support. That was clear—Battalion was throwing everything it had into the flanking attack by F Company and the Germans saw that. They knew Adam's platoon was no threat so they kept it pinned to the ground with a single machine gun, turning every other weapon they had on F Company.

Adam did what he could; he got one squad moving forward but as soon as the German gunner spotted the movement, he hosed it down. When Adam and Talley tried to get another squad forward, the first one stopped moving and began digging. It was like trying to push a rope and the stalemate might have become permanent except for the instinctive German reaction to such a situation: they scraped up a counterattack and threw it at the weak spot in the American effort.

"Oh, Godalmighty!" said the soldier holding the field phone. Adam heard it: the roar of a tank engine, its tracks squealing and clattering as it emerged from Medell. A great squat thing spattered with whitewash to make snow camouflage, a long-barreled gun with a big muzzle-brake jerking ahead of it.

It advanced until the gun could fire down the slope and disappeared behind its own muzzle blast. The shell hit a house in Hochkreuz with a stunning explosion, flinging up stones and a window shutter that shed pieces as it sailed away. Medell disgorged what looked like a Ku Klux Klan rally: running figures draped in white bedsheets.

"Shoot!" Adam screamed at the machine-gunners. "For God's sake, shoot!"

The gun got off a long burst and Adam scrambled to a soldier who had an automatic rifle, the antique twenty-pound Browning issued one to a squad in the U.S. infantry ever since 1918. He got that going and the machine gun fell silent. The crew was pulling it off its tripod.

"What the hell are you doing?"

One of them jerked a thumb over his shoulder without looking at Adam. Three or four riflemen were running downhill toward Hochkreuz and as Adam watched, more joined them.

He tried. He couldn't stop them. Another horror joined the German tank: a self-propelled antiaircraft gun like the one that had blown Adam's company off the road in December. Its four automatic cannon opened up with a thumping roar and a pattern of flashing explosions marched down the slope. The 20mm shells were meant to tear an airplane apart if they hit it, so they exploded when they hit anything else.

The machine-gunner with the phone yelled something and then was gone, running. Panting, crying in frustration, Adam ran after him. He made it to the macadam road and flattened himself behind a shattered wall. The best thing you can do, Talcut, he told himself, is get a hole in you quick before that captain finds you. That way maybe he won't court-martial you for running away.

A jeep came up the macadam road from the south, spinning wheels throwing a fan of mud and slush into the air. As it passed Adam, the German tank slammed another big shell into the village and the driver stood on his brakes. The jeep made two complete turns on the slick macadam before it spun into the ditch. Some-

one jumped from it and crossed the road in a crouching run to join Adam in his scant shelter.

"Hey . . . what the hell's goin' on?"

Adam looked at him dully. A real boy lieutenant,
this one. All clean and shiny, holding his helmet on
with one hand, clutching a map board in the other. He
looked like he was about eighteen years old. Adam
pointed up the slope.

"Oooh . . . Jeez!" said the youngster.

"A fuckin' Tiger tank!" said one of Adam's men,
crouched behind the wall.

"No Tiger . . . that's just a Mark Four," said the
shiny lieutenant.

"Who the hell are you?" demanded Adam. The
German tank looked as big as a boxcar on tracks to
him—big enough to be a Mark Six Tiger.

"Worden, 18th Chemical Battalion. We got a company in the railroad cut." He jerked a thumb to the
south. "Down the road a way."

"Chemical? What are they . . . Flit guns?"

"Hell, no! Mortars . . . four-point-twos!"

Adam rolled over and stared at him in wonder. Four-
inch mortars? "Can they shoot that far?" He pointed
at the nightmare crowd spilling out of Medell.

"Sure! Haven't you got any artillery?"

Adam spat. It wasn't easy. His mouth was so dry he
could only make a noise. "I can't get it . . . somebody's got it all."

The boy lieutenant yelled at his jeep and a soldier
with a radio came across the road and flung himself
prone. The German flak wagon was spattering 20mm
shells against the houses and both the lieutenant and
his soldier watched openmouthed.

"Jeez!" said the soldier. "They blow up when they
hit!"

His lieutenant fiddled with the radio. "Ruby three-
niner! Ruby three-niner, this is Ruby two-one Charlie. . . ."

"Yeah!" he exulted privately. "This is Two-one Charlie. Fire mission . . . infantry and tracked vehicles in
the open. Can you shoot?"

There was a long pause while the lieutenant traced something on his map with a forefinger. "From base point left one thousand eight hundred . . . up six hundred. Can you shoot?"

He held up a triumphant thumb. "Gimme one round Willy Peter . . . will adjust . . . and make it quick, they're movin' out!"

In an incredibly short time a great creamy fountain of smoke erupted from the hillside, glowing orange fragments of phosphorous scattering from it. Worden shouted a correction into his radio and abandoned any pretense of formality. "Hell no, they're not runnin' away . . . they're comin' down here! Hurry, will you? Pour it on . . . I'll tell you when to stop."

The result was apocalyptic. Eight more eruptions, black and orange and thunderous, bracketed the German tank and flak wagon. White camouflage smocks flapping, the infantry scattered.

"Good God, Miss Agnes!" muttered Adam. Eight more, another eight, and two more volleys faster than he had ever seen artillery pump it out. The harsh barking explosions merged in a rolling thunder, reverberating against the houses of Hochkreuz.

Unbelievably, the German tank, infantry clinging to it, came on. The flak wagon didn't. It must have taken a direct hit. Slewed sideways, it sat forlornly silent, its pot-shaped turret opened up like a shattered egg. Worden howled at his radio, trying to get his fire in front of the advancing Germans.

Adam's people were some help. They put up enough fire to keep the attacking Germans clustered behind their tank but it came on and they broke, running for cover in the houses. Some stayed. The bazooka team rose from cover—and turned the war at Hochkreuz around.

The German tank reached the first house on the eastern edge of the village, shed its infantry, and edged out to fire. The bazooka gunner got off two rockets— one missed but the other hit its target with startling effect. It jammed the turret of the German tank so its commander couldn't traverse his gun.

Like a great demented bug the tank lunged at a concrete telephone pole, the driver locking first one track, then the other, slamming his jammed gun against the pole trying to free the turret. The pole snapped off. If the turret broke its lock, no one would ever know. Sitting cross-legged in the snow, Worden coached his incredibly accurate mortars and they dropped eight twenty-pound high-explosive shells in a cluster around the tank.

"Bull's-eye!" he crowed. Adam was doubtful but Worden was right. The long gun muzzle sagged onto the front plate of the motionless tank. It was dead—stone cold dead in the market—and all the steam went out of the attacking German infantry. They fell back, took cover in the cluster of farm buildings where their armored support sat silent. Worden's terrible mortars blew the houses apart and the surviving Germans ran away, followed by the mortars.

13

THE SLOPE looked as if some terrible subterranean disturbance had occurred beneath it, leaving a field of blackened, smoking craters. The German infantry left some dead among the craters, identifiable because the white camouflage was blown off them. They left a wounded man too, who cried for help: "*Sanni . . . Sanni! Hilfst du mir!*"

"What's he want?" asked Worden's radioman.

"Medic." Adam looked at the Chemical Service lieutenant. "Jeez! That's a piece of work!"

"Too bad we didn't have the whole battalion. We could lower that hill a couple of feet."

"That was one company?" asked Adam in disbelief.

"Right . . . eight mortars. Lucky we were in position . . . didn't have to shift the base plates."

"Nobody told us there was anything like that around here."

"We were supposed to shoot for the 517th—the paratroopers—but they didn't need us. They got Wallerode before noon."

Adam studied the deserted slope. "You got any more of that smoke . . . or you just use it to spot targets?"

"Man, I told you we're Chemical. We invented smoke."

A wild exultant hope gripped Adam. "Will you help me? Can you shoot for me?"

"That's what we're here for. What d'you want?"

"Smoke that crest, Junior! . . . Smoke it till those bastards can't find their ass with both hands!"

Worden's Chemical Company spaced eight great blossoms of white along the crest of the slope and methodically filled in the gaps. In minutes they had an impenetrable wall of smoke erasing Medell, spilling down the slope like some kind of heavy liquid.

"Where's the bazooka, Talley?" demanded Adam.

"Right here!"

"Tell 'em to shoot! Hold high an' drop it in that smoke and get the company mortars on it too." Sixty-millimeter mortars would have small effect in the village but falling through the smoke screen they would keep the German infantry under cover.

Adam could hear the German machine guns hammering behind that great wonderful wall of smoke but the kraut gunners must have been city boys—shooting blind, they shot high. A hunter would know better. Shoot downhill—shoot low, was the gospel old Cap Simmons preached when he took Adam boar hunting in the mountains of Tennessee. He remembered something else Cap Simmons said when they didn't even see a wild boar for three days: things get so bad they got to get better.

They just got better, Adam exulted. To hell with the artillery—we got our own. He stood up and nudged a rifleman with his boot.

"Come on, soldier . . . let's go!"

He grinned at Talley and the sergeant scrambled to round up the scattered riflemen. "Come on, Junior!" Adam told Worden. "Maybe we can get you a Combat Infantry Badge."

The light machine gun was in action again and Adam admired the stream of tracer bullets arching over his head. He walked forward, not crouching, standing straight up, firing his carbine from the hip. Like farting in a whirlwind, Sergeant Buell had said, but his men went with him, their rifles banging. Didn't matter if they couldn't see anything to shoot at. It made them feel better, and wild slugs punching into the smoke would pucker up the krauts. His men were yelling at each other now, breaking into a stumbling run—up the slope this time. Not down it.

A hundred yards from the crest, Adam yelled into Worden's ear: "Can you move into the village? Get some H.E. with it?"

"You got it, Dad! Don't stop . . . I'll keep it ahead of you."

The smoke screen thinned, grew ragged, but Medell was like a peek into hell: when a four-inch-high explosive mortar shell hit a house it shucked off the roof in a fan of flying tiles; white phosphorous shells gouted creamy smoke and a spray of incendiary fragments that sent kraut infantry scrambling for cover. When one of those glowing scraps hit a man it clung, burning through clothing to the flesh, where it kept on burning.

To his astonishment, Adam found himself among the houses, his riflemen suddenly fighting like veterans, paired off in competent teams: one man firing when the other rushed. They were moving well and Adam saw the first captured Germans; younger than Worden—terrified kids who threw away their helmets and held their hands high in surrender. But there were others who did not quit. A machine gun dug into the cellar of a house swept the main street of Medell.

A bazooka team tried to get it. The gunner pushed his launcher around the corner of a house and got off a rocket that hit the cobbled street, spun high and useless. His loader shoved another into the tube, slapped him on the helmet to tell him he was armed, and the gunner stepped into the street, took careful aim, and was cut down before he could fire.

Adam led three riflemen, scrambling and panting, behind the houses, climbing walls and falling into cellar ways. When he thought they were behind the German gun they broke in a door, ran through the house to its front on the street. They were behind it; they could see the orange flame of its muzzle blast across the street.

"Cover me!" he yelled, and jumped from a window onto the cobblestones. There was a window in the cellar where the gun was sited. If he could reach it he could get at them with his carbine, and he ran for it, slipped, and went sprawling on the stones. A German stick grenade bounced toward him, stopped rolling so close he could hear the fuze hissing.

Convulsively he struck at it with the muzzle of his carbine, sent it spinning just out of reach, and buried his face in his arms. Someone ran past him, lofted the grenade with a soccer player's expert kick. It was Frenchy. The explosion of the grenade was lost in the roar of his weapon—as irregular as his status in the American army—a short-barreled pump shotgun. He jammed it into the cellar window and emptied it, the twelve-gauge riot gun booming savagely. The stutter of the German gun stopped.

On hands and knees Adam stared in astonishment at the Belgian, who grinned at him, stuffing shells into his shotgun.

"You are all right, sir?"

"Bet your ass, Frenchy! Good goin', man!"

After that it was easy—nothing but a few scared German boys who surrendered if they could. The anti-tank gun was gone; they must have got it out under cover of the smoke. One smart bastard, Adam thought. That kraut commander got his heavy stuff out and left the green kids and one diehard machine-gun crew to cover his ass.

Suddenly the village was full of Americans. F Company stormed in from the north and the remainder of Adam's company—the battalion reserve—came in riding on four Sherman tanks. It took a while to flush out the last German riflemen and make sure there were none with a *Panzerfaust* and the guts to use it against an American tank. The Shermans reached the last houses below the wooded ridge and fired blindly into the forest with no response. The F Company commander pushed a patrol forward and it drew machine-gun fire a hundred yards inside the woods. The Germans had not gone far and the patrol came back.

"We're supposed to be on top of that thing," Adam told Talley, gesturing toward the wooded ridge, but the sergeant shook his head.

"Nearly dark, Lieutenant. Don't want to mess with those woods in the dark."

Adam looked at his watch and laughed. Something had smashed it and Mickey Mouse's gloved hands were frozen at two o'clock. He studied the thick forest and knew Talley was right. Battalion must have thought so too, because the lieutenant commanding F Company appeared grinning.

"Stop here . . . we got orders to hold what we got. Take the goddamn ridge tomorrow. Hey, buddy . . . where the hell did you get all that artillery?"

Adam grinned at Worden. "We got friends in high places. Wasn't artillery . . . it was mortars."

"Shit! What kind of mortar does that?"

"Four-point-two-inch chemical mortars," said Worden happily. "A whole company of 'em."

The F Company lieutenant shook his head in wonder. "Stick around, Junior. We'll need you tomorrow. Talcut, haven't you got a radio?"

"No, but we got a telephone line to Battalion. Where is it, Talley?"

"Lost it, Lieutenant. Guy that was carryin' it got hit."

"Didn't you bring the phone?"

"Yessir, we got the phone but the line's cut an' there wasn't no time to find out where."

"Well . . . soon's you get sorted out," said the first lieutenant, "you better get on my radio. Battalion commander wants to talk to you."

"Oh, hell! Have I got to go back to Battalion?"

"You're still attached to my company. Stay here. You can help me take that ridge tomorrow."

"That's a hell of a choice!"

"Stick around. I doubt he'll come up here looking for you . . . not till we get on top of that ridge. You think those bastards will hit us tonight?"

Adam shook his head, delivered his opinion with

newborn confidence. "Nope. That infantry is just green kids. He's too smart to waste what good men he's got in those woods tonight."

"Who? Who're you talkin' about?"

"The kraut commanding that bunch."

The lieutenant took off his helmet, scrubbed his head with his knuckles. "Well . . . I reckon you know him pretty well by now. You threw him out of town but if it was me on that ridge in the snow I'd fight to get back in these houses."

"That's true. We damn sure can't take a chance on him . . . better dig in good and get some listening posts up there in the edge of the woods. Can we get some trip flares?"

"Good idea! We can set 'em up between here and the woods."

He assigned Adam three houses on the eastern edge of Medell and Adam put a squad in each, two-man fighting positions to be found outside the houses facing the threatening forest. It would take all night to dig real fighting holes but the riflemen could punch loopholes in the little stone outbuildings behind the houses.

"We need a two-man listening post just inside the woods. They'll have to stay till daylight . . . too risky changing 'em at night. Make sure everybody knows they're out there, Talley."

Half of each squad would man the fighting positions; the other half could get warm in the houses. Squad leaders would make sure each man got a turn at that luxury during the night. Adam checked the squad positions, made sure every man knew about the listening post, and when he returned, Talley was waiting for him.

"They want platoon leaders at the F Company C.P. in the church," Talley told him. "Attack order for tomorrow, I reckon. You want me to go with you, Lieutenant?"

"I reckon I can handle it," said Adam. "Have you got a casualty report?"

"Turpin's dead . . . I saw him. Gulick's gut-shot. Bad. Battalion aid station says he won't make it. Cobb and Hayes got hit but not bad. They walked back and I doubt we'll see that pair again. They'll make it to the hospital before I can get 'em. Two missing . . . Luikart and Holman."

"You talked to Battalion? You hooked up that phone?"

"No, Lieutenant. I got the word on F Company's radio."

Adam heaved a sigh of relief. "Don't fix that phone till I tell you to. What d'you mean Luikart and Holman are missing?"

"They ain't here and the aid station hasn't seen 'em."

"How can they be missing? What happened to them?"

"I don't know, sir. Nobody else either. Maybe they're dead or maybe they just took off."

"I'll be damned. Is that all?"

"Weiler says he got a shell fragment in his leg but I can't find it."

"You looked?"

"Yessir."

"Where is he now?"

"With his squad. Where else, Lieutenant?"

"All right. Keep him there and tell the medic to give him a tetanus shot and a Band-Aid."

"Hell, sir . . . you do that and the medic's got to write it up. The doc will make us send him back."

"Tell the medic to say it's a slight wound. That way he'll get a Purple Heart anyway."

"They'll want him at the aid station," said Talley stubbornly.

"Tell the damn medic to write down Weiler doesn't want to go back. He wants to stay with his squad. Maybe they'll give him a Bronze Star."

"Weiler? That meathead?" Talley was appalled.

"Somebody," said Adam, "ought to get something out of this mess. I don't care if it's Weiler."

At the battered church in Medell the first lieutenant

commanding F Company and Adam's platoon issued the battalion attack order for the next day, the twenty-sixth of January.

"Sixteenth Infantry took Amblève. They're in Mirfeld . . . a day ahead of schedule. Paratroopers on our right took Wallerode before noon. We're screwin' up the exercise. Third Battalion stopped outside Meyerode and we haven't got that goddamn ridge like we were supposed to."

He scowled at his platoon leaders. "Tomorrow, first light, we got five minutes artillery prep on Deperts Berg and we're on top of it by 0900 . . . nine-fucking-ayem! You got that?"

There was no answer and he was moved to cold anger. "We're all that's left of the Hungry and Sick . . . the poor-ass 106th Infantry Division. They don't think we can hack it and if we don't take that ridge they'll send somebody to do it for us."

He folded the map he had spread on the floor of the sacristry of Medell's ancient church. "No goddamn pack of hoodlum paratroop infantry is goin' to climb over my ass tomorrow. We're going to take that ridge and I swear to God I'll hang a court-martial on anybody who doesn't go for broke. You got any questions?"

He got his answer that time: "No, sir!" in chorus.

"All right. Talcut, you're on the right again. Make contact with the paratroopers before we move out. Hyde, you're on the left and you hold hands with the 3rd Battalion. You both report contact before dawn but if you don't have it, we're going anyway. Battalion says chow and ammo is on the way. If you're short anything, let me know. Talcut, I want to talk to you."

When the others had gone, he looked at Adam: "Did you get on the radio to Battalion?"

"No, sir, I didn't."

"Why not?"

"I don't want to get my ticket pulled . . . not now. I'll do it tomorrow if it's all right with you."

Adam held his breath until the lieutenant grinned. "You damn redneck! I like the way you fight. You can stay here till they come and get you. Go back to your platoon and I'll give 'em some kind of bullshit."

Talley had set up a command post in a stone barn and when Adam returned to it there was a marmite can—a big thermos container—of cooling C-ration stew and a jeep-trailer-load of ammunition outside. Each of the squads had sent a couple of men to pick up their food and ammunition.

"We get some trip flares?" Adam asked.

"Nosir. We got everything else, though—rifle ammo, grenades, rockets for the bazooka, and belted ammo for the machine gun. I got 'em pullin' the tracers out now."

"Good!"

"That captain at Battalion wants to talk to you, sir. He sent word by the jeep driver."

"So does the battalion commander. Everybody wants a piece of my ass. Have we got a phone line now?"

"Yessir, we ran a line to F Company. They're in to battalion and they gave us a drop on their switchboard."

"All right, but don't hook up till just before we move out tomorrow."

Talley grunted. "I don't see why they got their bowels in a uroar. We took this goddamn town, didn't we?"

"Yep. It's the one before this one they don't like. Have you been on that radio again?"

"Just to the aid station, Lieutenant. Asked if they had any word on Luikart and Holman—they haven't— and I told 'em Weiler don't want to be sent back."

"What did they say?"

Talley shook his head disgustedly. "I bet they put that eight ball in for a medal." The soldier at the field telephone put his hand over his face, laughing.

"Is Weiler that bad?" asked Adam.

"Sir, he's the champion fuck-up of the U.S. Army!"

"Well, now," said Adam solemnly, "he's a fucked-up hero. What's to eat?"

He summoned the squad leaders and gave them the attack order for the morning, not as dramatically as the F Company commander, but he made their objective clear: on top of Deperts Berg by nine o'clock.

"Second and third squads go for the top. First squad and the machine-gunners in reserve. If we hit anything, get around it and keep going. Talley will clean up with the First Squad."

"I got a mortar squad now, Lieutenant," said Talley proudly.

"From the company weapons platoon?"

"Yessir, 60-millimeter and a trailer-load of ammo for it."

"Did they bring a radio?"

"Nosir. They say they can't get any."

"All right. You bring the mortar with you tomorrow and if we need it I'll send Frenchy to tell you." He looked around the barn. "Where's our Comical Warfare lieutenant?"

"Went back to his company, sir," said the soldier at the telephone. "Said we got artillery tomorrow and we don't need him anymore."

"That's all he said?"

"Nosir, he said tell you thanks, but he don't want no Combat Infantry Badge."

Adam laughed and looked at his ruined watch. "What time is it?"

"Nine o'clock, sir."

"All right. Talley, you're on till midnight, I'll take it from there. I guess we better hook that phone up after all so we can check in with F Company. If Battalion wants me, say I'm out checking positions. We'll walk the line every hour . . . make sure one man's awake in every position. Where'd you put the machine gun?"

"Turn left when you go out the door, Lieutenant. Right at the end of the barn. Tied in with a gun in F Company."

"The mortar?"

"Got here after dark, sir. No chance to register it."

"To hell with that. Set it up behind the house. If the krauts hit us they can give us flares, can't they?"

"No sweat, sir. I'll take care of it."

It was still hard to tell from his face what Talley was thinking and Adam didn't know how to deal with that. He searched his pockets fruitlessly and the sergeant held out a pack of cigarettes. "Keep 'em, Lieutenant. I got plenty."

"Thanks. I reckon I better take a look around."

"Get some sleep, sir. I'll check 'em."

Adam decided he had better get one thing cleared up before morning. "You with me, Sarge?" he asked softly.

"All the fuckin' way, Lieutenant!"

There was no doubting that response, and Adam grinned happily. Just like Cap Simmons said. Things get so bad they got to get better. No matter what Battalion did to him, he had Talley's faith and that was no small thing. He got himself a cup of coffee and field-stripped his carbine.

"I will clean it for you, Lieutenant." Frenchy was cleaning his own weapon, the short-barreled twelve-gauge pump gun, and Adam winked at him.

"You know that thing's against the law? Krauts catch you with it, they'll put you against a wall."

"First they got to catch me," muttered the Belgian.

"Your home," asked Adam, "is Saint Vith?"

"No, sir. I am *Gendarmerie* . . . Belgian police. My post is Sankt Vith." He said it with a K, just like Anneke and Josef, and he must have noted Adam's reaction.

"Lieutenant," he said, carefully, "in this place, some people are German, some are Belgian and some do not know what they are. I am Belgian."

"I believe you, Frenchy. What's your real name?"

"Jean Paul Noel, sir, but in this company I am Frenchy."

"Frenchy it is, then. You were in Saint Vith when the Germans came?"

"Yes, sir. When they take Sankt Vith I go with the Americans. They give me a rifle and I stay with this company."

"When did they make you a corporal, Frenchy?"

"After the fight at Ennal, sir."

"It was bad?"

"Very bad. We try and we don't take Ennal and next day we go again. They say bad things about us so we got to take that town. The general of the division and the colonel of our regiment they go with us." He grinned. "They don't talk bad about us now. The colonel is wounded and the general he kills a German with his pistol."

"Sergeant Talley says they made you a corporal because you knocked out a German machine gun."

"Ah, was not much, sir."

"Yeah, but you got another one in Medell. You ought to be a sergeant for that."

The Belgian said nothing and after a moment Adam asked another question. "Do you know a girl named Anneke in Saint Vith?"

Frenchy shrugged. "Many girls are called Anneke in this canton. You know her family name, sir?"

"Hoffrion . . . Zhoffrion . . . something like that."

"Ah!" Frenchy lit a cigarette and Adam watched him curiously.

"You know her?"

"Maybe. She was with Virginie?"

Adam stared at him in surprise. "How do you know about her?"

"I go to Sankt Vith the day before we make this attack, sir. Many people know you stay with Josef and Virginie. That Josef . . ." He chuckled. "It don't matter who lose the war, Josef he wins."

"What about Anneke? You know her?"

"Maybe, sir. Can I know why the lieutenant asks about her?"

He may be a jawbone corporal in the 424th but he's still a cop, thought Adam. Well, Anneke said the Belgians were after her.

"She wasn't with Virginie. I knew her before, when I was hiding from the Germans in the woods . . . the forest by Meyerode."

"Oh, yes, sir. In Sankt Vith they say you are *partisan*.

You kill many Germans by Meyerode and Herresbach. They say Oberstgrueppenfuehrer Dietrich will give five hundred marks to any German soldier who kill you."

I'll be damned, thought Adam. Maybe Julian was worth five hundred marks—not me. But he wanted to know more about Anneke. "What do you know about the girl?" he persisted.

Frenchy was a cop again. "You know where she is now, sir?"

"Dead. The SS hanged her from a telephone pole in Meyerode."

"Why they have done that, sir?"

"Hell, I don't know. She said she was in the Belgian resistance in Liege . . . maybe they knew that."

Frenchy looked puzzled. "It is possible. I have heard she is with the Secret Army one time. But they say . . ." He watched Adam carefully.

"What do they say?"

"That she is maybe a spy for the Germans, sir."

"Then why the hell would they kill her?"

"I don't know, sir."

"What do you know?"

The Belgian shrugged. "Only the *Gendarmerie* want to talk to her about what she do in Liege. It is too bad the Germans kill her."

Adam was baffled. "If you knew she was in Saint Vith before the Germans came, why didn't you ask her about it?"

"She don't tell you she is friend of your secret police?"

"We don't have a goddamn secret police, Frenchy!"

He shrugged. "Maybe it is not secret, sir, but it is police. The *Gendarmerie* don't make trouble for friend of your CIC."

Adam shook his head in wonder. If I get out of this, he told himself, I swear I'm going to find out what that damn Counter-Intelligence Corps is all about. He doubted he would get any more about Anneke from the Belgian policeman though. That was finished now, just like Anneke. All I got out of it was a price on my head. Wonder if they printed up some posters? Be fun to send one home.

"What is a 'Groupenfewrer,' Frenchy?

"*Oberstgrueppenfuehrer*, sir. Very high general in the SS."

"Five hundred marks, eh? That's a lot of money?"

"Oh, yes, sir. Our company commander says it is."

"Frenchy, the company commander is dead. That lieutenant in Hochkreuz said he was killed this morning. How could he have known about me?"

"Peter Esselen tell him, sir."

"Who is he?"

"*Belgique* like me. He go with the Americans from Sankt Vith and he is cook for our company. He comes tonight with the jeep that brings food in the big cans."

"So when did he tell the company commander about me?"

"Yesterday, sir, before we make this attack. He tell the captain you are good *partisan*. You kill so many Germans they will give five hundred marks to any soldier who kill you."

"And how," asked Adam, "does this friend of yours know what happened at Meyerode?"

"He goes with me to Sankt Vith and somebody tell him. They say when the Germans are there the *Feld Gendarmerie*—German military police—they look for you every day. They will shoot anybody who help you."

"If everybody knew about me, why didn't the Germans find me?"

"Ah! The people who know about you don't tell the Germans. They know you are with Josef and Virginie but they don't tell."

Adam chuckled. Just like Laurel City, Tennessee. Gossip goes in circles but the circles don't touch. "They know about Josef?"

"He is deserter? Sure, sir, but if it got a motor, Josef make it go. Everybody like Josef. They are happy the German Army don't catch him and they are happy you don't put him in the camp for prisoners."

He's right, thought Adam, grinning to himself. No

matter who loses the war, Josef will win. Josef and Virginie—born winners. I wonder, he mused, if the company commander told anybody at battalion about this before he was killed? It might help if he did. If I get back there in one piece, I'll get a bottle of whiskey for Frenchy and his friend Peter. Won't hurt if they talk it up a little.

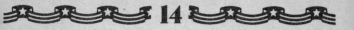

14

THE TWENTY-SIXTH of January came without a dawn, another slow change from darkness to a leaden gray light with flurries of snow sifting down to hide what had happened to Medell. Finally there was artillery support, late but infinitely welcome as the shells rustled overhead to burst with muffled unseen violence in the forest.

The F Company commander knew his business. He did not wait for the barrage to end, he sent his men scrambling up the bare slope to the forest edge while the shells still came. Adam took his platoon with them, knowing it was canny though dangerous—a shell falling short would fall among the attackers, but as soon as the barrage stopped the krauts would come out of their bunkers and man their fighting holes. Far better to gain the cover of the forest before that happened.

They made it, unscathed, and he scrambled through the inevitably thick firs to straighten out his line, sort out the mixed squads and get them ready to move on. When the artillery stopped firing, word came from man to man, "Go!"

Third Squad on the right found trouble a hundred yards up the wooded ridge, the sudden outburst of firing muffled by the snow-covered trees. Adam struggled toward the noise, everything he touched dumping thick wet snow on him, blinding him. He sent Frenchy for Talley and the reserve squad, meaning to pull the embroiled Third Squad out of its fight, keep it going. He knew if his attack stalled the Germans would pin it down.

There was no need for Talley. It was only a forward outpost, two scared German boys in a shallow hole who fired a couple of shots at the Americans laboring up the slope and surrendered at once. One of them was wounded; a freak hit by a rifle bullet had punched through the front of his helmet, deflected upward so it did not kill him, only half-scalped him.

An incredible amount of blood spilled over his face, dripping from his nose and chin, and the youngster sobbed convulsively. One of his captors was trying to wrap a bandage around his head but every time it threatened to blindfold him, the German shouted incoherently, fighting off the helping hands.

"Shit fire!" swore the G.I. "Hold still, dammit, or I'll hang your ass on a tree an' let it all run outta you. Hold this simple bastard, will ya?" he appealed for help.

Talley, Frenchy, and the reserve squad arrived, sweating despite the cold. The sergeant had driven them fast up the ridge. "Stay here," Adam told him.

"If I need you, I'll send Frenchy. You hear the First Squad get hung up, go help 'em. There can't be enough krauts in this goddamn woods to keep some of us from gettin' on top."

Talley looked doubtful but Adam had a growing conviction the Germans were fighting another delaying action. If the Americans stalled on the steep ridge, they might find a few men for the inevitable counterattack but if he could get a squad on top of Deperts Berg the defenders would pull out.

"What time is it?" he demanded.

"Little before eight. Don't get yourself dead tryin' to get up there by nine o'clock, Lieutenant."

Adam rapped his knuckles on Talley's helmet. "No sweat, Sarge. Take a break."

"What'll I do with these?" Talley jerked a thumb at the two Germans.

"Send a man to bring that mortar up here. He can take 'em back with him."

Talley looked at the solid roof of snow-bound branches

above. "Can't shoot through that. Goddamn shell'll go off right over your head."

"Chop down a couple trees, Sarge. Make a hole so if we get in trouble you can worry the bastards anyway. We got any smoke shells?"

"I never seen a smoke shell for a 60-millimeter mortar! If there was one, you could make more smoke with a cigar."

He was probably right but Adam was still entranced with the smoke screen the chemical mortars had provided. "All right, bring whatever they got. Let's go, men. Spread out and keep movin'."

F Company must have hit a hornet's nest by the uproar on his left and it sounded as if his own squad on that flank might have been sucked into the fight. That's all right, he told himself. Maybe it'll pull the krauts over that way. It would help. Even in these woods the Germans had to hear his men scrambling and sliding on the steep slope long before they could see them.

If they're as green as those kids they left back there, Adam told himself, gasping for breath, they'll open up as soon as they do, and that's good. If I know where they are, I can get around 'em. Being on top of Deperts Berg by nine o'clock obsessed him and very nearly killed him.

They were into rock now, great slabs of it thrusting up among the trees; good shelter but more difficult climbing. Adam wedged himself into a broad crack in a huge stone, spread his elbows on top, and tried to lever himself upward. The machine gun that opened up on him was so close he could see the orange flare at its muzzle as the cut branches hiding it were blown away.

He flung both arms straight up and let go, sliding down the crack like a gutter-ball in a bowling alley. At the bottom, he had no remembrance of how he got there. He was alive and that was a miracle he had to explore.

The German had missed him by inches, the burst of fire tearing off his helmet and slashing his face with rock chips. The helmet was a yard away, trapped by a bush, and he crawled automatically to retrieve it. Halfway, he stopped to watch the blood dripping from his face on the snow. Shaking fingers established there was nothing serious; then he picked up the helmet and whistled soundlessly.

The camouflage netting was torn away from the left side and there was a bright gouge in the metal where a bullet had ricocheted off it. He tested the side of his head gingerly and found a growing and painful lump. Frenchy crawled up to stare at him worriedly.

"You are hit, Lieutenant? Bad?"

Adam shook his head and groaned. "Look at that!" he said wonderingly, tracing the gouge in the helmet with a trembling finger. Frenchy let out his breath in relief.

"What you want to do now, sir?"

"Kill that sonovabitch!"

"Yes, sir . . . but how? We cannot see him from here."

This was no boy outpost—it was a main defensive position. Adam found that out when he gathered his squad and edged it away from the German gun until they could climb level with it. As soon as they did, the kraut opened up on them, firing in short, measured bursts, and when they tried to get above him, they uncovered a fighting hole with two riflemen in it. The machine-gunner had well-dug-in flank cover. Somebody lofted a grenade that looked like it went right into the hole but the explosion only blew away the evergreen branches stuck into the earth-topped log cover of the hole. The German riflemen were firing through a narrow slit under the logs.

Adam left four men with orders to keep firing, to keep the Germans fixed on them. The remaining two and Frenchy he took with him, clawing and struggling through the rocks. He could remember little of that nightmare scramble to get around and above the Germans. When he thought he was high enough he swung toward the machine gun and almost fell into another hole. Only a single German in this one—no kid this time—a mean-looking bastard in a white camouflage smock who leaned into his Mauser like it was an old friend. Adam, caught in a fir tree, fought to free his carbine.

Frenchy saved him. The German was so sure of killing Adam that he never saw the Belgian who blew him half out of the hole with a blast from his shotgun that got the attention of the Germans in the logged-over position down the slope. They turned their fire on Frenchy and Adam saw him haul the dead man from his hole and take his place. A roaring duel between two Mauser rifles and the American shotgun broke out.

Adam climbed higher, crawling through the rocks until he was above and behind the German machine gun. It was wonderfully protected: a deep pit with log cover impervious to anything but a direct hit by an artillery shell, and only a miraculous rifle shot would get into the narrow firing slit facing downhill. On the uphill side there was a tunnel framed with logs—the only entrance to the deadly burrow.

Adam had two grenades. He pulled the safety pin from one, let go the handle, and was glad the gunner could not hear the pop of the igniter in the uproar of his own weapon.

"One thousand-two thousand . . ." he counted, and tossed the grenade at the tunnel. He wanted it to explode on arrival and he was gambling he had wasted only half the four seconds it was supposed to burn before it did.

He was almost right, though he had counted a little too fast. The grenade tumbled down the slope, hit the side of the tunnel, and bounded onto the roof of the position. There it sat for a one-second century before it exploded, fragments shrieking over Adam's head.

"Shit-oh-dear!" he muttered. The Germans paid him no attention—they must have thought one of the American riflemen had thrown the thing at them.

On his knees, Adam armed his remaining grenade

and counted again: "One thousand-two thousand-three thousand . . ." before whipping it downhill like a baseball. Strike! he exulted. The deadly pound of serrated metal and explosive disappeared in the tunnel and the roof logs rose a little, then fell back in place. Smoke and a blessed silence came from the mouth of the tunnel.

Hoarse, triumphant yelling cheered the pitcher and his squad lunged forward. If the two Germans in the flank position tried to surrender, they didn't make it. There must have been a similar outpost somewhere to Adam's right but its defenders got away. He got to his feet and hauled himself upward from tree to tree. To his left he heard spaced, professional bursts from a German machine pistol.

He remembered something Ma used to say every Sunday dinner: you've had a piece of white meat, Adam, take a drumstick. We've had the white meat, the green Volksgrenadiers, now we got the old bastards—the dark meat. That's not all bad, he told himself—the kids stayed and died but if I can get a few men on top of this ridge I bet the old ones pull out. Too smart to die trying to stop a whole American battalion.

The German wasn't shooting at him; he was after F Company or maybe Adam's left flank squad. Exhausted and panting, Adam crawled into a deeply indented trail, the fresh snow trampled by booted feet; he crossed it and found himself peering over snow-topped firs falling away in a long convex slope.

I did it, he told himself, awed by the sight. I'm on top of the damn thing. One by one the men of the squad gathered around him and he waved them away. "Don't bunch up . . ." he said hoarsely, counting them. There were only four.

"Murphy got it," said the squad leader, "an' Zotz is hit. We got to get a medic quick."

"Frenchy . . . where's Frenchy?"

"I am here, sir." The Belgian, grinning like a fox, came out of the firs into the trail.

"Thank God for that," said Adam feelingly. "You get those two krauts?"

"No, sir. I keep them busy and Tilly get 'em with grenade."

"Tilly?"

"Till-ing-ast," said the Belgian, working hard at the name.

"Okay," said Adam. He had his breath back and he had stopped shaking. "One of you come with me. We'll ease down this trail a way and see if F Company is up yet. Sergeant," he told the squad leader, "cover this trail so they don't come at us from the south. Where's the wounded man?"

"Little way down the hill."

"Is his name really Zotz?"

"Bohunk, sir. Name's a foot long an' can't nobody say it, so we call him Zotz."

"All right . . . Frenchy, go find Talley and get him up here with his people. Make sure they bring a medic and a litter for Zotz."

A hundred yards north down the trail he encountered a cautious American soldier and minutes later the big lieutenant commanding F Company.

"We got it!" said the lieutenant. "Pretty good for the poor old Hungry and Sick, hey? What'd you run into?"

"Machine gun. Took us a while. D'you know where this trail goes?"

"Down a creekbed to Meyerode. Third Battalion got it this morning. We're tied in with 'em about halfway down."

"I've got one dead and one wounded. Can I bring 'em out this way? Got to be better than the way we came."

"Sure. We had two wounded and they're already started down. There's an aid station in Meyerode. They'll take care of your man."

"Good. What do we do now?"

"Regiment sent word we're to dig in here and they

want a patrol forward to find out if the krauts pulled out or just moved to the next ridge."

Adam dug a cigarette from a crushed pack, straightened it with his fingers, and lit it. He had dipped the case of his lighter in the gas tank of the jeep that brought last night's rations and the Zippo flared like a torch, the cigarette tasting strongly of gasoline.

He waited, knowing what was coming. It wasn't hard to figure out. The F Company commander needed every man he could find to organize even a small position on the ridgetop and he knew that as soon as battalion learned it was taken, they would want Adam's platoon sent back. The smart thing to do was get the patrol from Adam and send it out before battalion ordered him off the ridge.

"Say, Talcut . . ."

Adam shook his head. "I know. Soon as Sergeant Talley gets here."

"You don't have to go. Send Talley."

"No, I'll take it."

"Why, for God's sake?"

It would be easy enough to dump the job on Talley but he wouldn't do that. The reason was too complex to get clear in his head—he just knew he wouldn't. Rocks, he thought. You got rocks in your head, Talcut. First you're worried about the battalion commander and now you're worrying about a sergeant.

"I said I'll take it."

"Well, hell, man . . . you don't have to go to Berlin. Just find one kraut and get your ass back here on the double."

"Thanks, I'll do that."

"That's shit for the birds!" was Talley's comment when he reached the ridgetop with the reserve squad. "How come he stuck us with it?"

"Because he's got to dig in and hold this thing when the krauts come back and he can't spare enough men for a patrol."

"What about us?"

"I reckon you'll be gone before I get back. Battalion will pull us off. Report to F Company as soon as you've got the platoon together and send Zotz down this trail to the aid station in Meyerode. You can leave Murphy but tie a rag or something on a tree so the graves-registration people can find him if it snows again."

He took the four remaining men of his Third Squad down the east side of Deperts Berg, sliding most of the way; there was a foot of fresh snow on the ground. When they hit bottom Adam knew where he was—on the trail the Germans used from Meyerode to the Schönberg–Saint Vith road when the American planes drove them into the forest.

Julian and I scratched holes in the December snow to put mines on this trail—before the German patrol caught us. They killed Julian and I ran. Under the snow he could make out the deep ruts of the track and more—occasional humps and mounds beside it. One of those would be Julian. The krauts wouldn't waste time burying a woods guerrilla. Nobody would know which mound until the snow melted.

They crossed the trail and Adam spread his men to climb the next ridge. Not far up the slope they drew fire: spaced bursts from a German burp gun. Probably, thought Adam, the same canny old bastard that got off the last ridge just ahead of us. His riflemen watched him glumly until he waved them back.

"Is just one man," said Frenchy.

"No," Adam told him solemnly, "I am an old soldier now, Frenchy. That is the whole damn German Army. My orders were to find it, and I have. Let's get the hell out of here."

"A-men!" said someone fervently.

Frenchy grinned. "You get old quick, Lieutenant."

Adam studied the ridge they had slid down. "If we go north, can we get into Meyerode without climbing that thing?"

"Yessir, but 3rd Battalion is in Meyerode. They don't know we are here."

"We'll take a chance."

They probed cautiously north up the trail, climbed again, and from the crest Adam could look down a bare slope to the village. Frenchy was worried.

"We make them see us before we go down. It is better so."

"Yeah . . . we'll do that." But Adam was not looking at Meyerode, he was frowning, studying the bare knob they had reached. There, right at the top of that field . . . under the old stone cross.

He looked back down the trail they had climbed. They killed Julian there and I got away. Frenchy watched him, mystified. I thought sure they'd catch me so I hid it and ran.

"Stay here a minute," he told his riflemen. "I'll be right back."

"We don't go that way, sir," said Frenchy.

"I know, I won't be long."

Frenchy followed him and Adam found the cross in the trees at the edge of the field: the squat thick stone cross on a cracked concrete slab. He brushed snow from it with a gloved hand. "Heinrich Gerhardt von und zu Ahrens." Right. He patted the cross gently.

"I've come back, Heinrich," he said softly. "They didn't get me."

"Sir?"

He grinned at Frenchy and on his knees groped beneath the concrete slab for the badger hole he remembered. Brushing away the snow, he reached into the hole and felt the ammunition box he had put there in December. A month ago? It seemed a year. He pulled the box out, flipped up the bail latch, and opened it.

The bandolier was gone. Nothing left but pages torn from a notebook—his notebook. Penciled on one was a name, "Suter, John B., Pvt." and some numbers, "D/423, 68966718" and "516FF."

Private John Suter, E Company, 423rd Infantry. Army serial number 68966718, from whom he had collected 516 French francs. He wondered if Suter was still alive but that was lost in frustrated anger. Who got it? Why did they take the money and put the box back? He turned it over and shook it. The pages of his notebook blew away and something rattled, fell into the snow.

He threw the box away, pulled off his gloves, and sifted snow through his fingers until he found it—a little gold ring blackened by the wet paper it had nested in. He held it up and Frenchy leaned closer to look.

A woman's earring with a wire loop to hang in her ear. He stared at it baffled. One night in the lodge he had caught an earring like that in his fingers, tugged gently, and Anneke squeaked in protest. How could her earring be here?

"We got to go, Lieutenant," said Frenchy softly. "It is dark soon."

They went down to Meyerode, the riflemen in a column, Frenchy waving his helmet and shouting until two men of the 3rd Battalion came out of a house at the edge of the village and beckoned them forward. Adam looked at the earring, wondering how in God's name it had got into the ammunition box.

The only time I ever took that bandolier off was when she went to bed with me. Could she have lost it and it got into the bandolier? That was so improbable he couldn't believe it. She would have made a fuss when she found it gone. And whoever took the money—krauts or a Belgian farmer—they didn't see the earring in the box?

Among the outer houses of Meyerode they found a squad of American infantrymen, hacking out fighting holes in the frozen ground. A lieutenant appeared and wanted to know where Adam and his men had come from.

"Depert's Berg. Patrol. Krauts on the next ridge east . . . we got fire."

"You expected maybe Santy Claus?"

A comic, thought Adam bitterly. "Where's your battalion command post?"

The lieutenant jerked a thumb over his shoulder.

"In the schoolhouse. We ran the krauts out this morning but Battalion just got here. Don't make a noise or you'll scare 'em away."

They'll have radio contact with F Company, thought Adam. I don't have to go back up there. I'll get these people to tell Regiment we made contact with the Germans and pass that message to F Company on the ridge.

Finding Anneke's earring upset him but what he found in front of the schoolhouse sent him into a fury. He whirled on the lieutenant, who had followed him.

"You son of a bitch! You've been here since morning? Why didn't you take her down?"

"What're you talking about?"

Adam pointed a shaking finger at Anneke's body halfway up a leaning concrete telephone post, arms outflung, frozen there in the strangling agony of her death.

"You think that is your girl?" asked Frenchy in wonder.

"You're goddamn right I do . . . she's been there a month."

The aggrieved lieutenant shook his head, tapped his helmet with a finger. "You're off your rocker, buddy." He looked at Adam's men, gathered behind him. "Something happen to him on the ridge?"

"Lieutenant . . ." Frenchy tugged at his arm. "Look . . . that is no girl. Come close and look."

Adam went closer, his stomach knotted in sick rage. It was Anneke. Frozen. Head twisted. Feet stiff and shapeless beneath her long skirt. The bastards must have taken her boots. Blackened by weather, her clothes were unrecognizable but he knew it was Anneke. He had seen her on that pole when he came looking for the Belgian forester.

"See, Lieutenant?" Frenchy tugged at a frozen foot and the leg came away in his hand with a brittle snap. Not a leg, just a piece of wood with a rag wrapped around the end in Frenchy's hand.

"Only a doll, sir . . . a big doll. *Lu Popp*, we call it."

It was true—a life-size mannequin of a woman, arms and legs of wood in a dress filled with straw, a hideously realistic head made of a stocking stuffed with something, mouth and eyes painted on it with long hair of unraveled rope.

"Jesus!" said Adam. "Why would they do that?"

"Not the Germans, sir. The people in the town do it. In this canton they do this since a long time ago."

"Why? For God's sake why?"

Frenchy shrugged. "A joke, sir. A girl say she will marry a man but she runs away with another one. The friends of the first man they make *Lu Popp* and hang it by his house and laugh at him. You see the sign, sir?"

There was a placard tied about the waist of the puppet like an apron. Snow and rain had blurred the words written on it so badly he could not make them out. Frenchy puzzled over it.

"It say, 'Now is Ingrid run away. Raymund does not have her. Hermann-Josef takes her for his wife.' The people in the village they see that an' they laugh at Raymund. They make a big joke."

Adam stared at the puppet for a long moment before he began to laugh. His riflemen looked at one another.

"She's not dead," he said almost to himself. "They didn't kill her." He put the earring in his pocket and laughed again. I told her where I hid the money. She took them to it to stop them from killing her. Or she got one of them to take her and they got the money and took off. She left her earring in the box so I'd know if I ever ca..e for it. Anneke, the fox. She foxed those SS bastards.

He stared up at the shabby puppet and relished the fine pellets of snow stinging his face. No more soft silent snow—sharp and hard now.

"You are all right, Lieutenant?" asked Frenchy. "Is okay now?"

"Damn right, Frenchy!" He was laughing again and his men laughed with him—or at him. It didn't matter.

Anneke's alive and so am I. Yesterday I captured a town and today I got on top of that damn ridge. They caught me but I got away . . . and I didn't quit. By God, I won a little piece of this war.

He thought of Anneke and the kraut she must have tricked. Poor bastard, he won't have her long. She'll find a better one.

Maybe I'll even see her again. This war is a long way from over. Talcut, he told himself. If you live long enough, you may be one hell of a soldier.